Burning Bridges

Burning Bridges

CHRIS BEDELL

BLKDOG

CHAPTER 1

SASHA

Liars were everywhere.

Like when dentists told their patients the procedure wouldn't hurt. Or when children told their parents they brushed their teeth. Or when robbers told their victims they wouldn't kill them if they handed over the money. Or like while Sasha sat in the living room, drinking with her identical twin sister, Riley. There was no telling how Sasha would feel about Riley after the weekend because of everything that transpired between them over the last seven years.

Riley coughed. "Did you enjoy the train ride?"

"You already asked me that question," Sasha said.

"Fine." Riley sipped her drink. "I'll get to the point."

Sasha grimaced. No shit Riley should've told her what was going on. Riley randomly sent her a letter several weeks ago, and Sasha scoffed at the correspondence. If Sasha gambled, then she would've bet her life on never hearing from or seeing Riley again. Being related to Riley didn't mean Sasha absolved Riley of her sins—only time could.

Sasha furrowed her eyebrows. "I'm waiting."

Riley flipped her hair over her shoulders. "Sorry. Honesty is just easier for some people than others."

"If you're gonna lecture me, then I'll return to Manhattan. Even if that means dealing with Ivan." Sasha rose, then Riley grabbed her arm. The touch even surpassed someone dragging their nails across a chalkboard. Goosebumps were the only thing Sasha expected from someone that was a stranger to her.

Riley huffed out a sigh. "I'm not gonna complain about the past."

"Really?" I asked.

"You were a kid, and couldn't have been expected to deal with Vincent yourself."

Sasha looked Riley over. Riley hadn't stuttered, played with her hair, picked her nail, or displayed any other nervous tic—almost as if Sasha believed what Riley said. Yet whether she trusted Riley was another question.

"Please sit." Riley chugged the rest of her beverage, then grabbed the bottle on the table. She poured a more than generous serving of bourbon without adding ice to her drink.

Sasha sucked on her teeth. Riley never once said, "please" to her before.

"Fine." Sasha sat down.

Riley put her hands on her lap. "I should apologize."

"For sending me to prison for five years? Because we both know you set the fire that killed Vincent."

"Not exactly."

"Then what?" Sasha demanded.

"I was in New York City last year."

"So?"

Riley didn't speak. Instead, her gaze remained on Sasha. Almost as if Sasha once again believed Riley's hesitation was genuine.

"I saw your scuffle with Ivan when he shoved you against the taxi," Riley finally said.

The lump lingered in Sasha's throat. Hard to believe the incident Riley just mentioned wasn't that long ago.

"What's your point?" Sasha asked, raising her voice.

"You deserve more than being a victim of human trafficking."

Sasha averted her gaze. "The clients aren't the worst part."

"What do you mean?" Riley asked.

"I share a bed with Ivan." Sasha sipped her bourbon, yet didn't wince when the acrid taste pricked her throat. Perhaps she'd forget her past one day. She could hope, after all. No harm in deluding herself for one fleeting moment—the universe would remind her of how unfair life was soon enough.

Riley squeezed Sasha's hand. "I can't imagine what that must've been like."

"You're right. You can't."

Riley sobbed. "I know you don't have any reason to believe me, but I'm sorry for everything you've been through."

"I'm not convinced you didn't start the fire," Sasha said.

"What'd make you think that?" Riley asked.

"Disappearing after the fire was convenient."

Sasha wouldn't change her mind about Riley possibly killing Vincent unless substantial evidence emerged. Not wanting Ivan to harm her sister and Grandma was one thing, yet people might as well have been made of glass. Losing her innocence—both with going to jail for a crime she didn't commit and being Ivan's "girl"—taught Sasha the importance of living and dying by intuition. Gut instincts were the only thing she had left to hold onto.

Riley picked her nail. "I didn't wanna be blamed for Vincent's death."

Sasha grunted. "I was tried as an adult, and good behavior is the only reason I got out."

"It was manslaughter, not a murder charge."

"That's not the point," Sasha said.

"I'm sorry, but I can't change the past."

"Grandma stopped visiting me in prison after a while."

Riley gripped her neck. "How unfortunate. No point in being related to a real estate heiress if you can't enjoy the family money."

"Kind of odd you didn't mention anything about Grandma in your letter or when you picked me up at the train station."

"We don't speak anymore," Riley said without flinching.

Sasha slouched. "A part of me blames myself for what happened."

"Huh?"

"I went out drinking the day I was released from prison," Sasha said. "I mean, everything seemed fine—I was flirting with a guy. But I woke up the next morning at some mansion and he told me I was one of Ivan's girls now."

"Why not run?" Riley asked.

"He said he'd kill you and Grandma if I ever fled." Sasha's fingers tingled. She couldn't believe how she did the right thing no matter how much time passed since meeting Ivan. Most people would've only cared about saving themselves. Yet Sasha couldn't bring herself to run away from Ivan then. If roles were reversed, then Sasha wouldn't have wanted someone to risk her safety. Even if Sasha had no doubt about how Riley would've only cared about herself—some people just didn't care about doing the right thing.

Riley tossed back more bourbon. "You're welcome to stay as long as you want."

"What about Tyler and Cece?" Sasha asked.

"Doesn't matter. If they can't accept you, then I don't want anything to do with them."

Sasha blinked. "Really?"

"I'm not as heartless as you think I am."

"Actions speak louder than words."

Riley fanned herself with her shirt. "I'm serious. I don't wanna fight—I've got better things to do with my life."

Sasha counted to ten in her head. If Riley wanted to pretend their relationship was solid, then fine. Sasha would indulge her. Maybe, just maybe, she'd learn something about Riley in the process—something that would give her the advantage over Riley for once.

Sasha giggled. "I can't believe you have a stepson."

"Yeah, he's only five years younger than us."

Sasha laughed louder this time. "When did you realize you were bisexual?"

Riley spat out her bourbon. "Excuse me?"

"I never thought we'd have something in common."

"I'll try anything once."

Sasha elbowed Riley. "Are you sure you aren't using Cece for money?"

"Her hedge fund job is only one perk of our marriage."

"What's Tyler like?" I asked.

"Nice enough, but doesn't talk much." Riley stretched her feet on the living room table, almost knocking over the bottle of bourbon. "Something about not wanting anything to ruin his relationship with his boyfriend. Really, it's adorable. There's nothing like falling in love for the first time."

Sasha rolled her eyes. "You could pretend to care about him."

"I'd never hurt him."

"There's one thing we should get straight, though." Sasha pushed up her left sleeve, revealing a pink streak on her wrist. "Don't ever say I didn't feel guilty about what Vincent did to you. If I hadn't, then I wouldn't have cut myself."

Riley's mouth gaped. "Okay. I misjudged you."

"It's a little more than that."

"Tell me something. Why'd you respond to my letter if you hate me?"

Sasha snorted. "I'll try anything once. I can't make Grandma be a part of my life if she doesn't want to, so I gotta save myself."

"Maybe we're more alike than you realized."

Sasha almost laughed while the hallway clock chimed—Riley's suggestion couldn't have been more absurd. They'd never have much in common despite how some people might've thought identical twins were always in sync. Not when Sasha's instincts were opposite of Riley's, because Sasha didn't need anyone to tell her who was the good twin and who was the bad twin.

"Ever think about seeing a counselor for what Vincent did to you?" Sasha asked.

"That's in the past!" Riley exclaimed.

Sasha frowned. "Not if you act dysfunctional with Tyler and Cece like you did with me."

"I care about them."

"If you say so."

Riley cracked her knuckles. "Maybe this can be a fresh start for both of us."

"Do you actually believe that?"

"Anything is possible. You just have to want it bad enough. Anyway, I'm gonna start dinner." Riley stood. Evening sunlight glinted into the living room, accentuating her diamond's sparkle. Then, she flashed her wedding ring at Sasha. "Don't you love it? It's three carrots."

"The ring is beautiful," Sasha mumbled.

There Riley went again. One second Sasha chatted with Riley like they were girlfriends or real sisters, and the next she behaved like that seventeen-year-old girl who wanted the whole world to revolve around her.

***

Outside birds cawed, then Sasha yawned and rubbed her eyes.

Somehow, Sasha was still on the living room couch. Yet Riley wasn't nearby in addition to how no noises echoed from the kitchen. Sasha's mind returned to the issue of the couch, though. Dinner was the last thing she remembered. However, she couldn't have drank that much—her head wasn't throbbing.

But Sasha would stop stalling. Time to see if Riley embraced the loving sister role and already had breakfast prepared or if Sasha and her would go out for breakfast. So, Sasha hurried out of the living room after her stomach grumbled, only to halt between the kitchen's entrance, foyer, and living room.

The front door was open, and a gust of wind swooshed into the mansion.

"Riley?" Sasha called out.

Riley might've been too shallow to worry about security, but Sasha couldn't understand why the front door was open. A mouse, raccoon, squirrel, or other animal could crawl into the mansion without hesitation.

Sasha trekked down the front steps—perhaps Riley already made a cup of coffee and wanted to enjoy the drink outside. It was only the third week of September, and a distinct chill hadn't permeated the air yet.

Except Riley's Mercedes wasn't in the driveway.

Sasha scurried down the street before stopping at the bridge. Riley's Mercedes was parked by the edge of the bridge in addition to how a piece of paper was tucked under the windshield wipers.

Sasha ran to the car and grabbed the piece of paper. Then, she unfolded it:

Dear Sasha,

I know you can't possibly understand this, but I don't feel like going through life anymore. Even if you might think I've got the perfect life with Cece and Tyler.
Please remember me fondly,
Riley

Sasha's shoulders tensed. No neat phrase accounted for how Riley was alive one minute and gone the next. No matter how Sasha felt, Riley was dead, and she'd have to figure out what to do next. According to Riley, Cece and Tyler would return home tomorrow—Sunday—night, and Sasha wouldn't be blamed for another death she wasn't responsible for. It wasn't like Riley could've survived jumping off the bridge. Sasha's heart lurched from how the drop between the bridge and the water must've been a hundred feet.

Sasha could solve two problems at once, though. Assuming Riley's life meant nobody would discover Riley killed herself, and Ivan couldn't harm her if Sasha became a "ghost."

So, Sasha would be fine—she just had to give the performance of a lifetime.

CHAPTER 2

TYLER

Caring. Loyal. Reliable. Spontaneous.

Those were just some of the traits that Tyler loved about Jake. And that was why Tyler's Adam's apple throbbed while him and Jake drudged through the commuter parking lot towards an academic building on the other side of campus. Tyler didn't need a PhD for understanding how Jake wouldn't be happy about his secret.

Jake tilted his head, then ran his fingers through his spiked hair. "Something wrong, Ty?"

"Why would you ask that?"

"You're rather quiet."

Tyler craned his neck when nearby laughter echoed. Several girls strutted by him and Jake, and Tyler's stomach churned. He wanted nothing more than to have a carefree life, and not worry about what image he projected of himself. Living long and feeling life was long were two different things—life shouldn't have exhausted him so much. In fact, serendipity was why he gawked over Jake in the first place—Jake chatted him up a little over a year ago when they both attended the same party.

Tyler bit his lip. "That doesn't mean something is wrong."

"It's my job to care about you."

Tyler snickered. "I can look after myself."

"Nobody is accusing you of being weak."

"That's not what it sounds like."

"Tell me what's bothering you, because I can't help unless you do."

Tyler rubbed his neck. "It's Riley."

"What happened to not paying too much attention to her?"

"We share the same house," Tyler spat.

Jake exhaled a breath. "My bad. Anyway, please continue."

"She chatted with me yesterday, which was odd. Riley didn't even wanna go with Mom and me on the weekend getaway to Savannah."

Tyler couldn't get over Riley's friendliness the previous evening anytime soon. Nobody else would look after his mother if Tyler didn't appoint himself to the role. Riley would always be one of those people who fucked others with a smile. Assuming the worst in Riley was simply a survival skill. Especially in light of something that happened between them a long time ago—something nobody could never know.

"And why is that?" Jake asked while him and Tyler walked by a red, brick building.

"Don't you ever listen when I'm talking?" Tyler remained silent for a second. "She hasn't even said twenty words to me since she's been married to my mom."

"It's been several years," Jake said.

"Your point?" Tyler demanded.

"Maybe she's trying to be a different person. People can change."

"How astute of you—maybe you should write about that topic for an English paper."

Trees bobbed in the whistling wind, nipping Tyler's face. And Tyler cringed a little. Before Tyler could blink, it'd be Halloween. And then it'd be Thanksgiving, Christmas, and New Year's. And that meant another year of holidays without his stepmother. Kind of hard for him to enjoy the holidays when the image of blood spilling out of his stepmother's mouth would remain etched in his mind for the foreseeable future. Nothing said Merry Christmas more than death by a drunk driver. Even if five years passed since the event.

Jake winked. "Maybe."

Tyler pulled his backpack strap harder. "I'm not trying to be a buzzkill."

Jake ruffled Tyler's slicked back hair. "I'm only giving you a hard time. Besides, I meant what I said—be glad somebody cares about you."

Tyler didn't respond. Instead, he whistled while him and Jake passed another building. His mind returned to his deceased stepmother. Perhaps she was the reason why he held Riley to a high standard. If one stepmother challenged the Disney stereotype of the wicked stepmother, then Riley should've pretended to be decent. Doing so was the least he deserved—Tyler wasn't asking for a miracle.

"I'm sorry. That sounded worse than I meant it to," Jake continued.

"Don't worry—it takes more than attitude to scare me away.

"Good to know." Jake undid the top button of his Polo shirt. "Can I ask you a question?"

"You don't need my permission for that."

"Just trying to be considerate."

"Go ahead," Tyler said.

"Do you want things to be different with Riley?" Jake asked.

Tyler shrugged. "It'd be nice. But it's important not to get my hopes up."

"Interesting." Jake shifted left, avoiding a puddle. "Anyway, one more thing."

"I'm listening." Tyler's pulse blared in his ears. He kind of inferred where the conversation was headed, yet he inhaled several deep breaths. The universe might surprise him for once in his life.

"I nearly believed your babbling."

Tyler averted his gaze. "I'm not following."

Jake halted, then stood in front of Tyler, blocking him. "I'm not as oblivious as you might think."

"You're gonna have to be more specific."

"I know more than Riley is bugging you."

"You're reading too much into things."

"Not this time." Jake straightened Tyler's collar. The sweet and earthly scent of Jake's cologne wafted through the air, prickling Tyler's skin. "But it's okay if you can't be honest right now. Just know I'll be here for you whenever you're ready to tell me what's going on."

Dread once again filled Tyler's insides.

Tyler cursed under his breath while him and Jake entered the building for their first morning class. If Tyler wanted his boyfriend to believe him, then he'd become a better liar. And that fact made Tyler tremble. If he wanted to be more deceptive, then he might have no choice with spending time with Riley. Even if Tyler always shook his head from how Riley never met a price that was too much.

***

Tyler shoved his notebook, pencil, calculator, and textbook into his backpack the following day after his math class ended when Jake grinned at him.

"Wanna go off campus to Starbucks before our next class?" Jake offered.

"That won't be possible," said someone.

Tyler lifted his gaze off his beige desk—his teacher, Mr. Parker, was the one who had butted into his conversation with Jake.

At a first glance, Tyler should've made fists. His professor shouldn't have interfered in something that didn't involve him. Yet Tyler couldn't bring himself to do so. Having rage flare through him wasn't possible when Mr. Parker could've been a model. Whether it was his smooth face, parted hair, or green eyes didn't matter. Mr. Parker couldn't have been more than ten years older than him and Jake, i.e. only a few years younger than Tyler's mother.

Jake glared. "No offense, but this doesn't involve you."

Mr. Parker rose from his desk before rolling up his sleeves. He grinned, revealing his sparkly white teeth. In fact, Tyler should've had sunglasses—he would've been blind if Mr. Parker's teeth were any shinier. And Tyler kind of envied how snakes shed their skin. Attractiveness was one thing, yet Tyler couldn't help fretting over how Mr. Parker's appearance seemed too perfect.

"I'm not trying to ruin your plans—Tyler just emailed me about discussing a previous homework problem in greater depth than class time allows," Mr. Parker said, rubbing his dishwasher blond hair.

Jake glanced at Tyler. "Really?"

"Yes," Tyler said, nodding.

"Okay. We can go to Starbucks after our next class." Jake said.

"Good job today, though, Jake. You may have the highest average in the class," Mr. Parker said.

"Thanks." Jake marched out of the room without another word, leaving Tyler and Mr. Parker alone.

Tyler's backpack remained looped around his shoulders while Mr. Parker walked towards the door. The lock snicked after another beat.

Mr. Parker chuckled. "Take your backpack off, because we both know this is gonna be more than a second."

"My bad." Tyler placed his backpack on his chair while his heart thumped louder with each passing beat. Just because Tyler knew what came next, didn't mean he enjoyed keeping this secret from Jake. If anything, he'd stare at his bedroom ceiling a little longer tonight.

"There's something you should understand." Mr. Parker extended his hand, caressing Tyler's chin, yet Tyler didn't flinch. Not keeping a secret from Jake was one thing, yet this situation still defied labels. "You shouldn't feel ashamed for what you're about to do. You're doing what you need to in order to pass."

"Yeah."

"You therefore shouldn't feel like you're going to your execution." Mr. Parker's hand traveled from Tyler's chin to the top of his head. After that, Mr. Parker pushed a lock of Tyler's hair to the side before kissing him.

Tyler didn't push his professor away, though. The next sequences of events would happen with the same accuracy and precision a doctor used when performing surgery. Doing so was Tyler's only option. If he pretended that he was about to have fun with Mr. Parker, then he might actually enjoy the experience.

Mr. Parker unzipped his fly before returning his attention to Tyler. "You know what to do."

Tyler bent down, then leaned forward, mouth in front of Mr. Parker's waist. But no big deal if he'd blow his teacher in exchange from changing his D on the most recent quiz to a B+. Tyler was doing what any adult would've done in the real world—doing what needed to be done for survival. Sometimes, the best effort wasn't enough.

Tyler yanked his head away sometime later. "I hope you enjoyed yourself."

"I did." Mr. Parker moaned again. "But we're changing the game."

Tyler didn't know if he should be scared or happy—his arrangement with Mr. Parker couldn't get worse. Yet Tyler wouldn't tempt the universe. An invitation to make his life more complicated was the only thing the universe needed for doing so. It was a universe law—speak of something unpleasant, and the event would come true.

Tyler scrunched his eyebrows. "I don't understand."

"We both know you're gonna continue failing subsequent quizzes and tests."

"Okay…"

Mr. Parker licked his lips. "But I'm still gonna change your grades."

"Then what's the problem?" Tyler demanded.

"I don't want you dating Jake any longer, and I wanna meet at a motel next time." Mr. Parker plucked a loose eyelash from his right eye. "Nothing wrong with pushing the boundaries of our dynamic more."

In a perfect world, Tyler would've slapped Mr. Parker or stormed out of the classroom, yet he couldn't. Not if he wanted to pass math—a general education class he needed despite being a Creative Writing major. Mr. Parker had been right, and Tyler couldn't argue with him. His three tutoring sessions during the first week of the semester hadn't helped at all.

"Fine," Tyler mumbled.

"That's the spirit, but try to sound more optimistic next time," Mr. Parker said. "You should enjoy this arrangement too."

Tyler saved his energy, refusing to argue. As if he'd sleep with his professor if grades weren't at stake. Like everything else in life, his arrangement with Mr. Parker would be fleeting. And the situation could've been worse—at least Mr. Parker wasn't ugly.

So, Tyler would be fine one day—that day just wasn't today.

CHAPTER 3

RILEY

Perception was everything.

Like when a callous jock pretended not to care, yet would kill for his younger sister. Or when a woman said nice things to her daughter-in-law's face, but cursed her out in private. Or even when a cheerleader bullied a nerd, yet secretly lusted over the guy in private. Or like while Riley sat in the front passenger seat while the guy driving their car barreled down a new stretch of highway. Riley couldn't help smirking as her face remained pressed against the window. Sasha might've thought she killed herself several days ago, but that assumption couldn't be further from the truth.

Riley giggled. "Thank you for not judging me."

Josh took his gaze off the road for a beat. "What did I tell you about apologizing? You know I'd do anything for you."

"Thanks."

"I'm serious."

Riley sighed. "I'm not an idiot. You must hate how our interactions are limited to seedy motel rooms."

Someone should've given her a medal. If Riley didn't need Josh, then she wouldn't have ceded something. But no. Telling Josh what he wanted to hear, would only make him love her more.

"I'm a big boy," Josh said.

"Most men wouldn't be patient."

"There's one thing I've been wondering, though."

"And what's that?" Riley asked.

"Being with Cece doesn't freak you out?"

"You're gonna have to be more specific."

"I'm talking about sleeping with her."

Riley almost choked. "Oh, that…"

"You don't enjoy pretending with her, do you?"

"I've kissed girls before." Riley hadn't clenched her jaw. She had no problem using sex to get what she wanted—doing so meant she had the guts to do something most people wouldn't have. And that fact was great. Life got simpler for her once Riley discovered people were only as good as what they offered. And if that person was a woman, then fine. It wasn't like someone coerced her into kissing a toad.

"Okay." Josh sped faster when the driver behind him and Riley honked their car horn.

"I hope that isn't a big deal."

"I'm all for equality—I just don't want you to live a lie the rest of your life."

"I'm not gonna be married to Cece till I die."

"You must've thought about what's gonna happen after we're done with our mission in Los Angeles?"

Riley closed her eyes for a moment—time for deep breaths. Annoyance was a luxury she couldn't afford. Josh wasn't like her and required patience.

"Not really." Riley gripped her hair, which remained in a bun. "Just trying to take life one day at a time."

Josh chuckled. "Promise me one thing."

"And what's that?" Riley asked.

"Tell me that you aren't conning me."

"Why would you think that?" Riley drummed her fingers against her lap. If she wanted to control Josh, then she should've figured out what he was thinking no matter how difficult doing so might've been. Ignoring the issue wasn't an option. Then, Josh wouldn't know what happened when she moved onto the next person—whenever that day was.

"You disposed of Cece, and you could do the same to me."

Riley shifted her posture, then loosened her seatbelt. "It's not like I wanna hurt Cece—she was only a ticket to a better life. Besides, she's doing fine."

"What makes you think that?" Josh asked.

"I know my sister—she won't hesitate with assuming my life."

"How can you be certain?"

"It's the only way she'll escape being a human trafficking victim." Riley picked her nail. "And if she knows what's good for her, then she won't fuck up this gift. But this is Sasha we're talking about."

"Gift?"

Riley relished her victory over Sasha. To think Sasha assumed their relationship was mended provided Riley with more amusement than students having an unexpected snow day. If she got her way, then Sasha and her would never be real sisters. They couldn't—not after everything that happened. Things Sasha didn't even know about. Things Josh wasn't privy to either.

Only one person knew the real Riley, though. And that individual was long gone no matter how much Riley might've wished she could wave a magic wand and change the past.

Riley cackled. "I didn't have to extend her a lifeline, but I did."

"Being you must be nice."

"I don't follow."

"No offense." Josh stopped at a red light. "But you think you're perfect."

"I never said that."

"You didn't have to—I'm savvier than you realize." Josh resumed driving before turning left at the nearest EXIT sign. "Being a lawyer taught me a thing or two."

"Thanks for taking the leave of absence—that must not have made the senior partners happy," Riley said.

Telling Josh what he wanted to hear was easier for Riley than manipulating a kid into doing chores by offering candy. The only question was how long she could keep her dynamic with Josh going. No matter how much she might've wanted Josh to be clueless, Riley couldn't rely on that forever. If Josh shuddered from being tossed aside—even for a second—then Josh was smarter than Riley preferred.

"You might not be evil, but you're a bad listener," Josh said.

"Excuse me?"

"Were you paying attention several minutes ago? Being with you means accepting all of your flaws."

Riley's heart fluttered while the neon sign of an adjacent convenient store glowed. If the circumstances were different, then Josh would've been perfect for her. Someone's unconditional love was the one thing Riley wished she'd experience again. Like everyone else, she deserved that special person—someone who gave her permission to embrace the darkest parts of her.

***

Riley scooted to the edge of the bed the following evening.

The shrills of nighttime life roared outside the motel window. However, Riley hadn't given the issue of possible rowdy people a second thought. She also didn't regret sleeping with Josh—not even for a moment. Sex tricked Josh into believing their relationship was real, and was a consequence she could handle. And it wasn't like Josh wreaked of body odor—he didn't—so she could've done much worse for a fake boyfriend.

Arriving in LA tomorrow morning was why Riley hadn't looked Josh in the eye once since they checked into the motel room.

"Being human is okay," Josh said.

"I'm not some scared little girl," Riley interrupted.

"I wouldn't think any less of you if you wanted to vent—that's normal."

Riley scowled. "I don't actually want a relationship with my biological father. I just have to make him think I want patch our dynamic before ruining his life."

"Whatever you say."

"Let's go to bed." Riley clicked the lampshade on the table to the left of her off, then settled in bed, back to Josh. She wouldn't resume eye contact with Josh anytime soon. For now, Riley would be the woman who woke up in the morning without dark circles under her eyes. A good night sleep was the least she deserved. Believing in herself didn't mean she was oblivious to how her plan could be ruined. Almost as if her life was one, long game of chess.

CHAPTER 4

LOLA

Good girls didn't lie.

The idea was something Lola must've heard a thousand times since she was a kid. Yet she always reflected on that concept. Even if doing so passed being redundant a long time ago. Lola couldn't help herself—she often went back to how teachers and other adult figures over simplified life. Like while she remained on the right side of the bed with the comforter wrapped around her, matching Preston's frown with one of her own. It wasn't like she wanted to hurt him or that she was a bad person. Collateral damage was just an unfortunate part of life sometimes.

Preston grunted. "I'm serious. You can't use sex to distract me."

"You're making too much of a big deal out of this."

"I haven't met a single friend or relative."

"It's not my fault I keep to myself."

Preston tucked a lock of Lola's blonde hair out of the way. "It's more than that, and you know it."

"I just slept with you."

"I'm not an idiot," Preston said.

A scorching sensation jabbed Lola's stomach. Knowing where the conversation was headed didn't mean enjoying said fact. Once again, life would probably disappoint her, and she might end up alone and miserable. If she wasn't careful, that was.

"Come again?" Lola asked.

"You were hoping sex would distract me from continuing the argument."

Lola whimpered. "It's not my fault my parents died in a car crash."

"I never said that."

"I'm not sure what you want or expect from me at this point." Lola grabbed her night gown, which was folded on the table by the bed. She slipped into it in a matter of seconds. Like she was a ballet dancer sweating every step, because she couldn't have been naked for more than five seconds.

"Don't you understand why I'd be suspicious?" Preston demanded.

"Do you think I'm a serial killer, or something?"

"I didn't say that."

"But you were thinking that."

Preston let out a long breath. "I'm not asking for your whole life story. I just wanna know something. Something you haven't told me before."

"You've been reading too many romance novels."

"I'm serious."

Lola hung her head lower. "Don't you know how much I love you?"

"Saying you love me and actually loving me are two different things."

Lola expelled a nervous laugh. "Now I'm really cutting off your television—you've been watching too much *Dateline*."

"This isn't a joke."

"You're treating it like one," Lola said. "I've never given you a reason to doubt me before, and it'd be nice if you appreciated that fact."

"You're 24 years old," Preston said.

"Thanks for stating the obvious."

"I'm being serious." Preston wiped a bead of sweat from his forehead with one flick of his arm.

"Fine. What's your point?"

"I can accept if you don't have any family— tragedies happen. But you've gotta have one friend."

"I don't."

"Then you must be keeping something from me."

Lola jumped out of bed, then pointed a finger at Preston. "Get the hell out of my apartment. I don't have to stand here and take this."

Preston grunted. "Gladly."

"If you can't accept me, then that's your problem."

"I'm trying to be real with you." Preston shoved the comforter off him before grabbing his jeans and boxers, which were to the left of him. He slid into his boxers, jeans, and tee-shirt in a matter of seconds. After that, he lunged out of bed and put on his flip flops. "I hope you know what a big mistake you're making."

"It's not your job to lecture me," Lola said.

Preston sneered. "Maybe not. But you lost your one chance at happiness, and you'll have to accept that one day."

"Leave!" Lola exclaimed.

"Have it your way." Preston exited her bedroom and the door's slamming echoed several seconds later.

The pinewood aroma from whatever herbal deodorant Preston used lingered in the air. Lola closed her eyes before tears welled in them. More rage currently shot through Lola's body than the anger a child might've felt if finding out their birthday was canceled. Her complicated life wasn't her fault. But it wasn't like Preston would ever understand that fact—some truths were stranger than fiction. Lola didn't know how she would've explained her past to Preston even if she wanted to.

Deep breaths for her, though. She'd be okay one day. And she would do whatever she did in the past when life disappointed—live with the pain.

Lola shook her head. She didn't have to accept how she'd never be happy. Instead, she'd call someone.

So, Lola opened the drawer from the dresser next to her bed, and grabbing her burner phone.

"Hello?" said the other person on the other end of the line.

Lola swallowed the lump in her throat. "You've gotta come to Los Angeles immediately, Grandma. I've got a big problem."

"Fine. I'll be on the next flight."

***

"Thanks for meeting me." Lola stood the following afternoon when a woman with blonde lowlights and highlights approached her table at the outdoor café.

Vanessa rolled her eyes. "Don't be so formal."

Lola forced a grin. "Sit. I ordered you a cappuccino—I even remembered to ask for cinnamon on top of the foamed milk."

"Thanks." Vanessa obeyed Lola, then sipped her beverage. Except she spat it out. And Lola could've kicked herself. So much for warning her grandmother about the drink being hot.

"You're lucky I don't have a problem visiting you on a whim," Vanessa said.

"Don't make me feel guilty."

"What couldn't you tell me over the phone?" Vanessa asked.

"I had to break up with another guy." Lola rubbed her headscarf and pushed her Aviator sunglasses further up her nose. As if any distraction saved her from grappling with the truth she'd be running from for the last seven years.

Vanessa clutched her pearl necklace. "Sorry to hear that."

"Don't get me wrong. Sending me money every month is amazing, but I can't keep doing this."

Vanessa did a 180 around the café—a couple of people sat in chair at an adjacent table—then leaned closer. "You made the choice to run away."

"What was I supposed to do?" Lola took in a deep breath. "That stupid bitch tried to kill me."

"You'll be interested to know Sasha is back in Connecticut."

Lola gave her grandmother a dirty look. "Why?"

"I don't know. The only thing I know is that Katrina picked her up at the train station," Vanessa said before sipping her cappuccino.

Lola's lips quivered. "God. This is so fucked up—it's not like I don't feel guilty for Sasha not knowing the truth after all these years."

"You can call yourself Lola all you want, but we both know you're the real Riley."

"Not so loud," Lola spat.

"It's not like I haven't made sacrifices too. Once Sasha went to prison, I distanced myself from her, because I didn't give her any family money. Or maybe that doesn't matter to you."

Lola counted to twenty in her head. She couldn't alienate the one person who'd been there for her that night. The one night she realized her family was more complicated than she could've ever imagined. The night she lost her innocence. The night her entire life changed.

***

Lola's back hairs rose while walking through the woods a couple of weeks after her seventeenth birthday.

She would've rather been buried alive than walk through the woods when it was pitch-black, yet she didn't have a choice. When her stepfather—or Vincent as she referred to him, because he'd never mold into the stepfather role—summoned her, she couldn't say no.

The wind howled and a tree branch snapped, then leaves crunched under Lola's sneakers. Except Vincent wasn't standing in the clearing. A girl with a similar weight and blonde hair as her stood in Vincent's place.

"Sasha?" Lola asked. "I thought you were out of town with the debate team?"

The girl remained silent.

"If this is your idea of a joke, it isn't funny," Lola continued.

The girl smirked. "Nice to meet you, Riley."

"Who are you? And why do you like Sasha and me?"

"The name's Katrina."

Lola pouted. "You didn't answer my question."

"Have some patience."

Lola stomped her feet. "I'm serious."

"You're rather rude, aren't you? Apparently, some stereotypes are true, because your grandmother being a real estate heiress hasn't helped you."

"You don't know anything about my life."

"I know it's a life I should've been a part of—something that was denied to me because of dumb luck. But that's about to end," Katrina said.

"What are you talking about?"

"Look alive."

Lola cocked her head, yet she was too late. Before she could respond, Vincent smacked her in the back of her head with a rock and she was out cold.

***

"Are you listening to me?" Vanessa pressed, snapping Lola out of her digression.

"I'm sorry." Lola removed her hair tie, letting her locks down—they extended a few inches beyond her shoulders.

Vanessa's nostrils flared. "You're something else. It'd be nice if you acknowledged me sacrificing my relationship with Sasha just this once."

"That can wait till later."

"Sometimes I wonder why I bother." Vanessa finished her cappuccino. "I'm beginning to think I shouldn't have come here on a whim."

Lola's hair bobbed in the wind. "That can wait. I'm concerned about what uou said about Sasha and Katrina at the train station. You don't think Sasha knows Katrina isn't me, do you?"

"I don't think so—she'd never willing speak to her if she finds out the person she thinks is you is really someone else."

Lola continued biting her nail for the longest time. The idea forming in her head might've been crazy, yet the plan might work. Sometimes, the most radical ideas were the ones worth pursuing—her life couldn't get worse.

So, Lola didn't have any doubt for once in her life.

Vanessa's face lit up. "What's going on?"

"Maybe it's time we end this sham, and Sasha finds out how her, Katrina, and me are really identical triplets."

CHAPTER 5

SASHA

Sasha had been "Riley" a little over week.

The shift in her life was easier than anticipated. Like with how Riley's iPhone, credit cards, car keys, and driver's license were in Riley's purse inside her Mercedes parked by the bridge. And said fact was great—her arrangement could've fallen apart before it began if she couldn't eat, sleep, and breathe the role.

Sasha wasn't stupid, though. One false move, and Cece and Tyler might discover the truth, so that was why she remained silent while sitting at the dining room table with Cece and Tyler. Even if the atmospheric setting from the two lit candles on the middle of the table should've calmed Sasha.

Cece looked up from her plate. "Something wrong, Riley?"

"Probably figuring out how to take more of your money," Tyler said.

Cece shot Tyler a look. "Don't be like that."

Sasha's stomach sank—she couldn't fault Tyler's attitude no matter how positive she might've wanted to be. If circumstances were different, then her and Tyler could bond over how Riley wronged them.

"It's fine," Sasha mumbled.

Cece twirled a strand of her cherry red hair. "Don't make excuses for Tyler. He'll never learn his place in life if you coddle him."

"You're one to talk," Tyler snapped, sliding his elbows onto the velvet tablecloth. "You resent me because of getting pregnant at fifteen."

"That's not true," Cece said.

"Yeah, it is." Tyler took in a deep breath. "But you know what? It's not my fault you were too stupid to use a condom or weren't on the Pill."

"I don't know what's gotten into you." Cece wiped her lip, then placed the napkin next to her plate. "This isn't appropriate conversation."

"I'm not offended," Sasha said.

Tyler snorted. "First time for everything."

Cece finished the rest of her white wine. "If you have a problem with something, then I expect you to communicate your feelings in a mature fashion— not cause a scene."

"Not everyone is well adjusted like you," Tyler said.

"Let's not fight." Sasha broke off a piece of chicken with her fork, and dunked it in sauce before devouring the bit in a matter of seconds. The lemon flavor even electrified her taste buds—not too tart or too bitter. Almost as if Sasha making the perfect sauce resembled *Goldilocks and the Three Bears*.

"What's wrong with you?" Tyler asked.

Sasha gasped. "Pardon me?"

"It's like you're a whole different person," Tyler replied.

"Don't be rude—Riley is still my wife no matter how much you might disapprove of me remarrying." Cece poured more wine.

"You're right—stepmother number one was best," Tyler said.

Sasha didn't need to know much about Tyler's life for empathy—it was called being a good person. She had enough sleepless nights over the years for appreciating how palpable emotional scars sometimes were.

"It's not my fault she died," Cece said.

Tyler raised his eyebrows. "Never said it was. By the way, her name was Janice."

"It'd be so amazing if we got along," Sasha said.

"It's also not my fault your father overdosed before you were born," Cece said.

Sasha clapped her hand over her mouth. Losing a stepmother proved challenging enough, yet Sasha didn't wanna begin contemplating what psychological wounds Tyler might've had from never meeting his father. Perhaps the daddy issue was why Sasha sympathized with Tyler even more than she had at the start of dinner—Sasha's father abandoned her and Riley when they were only four years old.

"Never said it was," Tyler said.

Cece wrinkled her nose. "You might as well have. I see the resentment in your eyes."

"You aren't innocent. Riley might be greedy, but you only married her because having a blonde wife looks good," Tyler said.

Sasha pursed her lips. Perhaps Tyler was meaner than she first anticipated, and might've had something in common with Riley. No matter how much Sasha might've wanted to believe Riley was capable of being a good person, that wasn't the case. And any hope for having a good relationship with her sister vanished ages ago—it wasn't like she could enjoy their brief reconciliation—Riley's suicide tainted that.

Cece shuddered. "That's not true, and you know it."

"Then maybe you should practice lying more, because you're terrible at it." Tyler stood, yet didn't push his chair in. Instead, he raced out of the room so fast that the painting on the wall behind Sasha almost fell off.

"I'm sorry you witnessed that." Cece chugged more wine. "But I should thank you for one thing."

"And what's that?" Sasha gripped her glass tighter, yet didn't sip her wine. Staying sober for this conversation might've been best. No telling what would happen later in the evening since it was only a few minutes past seven o'clock. "I didn't do anything."

Cece giggled. "Don't be modest—your attitude was wonderful tonight. Almost like you really care about Tyler."

Sasha patted Cece's hand. "I do."

"Good. Maybe one day the lie will be true," Cece said.

***

Deep breaths were the only thing Sasha needed.

Sasha knew she'd be okay—eventually, that was. She was only knocking on Tyler's bedroom door—not entering a warzone. It wasn't like Sasha played the situation stupidly. Waiting a full twenty-four hours before chatting with Tyler might've meant he calmed down.

So, enough stalling for her. She made a fist, then beat it against Tyler's bedroom door.

"Who is it?" Tyler asked.

"It's Riley."

"I don't wanna talk to you."

"I promise I won't judge."

"Leave me alone."

Sasha's throat constricted—she couldn't give up on Tyler. Perhaps if someone had been there for Riley, then she wouldn't have been abused in addition to how she wouldn't have committed suicide. The idea was worth a thought, at least—her life couldn't get worse than it was.

Sasha knocked for a second time. "I'm not leaving until you let me in."

"Fine," Tyler barked.

The door clinked, and Tyler opened it. He gesticulated at Sasha before sitting down on his bed.

Sasha wouldn't judge him for the clothes seeping out of the hamper, the dust coating his bookshelf, or the books and papers cluttering Tyler's desk on the other end of the room. Tidying up could wait no matter how much she almost ran to the hallway closet and grab the cleaning supplies.

Tyler's face drooped. "Well? You wanted to chat."

Sasha coughed. "Right. I'm not gonna pretend to understand your life, but there's no reason why we can't get along."

"You've never taken an interest in my life."

Sasha resisted rolling her eyes. Riley's past with Tyler was just that—in the past. So, she and Tyler would get along soon enough.

"If something was bothering you, then I'd want to know," Sasha said.

"Why?"

Tyler just couldn't make things easy for her, and Sasha had to hold onto her patience as long as possible. If she didn't, then she wouldn't be able to help Tyler. And if she couldn't do that, then no absolution for not helping Riley deal with Vincent's sexual abuse or being unable to detect Riley's suicidal tendencies.

"It's called being a decent person," Sasha said.

"Never stopped you before."

Sasha couldn't help her current regret. If she attended college and took a psychology class—then she would've known how to deal with a nineteen-year-old—because she'd say the wrong thing if she wasn't careful. But money was a luxury Sasha could only dream of when flipping through magazines and sighing at dolled up celebrities back in her Manhattan apartment—affording electricity proved miracle enough.

"Nothing you say will push me away, but go ahead. Give it your best shot," Sasha said.

Tyler grunted. "Have it your way."

Sasha crossed her arms. "I'm waiting."

"What if you had to hurt someone you loved if it was for the greater good?"

"Is this about Jake? Is someone making you do something you don't want to?"

No matter how sane Sasha might've pretended to be, her mind couldn't help going to dark places. Some people had no qualms about hurting others, and Sasha wouldn't fault herself for contemplating if someone was messing with Tyler's relationship. Stranger things happened, and Sasha was proof— like her assuming Riley's life.

"Doesn't matter. The point is, I asked you a question," Tyler said.

Sasha's blank expression didn't disappear. Giving bad advice was the only thing worse than not helping at all. And if Sasha had it her way, then Tyler would give more specificity.

"Forget it," Tyler said, shaking his head. "This was stupid, so just go—you can't help with this, and you're probably just bored from all your shopping."

Thinking twice about her response wasn't necessary for Sasha, so she exited Tyler's bedroom. She might not have been able to help him today, but she would someday. It was a promise, and the least Tyler deserved—his emotional stature just wasn't something that could be faked no matter how good a liar he might've been.

CHAPTER 6

TYLER

Forcing himself not to have an emotional outburst while sitting at a table in back of the local Starbucks was the only thing Tyler could do the following afternoon after Sasha tried chatting with him. Tyler might not have known how the remainder of his life would unfold, yet he'd trust life would be okay. Doing so was his only option. Math was one semester, whereas he had the rest of his life to fix his relationship with Jake.

Tyler should have made eye contact with Jake, though. They could only sit in silence for so long.

"What's with the impromptu outing, Ty?" Jake asked.

Tyler quirked his eyebrows. "You were the one who proposed going to Starbucks between classes the other day."

Jake chuckled. "That's my point—we both know I'm the spontaneous one."

"Can't I surprise you once?"

"Just tell me what's going on."

"You were right." Tyler sipped his Venti Caramel Macchiato, yet the mixture of the bitter espresso and sweet caramel flavors escaped him. Certain situations were beyond comfort, because the knot in Tyler's stomach only grew larger since him and Jake arrived at Starbucks. "I'm keeping something from you."

Jake rubbed Tyler's hand. "It'll be okay—I promise I'll listen."

Tyler couldn't swallow the lump in his throat. Listening was the least of his problems—he had to do most of the talking, not Jake.

"Are you in trouble?" Jake asked, lowering his voice.

"Not exactly."

"Then what?"

"I want to break up with you," Tyler blurted.

Jake's eyes bulged. "I don't think I heard you correctly."

"I'm serious." Tyler grabbed a napkin from the metal dispenser on the middle of the table, then ripped it into dozens of pieces. "This relationship isn't work for me, and we need to go our separate ways."

"Try again."

Tyler's jaw trembled. He should've known Jake wouldn't go away without demanding a serious explanation. Tyler was the one whose eyes almost popped out of their sockets from Jake's 4.0 GPA the previous year.

Jake's face sagged. "Did I do something wrong?"

"This has nothing to do with you—it's me."

"Yeah, right. Nobody means that when they use that excuse."

"I wanna focus on my studies."

"Is this because you're worried about passing math?" Jake demanded.

Tyler's pulse pounded in his ears. He didn't know what he would have done if Jake discovered the arrangement with Mr. Parker. The current sorrow in Jake's eyes had nothing on the vein on Jake's forehead that would've popped if he discovered how low Tyler stooped just to pass a class, and Tyler couldn't ignore that fact. Tyler hadn't recovered from the shouting match between Jake and his father last year when Jake's parents bickered over their divorce.

Jake's gaze remained on Tyler. "You didn't answer my question."

"I did—you just weren't paying attention. I'm gonna focus on my school work this year, but I wish the best of luck with the rest of your life."

Jake sobbed. "So, what? You're gonna pretend we don't know each other?"

"That'd be easier," Tyler murmured.

"I'm done. Come find me when you're ready for a real relationship." Jake rose, then dashed out of the Starbucks without grabbing his latte.

Tyler shifted his head for a second. A barista at the front of the store pressed a button on the blender, and a grinding noise—a sound Tyler would've expected from a lawnmower—echoed. Then, Tyler's mind drifted back towards Jake. Tyler might not have been certain of much, but there was one feeling he couldn't shake. The twisted irony of life. Jake once again gave him an opportunity for honesty, yet Tyler lied.

***

Tyler rolled onto his back several hours later, then crawled to the edge of the bed.

His focus remained on the comforter while Mr. Parker couldn't stop grinning. So, Tyler did the only thing he could. He reminded himself that the situation would be over one day and how this transgression might provide good fodder for a future short story. Doing so was the only thing he could do. The alternative to his positive spin was much worse, because his back hairs would've remained up.

Mr. Parker chuckled. "What? Nothing to say?"

"This is a business transaction."

"Whatever."

"I'm serious—I don't care about you."

"We can revisit that subject in several weeks once we've had more time to enjoy our exclusive relationship."

Bile almost seeped up through Tyler's throat. The idea of never being with Jake again was crueler than a kid attending summer school every summer until graduating high school.

"Are you kidding?" Tyler asked.

Mr. Parker made a pig-like snort. "Nope, I'm serious."

"Have you forgotten about your wife? Or maybe she doesn't mean anything to you?"

"I care about Rose," Mr. Parker stammered.

For a moment, Tyler could have skipped through town. Normally, he wouldn't take joy in someone else's hesitation. Yet Mr. Parker was the exception. If Tyler would agonize about ending his relationship with Jake, then Mr. Parker deserved to be miserable too. It was only fair. Tyler would have been damned if he was the only one suffering.

"There's something you should know," Tyler said.

Mr. Parker winked. "Oh, yeah? And what's that?"

"This is only for the semester."

"We'll see about that."

"I'm not kidding." Tyler made a clucking noise with his tongue. "Jake is the one I want to be with, not you."

Mr. Parker gave Tyler a mock frown. "Ouch. You know how to hurt a guy."

"Enjoy this arrangement while it lasts."

"Please. Nobody can resist me."

"Having a high opinion of yourself must be nice."

"Nothing wrong with knowing my worth."

"Keep telling yourself that," Tyler said.

"If you really cared about Jake, then you wouldn't have ended things with him."

Tyler forced laughter. "We both know the situation is more complicated."

"If you insist."

"Remember something." Tyler got out of bed, then put his boxers and jeans on before sliding his frayed, leather belt through the loop. "If you cause trouble for my eventual reconciliation with Jake, then I'll tell your wife everything."

"You wouldn't do that."

"Try me."

"There's something you should realize." Mr. Parker slid over to Tyler's spot on the bed. After that, he pulled Tyler against his body—so close that the lingering smoky odor from Mr. Parker's cigarettes practically burned Tyler's eyes. "This isn't only about my pleasure—you need to enjoy yourself as well."

Tyler scoffed. "Please. We both know you're only sleeping with me because your wife kicked you out of your bed. Could it be because she knows you're gay?"

"I'm not gay. I'm experimenting," Mr. Parker said.

"Fine," Tyler said.

Mr. Parker's pupils dilated. "What do you say? How about round two?"

"Interesting offer." Tyler put his head in front of Mr. Parker's face, lips almost grazing his professor's mouth. However, Tyler pushed Mr. Parker back onto to the bed, and his head thumped against the pillow. "But I should get home before my mother and stepmother wonder where I am. Have fun jerking yourself off, though."

Tyler snatched his shirt from the ground in front of the bed before putting on his sneakers. He even smirked while leaving the motel room. Just because Tyler didn't have all the power in the situation didn't mean he couldn't have fun. Doing so was the least he deserved—it was the only comfort Tyler had until reuniting with Jake.

***

Tyler returned to his family's mansion the following afternoon after arriving home from his last class. And his heart raced upon discovering who Riley was having tea with in the living room.

"What's going on?" Tyler folded his arms after approaching Riley and Jake.

Riley smiled at Tyler—like she actually cared about her stepson. "Jake wanted to chat with Cece, but she's at work."

A python might as well have wrapped itself around Tyler. He doubted how life could get more claustrophobic. If Tyler had it his way, then Jake would've forgotten both his name and relationship while returning to his life before their relationship. Having one event go right was the least he deserved if he'd stew in his own pain till the middle of December when the semester ended.

Tyler kicked his feet against the gray carpet. "You didn't answer my question."

"No need for tantrums," Riley said.

Please. Patronizing behavior was the only thing filling him with more disgust than not being with Jake. There was nothing worse for Tyler than an adult telling him how to feel. He wasn't some kid who needed protection from the truth about Santa Claus.

Jake brushed a piece of lint off his shirt before rising. "I'll be blunt. I'm more than a little worried about you."

"And you decided to talk to my stepmother?" Tyler demanded.

"I didn't have a choice even if you'd rather talk with the devil than Riley." Jake turned to Riley. "No offense or anything."

Riley tucked a lock of hair behind her ear. "None taken."

"Wait." Sweat dripped down Tyler's back. "Is your visit due to me breaking up with you? Because you've got no idea what's going on."

Jake's eyebrows knitted together. "I thought you were concerned about your school work? Or was that a lie?"

Tyler would learn how to greater resemble a sociopath later. He was even closer to making one wrong move, and he couldn't have that. Not now. Not ever.

Tyler drew in a breath. "I'm not pulling something. I meant what I said, you've got no idea what's going on, because my classes are more stressful than you can imagine. But, hey. Maybe you don't care—you just show up to class and get an A."

"Jealous of me?" Jake asked.

Tyler pointed a finger towards the front door. "This is my home, so leave."

"Fine by me." Jake rushed out of the living room and walked out the front door before Tyler could blink.

Tyler did something all too familiar while Riley sipped her tea. He closed his eyes, mind focusing on waves crashing into the shore and the warmth jolting his palms when picking up sand at Tide Beach, his favorite beach. Maybe, just maybe, his life would be okay if he wanted it enough.

CHAPTER 7

RILEY

Riley didn't think twice about ringing the doorbell.

Even if there was a hole in the roof, eroded shudders, and peeling paint on the house's exterior. She could scoff about the house being a dump later—only one thing mattered to her while her and Josh held hands, waiting. Manipulating herself into her biological father's life so she could eventually ruin said life.

The door creaked, revealing a man with stubble and an untucked shirt. His hair flopped in the wind, not helping his appearance. And Riley couldn't help being thankful for once in her life. She must have gotten her looks from her mother, because she wouldn't have been caught dead with shaggy hair.

The man grunted. "Can I help you?"

"There's no easy way for me to say this, so I'm gonna be direct. I'm your daughter, Riley." Riley shoved her hands into her jacket pockets.

"I don't have a daughter," Adam said.

"Yeah, you do," Riley said.

Josh bit his lip. "We aren't here to cause trouble."

"I've got no reason to be believe you," Adam said.

"You're the one who walked out on Sasha and me," Riley said.

Adam looked passed Riley and towards Josh. "Who are you?"

"He's just a friend," Riley interrupted.

Josh shook his head, and a scorching sensation jabbed Riley's stomach. No matter how much her relationship with Josh would never be real, she'd be more mindful of what she said. Believing a lie—such as how her and Josh were "dating"—wasn't enough. She had to live the lie, because she couldn't lose the support system in her life.

Adam forced in a breath. "What? Are you here to collect money?"

"I thought we could become better acquainted," Riley said.

"That's rather presumptuous," Adam said.

Josh rubbed his cheek. "No need for cruelty."

"It's the truth." Adam remained silent for a beat. "Look. I'm sure you're a nice woman, but I don't want a relationship with you and Sasha."

"Then you admit what you did?" Riley asked.

Adam scratched the stubble on his neck. "Fine. You're right. I shouldn't have walked out on your mother, you, and Sasha."

A bird perched on a nearby tree branch chirped, and Riley sighed. No matter how important her mission was, she couldn't deny how life would've been simpler if she were an animal. Her mind wouldn't have always been spinning. The situation with her father would go her way, and that was it. No discussion about it. Good things had been owed to her for ages, and she would collect ASAP. It wasn't like Riley wanted to live forever. She just needed the people who wronged her to pay.

"There's more than abandonment at play here, and you know it," Riley said.

"You're wasting my time," Adam said.

"Don't you wanna know me?" Riley asked.

Adam ran his fingers through his hair, accentuating its greasy texture. "Nope. Anyway, have a good day."

Her father slammed the door without another word, and Riley's jaw lowered. Screaming was the only thing she could do. She might have been a lot of things, yet Adam wanting nothing to do with her was one thing she hadn't anticipated. Manipulating her father wasn't a stretch—Sasha had been more than eager for a second chance—and she just couldn't fathom why hurting Adam had to be so difficult.

Josh patted Riley's shoulder. "I'm sorry."

"I'm not accepting defeat."

"I don't expect you to."

"I didn't give up my life in Connecticut for nothing." Riley brushed Josh's hand away. This moment wasn't the time for faking intimacy. Not when her plan might have ended before it began. "I'm gonna get what's rightfully mine."

"Do you wanna grab a drink?" Josh asked.

"Sure. That'd be great."

"I did have one question," Josh said, stuttering.

"And what's that?"

"Why didn't you introduce me as your boyfriend?"

"If you want me to spell it out for you, then fine." Riley played with her ponytail. "We can't risk anyone finding out about our affair—not even if we're on the opposite side of the country as Cece.

"Whatever," Josh whispered.

Riley's heart hadn't shattered from beating too much—she had plenty of time before worrying about Josh losing interest in her. Getting that drink was the only issue that mattered. An outing was the least she deserved.

***

Riley seized the nail file on the bedside table while a guy laid next to her on the motel bed, studying his biceps. Josh decided to visit an art museum, and Riley declined—she'd choose booze, sex, and money over something studious any day. So, Riley had the afternoon to herself, and she'd have fun.

Amusement was the least she deserved. Only a day passed since the conversation with Adam, yet Riley wouldn't stop complaining anytime soon. She'd inch into her father's life, and there wasn't anything he could do.

Ted looked her in the eye. "Something wrong?"

Riley's lips curled. If she bothered caring about anyone but herself, then she would've appreciated some random guy caring. But no. Riley would separate sex like she separated every other event from her emotions.

"I'm fine," Riley said.

"I wouldn't have pegged you as the seedy motel type."

"Looks are deceiving."

"No shit," Ted said.

Riley finished filing her nails. "This was fun, but you should leave."

"You're kicking me out?"

"I've got a boyfriend," Riley blurted.

Ted blinked. "Seriously?"

"I'm not joking, and you might wanna leave before he returns."

"Don't say another word." Ted dressed himself in a matter of seconds before looking back at Riley. "Wanna do this again sometime?"

Riley giggled. "I'm more of the hit and run type."

Ted winked. "No worries, but thanks again for a great afternoon."

"Don't mention it."

Riley was alone before she knew it, and she stroked her chin. A vile stench filled the air, so the hotel maid must've tidied when she picked up Ted at the bar across the street.

Whatever. It wasn't like anything was taken— her iPad remained tucked away in the drawer, evident by her spotting it before slipping into lingerie half an hour earlier. Her mind soon returned to Adam. There just had to be a way for conning Adam and making him see her vulnerable side before gutting him.

***

Josh's mouth gaped the following morning after he finished checking his email on his iPhone while standing by the motel room window.

"Don't tell me the senior partners are hassling you over taking time off?" Riley asked, sitting up in bed. "They must know you work hard and deserve a vacation."

"If only life was that simple," Josh said.

"I don't understand."

Josh smacked his head with his free hand. "Shit. I shouldn't have been so stupid."

Riley didn't respond—she couldn't twist the situation to her favor unless she knew what game they were planning. Instead, she met Josh's gaze. More specifically, the torn condom wrapper on the floor in front of the bed.

So much for her discretion. If Riley got her way, then Josh wouldn't have detected any hint of malicious intentions. Yet Riley would remind herself later how she should've known better than for hoping life would go her way. Even if having the entire universe wrapped around her finger provided more intoxication than any drug could have.

"I can explain." Riley's fingers tingled, blood pumping through her veins faster. She'd definitely curse the universe out later. Having her father not cooperate proved bad enough, and Riley didn't know what she would've done if Josh ditched her before she was done with him.

Her life would be okay, though. People didn't leave Riley—she left them. So, she'd do what she always did. Make up such an outrageous lie that Josh wouldn't have a choice with believing her. Yeah, she would be fine. Lying was easier than breathing for her.

Josh put his hands on his hips. "Give it your best shot."

"The maid must've had a quickie when she cleaned the room," Riley said. "I grabbed several drinks at The Falcon yesterday while you were at the museum."

Riley could have squealed. She just didn't understand why some people had trouble lying. The best lies weren't completely false—those misdeeds were busted first. The best lie contained a shred of truth. Like her drinking at the bar yesterday—Josh couldn't prove that hadn't happened.

"Give me one reason why I should believe you," Josh said.

"You mean more to me than Cece." Riley blew a lose strand of her hair out of the way. "You're helping me in ways she never would, because Adam is gonna pay for what he did."

"If you ever cheat on me again, then I'll leave," Josh said after a beat.

Riley didn't bother hiding her smile. No big deal if Josh discovered her indiscretion. The point was, Josh hadn't dumped her, so she'd see another morning with Josh. Besides, she would do what she always did when men doubted her. Use sex as a distraction. It wasn't like Riley would close her eyes. In fact, Josh seeing through her crap was all Riley needed for her tongue wetting her lips. Weak men were the only thing she hated more than her father. And maybe, just maybe, she'd believe her and Josh were in a real relationship—for a fleeting moment, that was.

CHAPTER 8

LOLA

Making a plan and following through with said plan were two different things. And that fact was why Lola suggested going out for drinks to her grandmother about a week into her LA vacation. It wasn't like they could fly back to Connecticut on a whim and expose Katrina for everything she did. Even if the idea would've given Lola a greater euphoria than eating pizza fresh from the oven.

Not even Lola was that impulsive. She might not have known everything about Katrina—yet she couldn't have been stupid after masquerading as her for all these years. And that was why Lola and her grandmother could only strike when they were ready.

"Something wrong?" Vanessa sipped her martini while she and Lola remained at their table in back of the bar. "I'll chat with the bartender if he didn't give you enough tequila in your margarita."

"Let's see." Lola gulped her drink. The mixture of the bitter tequila and sweet and tart flavors from the lime juice jolted her taste buds. Almost as if she couldn't have made a better drink herself. "No, it's fine."

"Good. There's nothing worse than someone making a stingy drink."

"Can I quote you?" Lola asked.

Vanessa giggled. "Sure."

"I hope you aren't mad at me for this outing—it's not like I attract attention. The Falcon is just a nice play for relaxing."

"I trust you." Vanessa finished her martini before shoving it to the edge of the table. "It's not like Katrina will track you down."

Lola couldn't help widening her eyes—she hadn't once expected her grandmother's confession about believing her. Even if their familial connection entailed having an innate sense of loyalty.

Lola didn't have to think about her response. "That's true."

"But I can't stay in Los Angeles forever."

"I know."

"Although a break from Connecticut is great," Vanessa said.

Lola rested a free hand under her chin. "Sometimes, I can't comprehend how my parents would do something so despicable."

"People make mistakes."

"You shouldn't be defending them selling a baby on the black market."

"I'm not." Vanessa frowned at Lola. "I'm pointing out how the situation might be more complicated than you realize. The decision also wasn't your mother's choice. Adam sold Katrina on the black market, not her."

"Doesn't make it okay."

"What was your mother supposed to do?" Vanessa demanded.

Lola shrugged, then took a more than generous gulp of her cocktail. "Don't ask me. I never wanna have children."

"Don't be silly, dear. You could change your mind in ten years."

"I don't think so."

"No harm indulging me." Vanessa loosened her collar.

"I wouldn't have children if someone put a gun to my head."

Lola's cheeks flushed while she soaked up her surroundings. Life might not have been perfect, but Lola didn't disagree with how there were worse places for having drinks than The Falcon. No questionable aroma—like the smell of piss and stale beer—lingered in the air. And none of the overhead lights flickered above Lola, which was another fact she appreciated. Lola watched enough indie films for understanding how bars were sometimes seedy like motels—like the one across the street from The Falcon.

"You'll change your mind—I just know it," Vanessa said.

Lola played with her straw. "My body; my life."

"There's one thing I can't get over," Vanessa said.

"And what's that?"

"It's kind of ironic how Sasha worked for the man who helped engineer the whole scenario."

Lola's eyebrows swung upward. "You shouldn't keep tabs on Sasha if you can't be in her life."

"The little things are the only thing I have."

Glass clanked behind the bar, and Lola jerked her head. Whether Lola accepted the truth or not, the noise brought back a certain event. Something that would have stayed buried for the rest of her life if she had her way.

***

An ache jolted Lola's head when she opened her eyes. She rubbed her head, then cringed from her blood caked finger.

She just couldn't believe how someone hit her hard enough for bleeding—tragedies were supposed to be read about in newspapers. Not played in real time as if Lola resembled a doll and had no control over her life.

Lola scanned her surroundings while sitting. A gust of wind pushed a pile of red, orange, and yellow leaves, which almost had a slight glow to them against the nighttime sky. Whatever. At least she'd been left to die as opposed to being buried alive.

A chill rolled up Lola's back. The person she chatted with before Vincent attacked her wasn't Sasha. Yet the person still looked like her and Sasha. Almost as if they Riley and Sasha were identical triplets, not identical twins.

An owl hooted, and she muffled her screams. For all she knew, the girl and Vincent were nearby, so she wouldn't make a sound. Not if she wanted to live.

So, Lola did the only thing she could—pass by the clearing and continue running until arriving at the highway on the other sides of the woods.

Except Lola didn't count on her belabored breathing when she arrived on the other side of the woods, trying to flag down a driver—someone, anyone, who would take her to her grandmother's house. Lola's grandma was the only person she could depend on.

A station wagon halted, then the front passenger seat window rolled down. A woman with gray hair wrapped in a bun, yet who still had wrinkle-free skin, was the driver. And she didn't have to think twice about hitching a ride with this lady—the chances were pretty good that the woman wasn't a serial killer.

Lola panted. "I can't explain, but I really need a ride."

"Sure," said the lady.

Lola paced back and forth on her grandmother's front porch, waiting for her grandma's appearance. Maybe, just maybe, Vanessa was home. Fuck patience. She'd ring the doorbell again. Then, Vanessa might understand she couldn't be ignored.

"What are you doing here?" Vanessa asked after opening the front door.

"You've gotta help me, Grandma."

Vanessa looped her hands around Lola. "Absolutely. Just tell me what's wrong."

"Someone tried to kill me tonight," Lola said, each subsequent breath requiring more effort than the previous one. "But I should start with the girl who looks exactly like Sasha and me."

Vanessa's jaw quaked. "Oh. I see you've met your third sibling."

***

Vanessa's slurping snapped Lola out of her digression.

Yeah. If Lola got through the night she almost died, then she'd get through anything. She would just remember to be patient.

Lola smiled. "I really am thankful for everything you've done for me."

"I know." Vanessa finished her second martini, then slid it towards the table's edge.

"Why give me a hard time?"

"That's my job."

Lola's cheeks burned. "Good point."

"I might go for a third martini."

"Do it," Lola said, slurring her words.

Vanessa wagged her finger at Lola. "You're a bad influence."

"It's my job." Lola's heart pulsed faster, preventing her from saying something else. The person who ruined her life was sitting at the bar counter with a guy. And Lola didn't have any doubts about her suspicions—she would have recognized the person's devilish grin anywhere.

"What? Do you think I'm a lush?" Vanessa asked.

Lola leaned into her grandmother's right ear. "We've gotta get out here now. Katrina is here."

"Okay." Vanessa threw on her coat.

Lola's heart hadn't stopped its increased beating. She hadn't made it this far, only for her life to end. So, she tossed a fifty-dollar bill on the table, and her and Vanessa would leave—even if Vanessa was taking longer than she should've with buttoning her jacket.

"How the hell did Katrina find me?" Lola asked after they stepped out of the bar and onto the sidewalk.

"I don't know."

"I've been careful," Lola said.

Vanessa gritted her teeth. "If Katrina really tracked you down to finish what she and Vincent started all those years ago, then you should consider returning to Connecticut with me."

"Maybe," Lola croaked.

No matter how much Lola would have rather laughed at her grandmother's suggestion, she couldn't. Nothing was more important than her life. So, she might have had no choice in fleeing again.

CHAPTER 9

SASHA

Life didn't get simpler for Sasha than watching *Days of our Lives*, and she wouldn't apologize for doing so while her feet remained stretched out on the living room table. Sometimes, Sasha needed time for herself no matter how trivial the task was.

So, Sasha more than relished this hour for herself. She never underestimated routines even when she whored herself out for Ivan and her clients. Catching *Days of our Lives*—often later on YouTube—was the one constant event in Sasha's life during that time when she closed her eyes, wondering how soon her customers would finish.

She didn't anticipate Tyler shuffling into the living room, though.

Tyler sighed. "Do you have a second?"

"I thought you left for class already?"

"I don't have classes today." Tyler drew in a long breath. "I don't mean to bother you, but I've got nobody else to turn to."

Sasha didn't have to contemplate her answer—not even for a moment. Tyler approaching her revealed a gift from the universe. She might not have wanted to push him too much, yet she had prayed Tyler would confide in her. Anyone with at least some common sense could've seen how Tyler was grappling with something, and how Cece hadn't been more observant baffled Sasha. A mother should have pretended to care.

"Sure." Sasha turned the TV off, then tossed the remote on the couch. "What's going on? Is it about Jake?"

Tyler snickered. "When did you start watching *Days of our Lives*? You're the one who said soap operas and reality television are for weak people."

So much for Sasha emulating every aspect of Riley's life. She could have yelled at herself—she couldn't have been so careless.

Viewing a soap opera wasn't exactly not having the same birthmark as Riley, though. So, she hadn't seen the harm in consuming a guilty pleasure. Although that was the problem with her dead sister being a stranger—filling in the details of Riley's life herself. And it was a miracle Riley didn't have any friends. Faking it with someone's spouse and stepson was one thing, yet friendships were different. Family loved you unconditionally whereas friendships encompassed lots of little things. Like the inside jokes nobody else knew about. So, a friendship's history couldn't be feigned in the same way certain intense emotions couldn't be fabricated.

"I didn't wanna break up with Jake," Tyler said.

"Come again?"

"Somebody made me do it."

"Is someone blackmailing you?"

"Not exactly, although the situation is far from ideal."

"No offense, but you're gonna have to be clearer. I can't help you unless I know what's going on." Sasha scratched her shoulder.

Tyler huffed out a bigger sigh. "I'm sleeping with my math professor."

"Are you joking?" Sasha asked.

"I wish I was, but I'm serious."

Sasha closed her eyes for a beat. Having a less than sheltered life—like spending a few years in prison—should've entailed not being surprised by Tyler's news. However, she still cringed. Perhaps it was the part of her that wanted to believe innocence existed in the world was why her contempt burned through her body. Whoring himself out wasn't something Tyler should've done because of his mother's hedge fund job. Yet here Sasha was, waiting for divine intervention regarding the perfect response.

"Does Jake know about the arrangement?" Sasha asked.

Nothing wrong with her question. Doing so proved she cared without accidentally saying the wrong thing.

Tyler pressed his arms together. "No, but you should've seen the look in his eyes when I ended things with him."

"Your professor didn't force himself on you?" Sasha asked.

"No. But there's more."

"Lovely."

The color drained from Tyler's cheeks. "He's married to a woman, so he's a closet case."

Sasha got off the couch, then walked over to Tyler. She placed her arms around him, looking him right in the eye. "Why would you do this?" Sasha asked.

"It's the only way to pass the class."

"What about a tutor?"

Tyler broke eye contact with Sasha. "I already tried that—it didn't work."

"I don't understand why your professor made you break up with Jake." Sasha drank the rest of her coffee from the chipped mug on the living room table. Not having caffeine wasn't an option if she would continue her conversation with Tyler.

"He wants me to himself," Tyler said.

Sasha snorted. "Yet he won't leave his wife?"

"He doesn't have the courage to do that."

"Do you wanna keep sleeping with him in exchange for a better grade?"

Tyler shrugged. "There are uglier looking people to be with. Anyway, what do you think I should do?"

Sasha nibbled on her lower lip, and a faint metallic taste filled her mouth a moment later. As awful as her advice would be, she didn't have a choice. Doing nothing always proved better than a solution someone remained uncertain about.

"Continue the arrangement for now," Sasha said.

Tyler elevated his eyebrows. "Really?"

"You'll figure out what to do eventually, and I'm gonna help you."

"Should I tell Jake the truth?"

"How would he react?" Sasha asked.

Tyler laughed. "Good point. He'd kill Mr. Parker if he discovered the truth."

"Thank you for being honest with me—that couldn't have been easy for you."

"I didn't have a choice…"

"Still means something to me," Sasha said.

"Talking to a stranger is sometimes easier than talking to a friend or family member."

"Is your opinion of me that low?" Sasha asked.

Disappointment wasn't something Sasha should have experienced in this current conversation—she knew she wasn't Riley, and Tyler's dynamic with Riley wasn't her fault. Yet Sasha would forever be that girl—the girl sporting an orange jumpsuit, yearning for something to hold onto while agonizing over imprisonment for a crime she didn't commit. So, she always latched onto even the faintest positive thing she could no matter how unrealistic the action was.

Tyler gaze narrowed. "Do you even have to ask?"

Sasha traced the right side of her head, fingers snaking through her hair. "You're right."

"The advice was helpful."

"Good to know I'm useful for something."

"I might have misjudged you," Tyler said.

"Are you for real?"

Tyler lifted the sleeves of his Henley tee-shirt up. "Yeah. Perception is everything, and false assumptions are easy to make."

Sasha almost responded, yet stopped herself. Impulsiveness created terrible situations more often than they led to innovations. And that reason was why Sasha couldn't tell Tyler she wasn't Riley. Even if she wanted to scream said fact more than somebody being locked in a sauna shrieked when calling for help. Sasha was protecting Tyler in a way. If he didn't know she wasn't Riley, then he didn't have to lie for her. And that truth was worth than all the money in the world. Sasha might not have attended college, yet only an idiot would've ignored how Tyler didn't need another reminder of how harsh life was.

"Were you gonna say something?" Tyler asked.

"It doesn't have to be like this."

"Pardon me?"

Sasha cleared her throat. "There's no reason our dynamic has to be so standoffish. I'm working on becoming a better person, and we should be friends. Having an ally never hurts—especially once you figure how you wanna handle your professor."

"I'd like that."

Someone should've pinched her. "Seriously?"

"Jake was my only friend; I'm not exactly Mr. Popular."

"Shake on it?" Sasha asked.

"Sure." Tyler extended his hand, then Sasha gripped it.

Sasha didn't stop at shaking on her newfound friendship, though. She opened her arms, inviting Tyler in for a hug. Because she didn't care how corny or cliché the sentiment was. A gesture—even a small one—told Tyler that he wasn't alone.

"I hope you know your situation will resolve itself eventually." Sasha continued rubbing Tyler's back.

"I know, I know."

***

Sasha's eyes remained glued to a magazine the following evening while Cece closed her book and adjusted her posture in bed.

Cece cocked her head. "We should talk."

Sasha so loved that phrase. For all Sasha knew, she could have fucked up her cover. Even if believing she handled being "Riley" well was her only option for ensuring no excessive yawning in the morning, almost unable to open her eyes.

"Hopefully, it's not bad?" Sasha asked.

"Don't be cynical."

"Okay, fine. What's up?"

"Tyler and I talked when you went for your jog earlier."

"What's your point?" Sasha asked.

"He said you had a nice chat."

Sasha flashed a smile. She hadn't intended on manipulating Tyler, yet he might have helped her in a way. If Tyler liked her, then Cece might keep her around. Speculating about what Cece and Riley's marriage must have been like wasn't far-fetched, because Sasha couldn't think of one reason why someone would marry Riley.

Sasha massaged her jaw for a beat. Tyler mentioned something about having a blonde wife boosting Cece's image. Yikes. Now, Sasha didn't blame Tyler for approaching her over his own mother.

"We did," Sasha said.

"That's better than my birthday and Christmas falling on the same day—we're gonna be a happy family, just you see."

Sasha didn't need coaxing for believing what Cece just said. Everyone should have experienced the comfort and safety of a family at least once. It wasn't like she ever had that stability. Not when her biological father left her, Riley, and her mother. Not when her mother died of cancer six years after that. Not when her stepfather, Vincent, never fit into the parental type no matter how much he might have deluded himself.

"Agreed," Sasha said.

Cece tossed the comforter off her, revealing how she still sported her lilac bathrobe. "I'm gonna go take a shower."

"Okay."

Cece winked. "Wanna join?"

"Maybe next time. I'm gonna finish reading my magazine," Sasha said.

"Fair enough."

Sasha kissed Cece without a second thought. Not having shower sex didn't mean she couldn't be affectionate. Especially when Sasha should have been more careful with her role than the FBI raiding a drug kingpin's headquarters. And the strawberry flavored lipstick coating Cece's lips helped—nothing like a fruity aroma. So, Sasha didn't have one tinge of nausea while making out with Cece.

"What was that for?" Cece asked after pulling back several minutes later.

"Never forget how much I care about you."

Cece gave Sasha a look. "I'm not blind."

"And what's that supposed to mean?"

"I didn't have any misgivings about you when we got married—I knew what I got myself into. I'm a big girl, and can look out for myself. Anyway, enjoy the magazine." Cece left the bed without another word, then strutted towards the bathroom, which was attached to the bedroom. The lock made a snick and the pattering of shower water echoed.

Sasha didn't resume sifting through her magazine, though. Instead, she couldn't stop staring at the bedside table next to her. More specifically, the drawer. Her phone—the one from her pre-Riley life—hadn't stopped beeping.

So, Sasha yanked open the drawer. But her shoulders didn't jerk after Sasha checked the caller ID.

"Hello?" Sasha asked after answering the call.

"It's me."

"I know it's you, Dylan."

"Ivan is furious with you—I don't know where you are, but you've gotta return to Manhattan," Dylan said.

The bathroom door knob's turning echoed, then Sasha pressed END. Sasha shoved the iPhone back in its hiding spot right when Cece walked out, towel covering her body from the waist down.

"Weren't you reading your magazine?" Cece asked.

"I got bored."

"Oh."

"How was your shower?" Sasha asked.

Cece let out a sharp giggle. "It was a shower…"

"Sorry. Stupid question."

"It was fine, thanks," Cece said.

"Good."

Cece smirked. "That's what I love about you, Riley. You don't miss a trick—only you would find meaning in the most innocuous thing."

She didn't respond. Not when her mind remained on Dylan's phone call. Only she would underestimate the universe. Dylan—the love of her life—couldn't check in to reminiscence. The conversation just had to be linked to Ivan—the person she hated most in life. Another reminder how nothing was free—the tiniest gift—and she couldn't help speculating after Cece finished dressing if Ivan knew she was in Connecticut.

"One thing," Cece continued.

"Oh, yeah?"

"I didn't wanna make a big deal out of it, but you haven't been wearing your wedding ring."

Sasha peaked at her left ring finger, then at Cece, then back to her finger. She was definitely clueless about her arrangement. If she had Riley's credits cards, driver's license, keys, then she should've considered the wedding ring. That piece of jewelry wasn't something someone forgot—Riley waved the bling in her face during Sasha's first night in Connecticut.

Getting stabbed with a knife wouldn't have wounded Sasha as much as the look plastered on her "wife's" face. "Well?" Cece pressed.

"I lost it when you and Tyler took that weekend to Savannah," Sasha said.

"Fair enough. We'll get you a new ring ASAP."

When all else failed, then Sasha could blame herself. Clumsiness was something everything everyone was guilty of at some point. Even if Riley had calculated every deception against Cece.

Sleeping with one eye open tempted Sasha, though. At least until she figured out what Ivan's plan was. Ivan was one problem she couldn't lie her way out of.

CHAPTER 10

TYLER

Tyler's head remained above his lap while he sat on the edge of the motel bed, knees grazing his chest. Somehow, he hadn't disagreed with Sasha's advice from several days ago regarding his arrangement with Mr. Parker. Making the situation worse would have only complicated his life, and Tyler couldn't afford that.

Mr. Parker cackled. "You could pretend not to hate me."

"I never I said I felt that way."

"You didn't have to."

"Excuse me?"

"Being a math teacher doesn't mean I don't know how to read people—I do."

"Then why make me do this over and over?" Tyler demanded.

"I've got needs."

"Lovely. Just want I wanted to hear."

Mr. Parker arched his eyebrows. "Don't pretend to be some innocent victim. You agreed to this arrangement, and now you've gotta accept the consequences. That's the adult thing to do."

Tyler didn't reply right away. Contemplating what Mr. Parker said couldn't be avoided. Tyler wasn't a victim, but he wasn't filled with joy because of his arrangement with Mr. Parker. And where that left him remained to be seen. If Tyler wanted to, then he could stop the arrangement anytime he wanted and accept failing math was inevitable. Yet Tyler didn't, and he wouldn't stop playing with metaphorical fire anytime soon.

"Okay. You agree adults must live with the choices they make?" Tyler asked, resuming eye contact. Wow. First time for everything.

"Duh. That's what I just said."

Tyler grinned. "Okay. You'd be fine with living the consequences if I told your wife about our trysts?"

"You wouldn't do that?"

"Maybe. Maybe not. But you probably don't wanna take the risk." Tyler picked the excess part of his nail, then bit it. "I'm not some weak boy."

Mr. Parker licked his lips. "That's right. You're a man."

An icy sensation pricked Tyler's skin. He couldn't get over the excitement radiating from Mr. Parker's face. Having sex was one thing, yet his professor couldn't have enjoyed their relationship. The affair wasn't permanent, and would end like everything else in life. It was a promise. Nothing good also wouldn't come from being with someone who evoked as much emotions as a bag of rocks.

"Making me end my relationship with Jake crossed a line," Tyler said.

"Then do something about it," Mr. Parker touted.

"I just might."

"Please. You weren't exactly closing your eyes when we were going at it earlier," Mr. Parker said.

"There are a lot of people who are attractive, but that doesn't mean I wanna sleep with them."

Mr. Parker winked. "Admit it. You think I'm hot, don't you? And don't lie. It's just the two of us, so your secret is safe with me."

"Fine." Tyler pouted. "You're physically attractive. However, that's got nothing to do with being a good person, because you're ugly on the inside."

"How noble—you should be a poet."

"I write short stories—I forget it if I ever told you this, but I'm a Creative Writing major," Tyler said without thinking. Someone should have kicked him. Letting himself become caught up in the moment—even with something like polite conversation. If Tyler wasn't careful, then he might actually enjoy kissing Mr. Parker at some point in the near future.

"You better not use our arrangement as fodder." Mr. Parker burst into a laughter. "But if you do, please change the names."

"If you're lucky."

"Who hurt you?" Mr. Parker demanded.

"What are you talking about?"

"Anyone can tell you get off on punishment."

"It's simple." Tyler put on his clothes in a matter of seconds before getting out of bed. "I don't care enough about you to share that piece of information."

Mr. Parker clapped his chest. "Ouch. I'm so scared."

"You should be, because you don't wanna know what I'm gonna do to you if you don't change my grade on yesterday's quiz from a 40 to a 95."

"Fine. However, we're doing this again sometime soon," Mr. Parker said.

Tyler cover his nose with his shirt for a moment. The same nondescript stench from his arrival in the motel room an hour earlier still permeated the air. And the motel's housekeeping should have done a more thorough job. Playing "Guess the Questionable Odor's Source" wasn't an aphrodisiac.

"Another thing. Pick a different motel next time," Tyler said.

"If you insist." Mr. Parker's grin widened, as if it was possible. "But you're gonna have to do something for me first. I want a goodbye kiss."

Tyler wouldn't clench his fists—not this time. The kissing and sex was more fleeting than a parent's lecture over their misbehaving kid. He trekked over to Mr. Parker's side of the bed, then leaned his head forward. His lips were now only an inch from Mr. Parker's mouth. But he wouldn't kiss Mr. Parker for several more seconds.

Mr. Parker panted. "What are you waiting for?"

Tyler gave Mr. Parker a quick kiss, not letting it linger. "That right there is another reminder of how I've got power in this arrangement. Kissing you just happened on my terms, not yours."

"Bastard!" Mr. Parker exclaimed.

Tyler scratched Mr. Parker's jaw, almost drawing blood from his nails digging into Mr.

Parker's flesh. "Maybe. But I've proven I'm a worthy opponent."

***

Tyler looked up from his book the next morning while he sat at a table in front of one of the academic buildings. The rushed squeaking of feet against the ground should have been his first clue about the impending confrontation.

Tyler raised an eyebrow. "What do you want, Jake?"

"We need to talk."

"I already told you I don't wanna see you."

"Bullshit."

"Little early in the morning for cursing, don't you think?" Tyler asked.

Wind roared, pushing a nearby crushed can across the grass. Tyler even laughed. So much for attending the highest ranked college in Connecticut. He would have thought people might've cared more about littering. Or maybe he didn't want to deal with whatever snide comment Jake was about to say as the trees whipped even faster in the wind. Because Tyler just couldn't escape Jake's bulging eyes.

Jake's nostrils flared. "Cut the crap. We both know there's more going on than what you told me. Besides, I'm the one who should be furious."

"And why is that?" Jake demanded.

Tyler snickered. "You had no right speaking to Riley."

"This might shock you, but your stepmother isn't as evil as you think," Jake said.

"How'd you feel if I meddled in your life?"

"I'd get over it if what you did was for the greater good."

Tyler's stomach twisted in ten different directions. A crystal ball wasn't required for predicting how his situation with Jake might escalate. So, he'd do the one thing that would push Jake away for the foreseeable future.

"You're right. I'm not being honest with you," Tyler said.

Jake jabbed his fist through the air. "I knew it."

"I'm seeing someone new. I left you for another guy—an older guy. Apparently, I've got daddy issues."

"You're lying," Jake replied, head still shaking.

"I'm really not."

"What does this mean?"

Tyler pursed his lips. "I'll be more succinct since you're too much of an idiot to get the hint. I never loved you. And I used you because I was bored. But don't fret. I wasn't lying when I said you were fantastic in bed."

Jake grunted. "You're something else, and I can't imagine what anyone would see in you."

"You might wanna get tested for an STD—I slept with the guy while we were still together."

"I never want to see you again. In fact, I hope you drop dead." Jake stormed off without another word, and was soon out of sight.

Tyler waited another few seconds before sobbing. Realizing he had no choice with what he said and living with his lie were two different things. And as far as he was concerned, December couldn't arrive soon enough. Even if some people might've chastised him for wishing part of his life away. A distant, vague future was the only thing Tyler could look forward to.

CHAPTER 11

RILEY

Riley's focus remained on her prime rib while she and Josh sat at a restaurant table. More specifically, the blood oozing from the meat. Nothing like a reminder about how life could be cruel—even in a small way. The cow was alive one minute and dead the next. And said fact proved great. Riley had the same fate in mind for her father. If he ever let her insert herself into his life, that was.

Josh sipped his wine. "Something wrong, dear?"

"I'm savoring the taste."

"That's my girl."

"I should thank you." Riley cut a piece prime rib, then chewed slower than a grandmother crossing the street. Nothing like the juxtaposition of salt's flavor against the rare meat. "Most people wouldn't have given their partner a second chance after discovering an indiscretion."

Josh laughed. "No need for formalities. But remember what I told you, because I wasn't kidding."

Riley almost choked on the next piece of meat she ate. She couldn't have forgotten Josh's warning even if someone gave her a lobotomy. She'd never witness such intense anger before—not even when she made Sasha's life impossible after assuming the real Riley's life.

"I wasn't trying to threaten you—I was standing up for myself," Josh continued. "My feelings matter, and it's time you realized that. Think how you'd feel if roles were reversed, and someone made a fool of you."

"I know."

Josh patted Riley's hand. "I have no doubt you won't disappoint me. Not when I'm your only source of money."

Riley almost excused herself so she could laugh in the restaurant's bathroom. Josh couldn't have been more naïve if someone pointed a gun at him. What Josh didn't know was that she still had her wedding ring—the one she gloated about in front of Sasha hours before staging her suicide. The item was her insurance policy. Riley refused to be stupid no matter how much she cherished getting her way the majority of the time. One wrong move was the only thing standing between her and poverty.

"Are you sure you're okay?" Josh asked.

Riley giggled. "Please stop worrying so much."

"You must be serious—I've never heard you say please before."

"True." Riley finished the last piece of her meat. "Some things are too serious to joke about."

"There's something else you should know."

"Fantastic."

Josh chugged his remaining wine, then gesticulated at the waitress for a refill. "Nothing terrible. Actually, this is a good thing."

Riley's face lit up. "Tell me now."

"We're gonna chat with your father tomorrow morning."

"What made you wanna try again?" Riley demanded.

"I'm not clueless. You'll never be happy until your daddy issues are resolved. Even if doing so entails revenge."

"Thanks, babe."

Glee filled Riley's body even if she had more in common with the Grinch than a hippie most of the time. Josh hadn't realized this truth, yet he showed Riley who he was by his comment. And for one fleeting moment, Riley's opinion of Josh improved. Still nothing sexier than a man taking charge. At least this way, Riley wouldn't have to pretend so much with Josh. In different circumstances, Josh might've been a perfect match for her.

And, just maybe, Riley would become more appreciative in the future. Only a week passed since Josh discovered the condom wrapper, proving life could change in a short amount of time.

The waitress swaggered to the table, whistling. She placed the glass on the table.

"Here you go," she said. "I even told the bartender not to be stingy with the pour—hope you enjoy."

Josh nodded. "Thanks. I appreciate the good service, and will leave a good tip."

She winked. "I'm just doing my job."

Josh waved his hand through the air. "Nonsense. Most waiters and waitresses wouldn't care about their patrons."

The waitress flipped her hair over her shoulders.

Riley handed her glass to the waitress after finishing her red wine. "Mind getting me another glass?"

"Absolutely." The waitress darted away without another, not even so much as one wrinkle on her face from what Riley just said.

"You didn't have to scare her off," Josh said.

"It's her job to get me more wine."

"Calm down." Josh grabbed his white napkin, then wiped the bits of mashed potatoes from his lip. "I was just chatting with her, not flirting."

Riley wiggled her eyebrows. "Were you trying to punish me?"

"I really wasn't."

"Good." Riley's tightened grip on her steak knife didn't vanish. If anything, the hold intensified. Not actually slicing the waitress's carotid artery didn't mean she couldn't contemplate doing so. One slit of the throat, and blood would gush everywhere. Josh was her doll, not the waitress's.

Knowing she could kill the waitress was enough for her, though. The real power remained in letting the waitress live—Riley couldn't get distracted from her endgame—making Adam suffer for everything he did. If she was gonna cut anyone's throat, then it'd be Adam's throat.

***

Riley stood by the front door with Josh the following morning after their prime rib dinner.

Deep breaths because Riley wouldn't become enraged unless she had to. It wasn't like she was alone. So, Riley would play Adam like she manipulated everyone else in her life—almost as if playing games was as natural as waking up in the morning.

"Now or never," Josh said.

"Right." Riley rang the doorbell.

No answer.

Riley pressed the doorbell again.

Footsteps echoed, then the door opened.

"What are you doing here?" Adam growled at Riley.

"Don't speak to Riley like that," Josh said.

Adam put his hands on his hips. "This is my property, not hers."

Tears trickled down Riley's face. "I wanna make a deal with you. If you give me five minutes of your time and you still don't want anything to do with me, then I'll leave you alone."

Adam grunted. "Fine. Let's see what you got."

"I can't force you to be my father if you don't want to. But I'd love to get a real chance to know you. Especially since I have no family left—Sasha and I don't speak, and Grandma died."

If Riley had a conscious, then sweat would have drenched her brow. Her grandmother being alive was something Adam could have verified. But maybe, just maybe, Adam wasn't motivated enough for verifying said fact—thicker stubble coated his cheeks, neck, chin, and skin above his upper lip than during Riley's previous interaction with Adam. So, if Adam didn't care about something like appearances, then he couldn't have been motivated to dig more.

"Why does this matter so much?" Adam asked.

"You should become a better listener," Riley said.

Adam rolled his eyes. "I'm sorry you and Sasha aren't on speaking terms in addition to how your grandmother is dead. However, that's not my fault."

"Never said it was," Riley spat, pulling her jacket's belt harder.

"Reconnecting with you means a lot to Riley," Josh said.

Riley pressed her hands together. "Please."

"You've got nothing to lose," Josh said.

Adam threw a gaze inside his home. "I was gonna make a cup of coffee, and you're welcome to join."

Riley stole a glance with Josh. He nodded at her, then Riley and Josh strutted into the house. Riley would definitely have more faith in the universe going forward regardless of whether Adam caved just to appease her. She got her way, and that was the only fact that mattered.

***

Riley exited Starbucks by herself the following afternoon after her first interaction with her father—Josh decided to check out another art museum, which still hadn't piqued Riley's interest.

Her "boyfriend's" temporary absence and the saturated gray shade dotting the clouds wasn't why she blinked several times, though. If she didn't know better, then she would've thought Sasha stood a few yards away in front the coffee shop.

But Riley needed to shake off her shock. The girl she thought was Sasha just accosted her.

"What are you doing here, Sasha?" Riley asked.

"Try again.

Riley's hair smacked her in the face after wind shot through the air. "What game are you playing? You're obviously Sasha."

The woman snorted. "Nope."

"You're wasting my time, so I'm just gonna get to the point," Riley said. "Why aren't you still in Connecticut? I gave you a golden opportunity for escaping Ivan."

The woman grimaced. "It's Riley, bitch."

"Come again?"

"Wow. Maybe I did a better job of staying hidden than I realized."

"I don't have time for this," Riley said.

The woman groaned. "Or perhaps you're a bigger idiot than you realized. Apparently, nobody warned you about hubris."

"I have no idea what you're getting at," Riley said.

"I'll give you a hint. Remember that night the woods with Vincent and the rock?"

"No." Riley stroked her chin. The thought that popped into her head couldn't be true—especially because of the blood trickling out the real Riley's head wound that night in the woods. Yet Riley couldn't argue with Sasha being out of town that night—said fact was indisputable. Her past couldn't have returned to haunt her. It just couldn't have. She always got what she wanted, including reprieve from stealing the real Riley's life.

"For the last time, I'm not Sasha. I'm the real Riley, and your con is over. You stole my life, Katrina, and you're gonna pay." The woman took out her pocket knife from her jacket pocket. She shoved Riley against the brick alley, and only several seconds passed until a chill tingled up Riley's spine from the knife's metal texture caressing her neck.

So, yeah. Riley might've been fucked for once in her life. Riley met a situation she couldn't run from.

CHAPTER 12

LOLA

Danger didn't always matter.

That idea was why Lola couldn't help herself with confronting Riley after exiting the coffee shop. Idealism was sometimes overrated—Lola couldn't let Riley continue living one second longer without informing her of how terrible she was. There was no forgiven how Riley stole her life, forcing Lola into adapting the "Lola" alias in the first place.

So, the anger coursing through her body over the last eight years was why Lola wouldn't stop pressing the pocket knife against Riley's throat. Hard enough so Riley might have flinched for once in her life, yet not forceful enough for drawing blood.

Riley's jaw shuddered. "You don't wanna do this."

"Give me one good reason why I shouldn't kill you?"

"We aren't alone."

"You're lying," Lola said.

"I'm really not. But maybe you hate too much to accept I might be right about something."

Lola tilted her head for a second.

Damn. No matter how much Lola might have wanted to kill Riley, she couldn't. A man with yellow teeth and a ripped shirt and jeans sat in front of a dumpster on the opposite end of the alley.

One second was all Lola needed for losing control of the situation. Riley shoved Lola off her in one swift motion, sending Lola backwards. Lola stumbled, then her body thumped against the ground. Her pocket knife even clanked against the ground.

"You're stupider than I thought," Riley said.

Lola rose, then brushed the dust off her. "You're a terrible person and deserve to rot in Hell for what you did to me."

"Your life can't be too bad."

Lola's brow arched. "I don't know where you got that idea."

"Somebody must have helped you. You couldn't have ended up in Los Angeles by yourself."

Lola locked her arms together. "You're right— Grandma sends me money every month. Five thousand dollars to be exact."

"Lucky bitch."

"Just confess the truth already. You came to Los Angeles to kill me."

An ambulance siren blared down the block, and the vehicle was soon out of sight.

And Lola could only wonder about what the emergency was. Like if someone was about to die unless the ambulance she just saw arrived its destined location in time. Wow. Another reminder of how precious life was.

Riley ran her fingers through her hair. "Wrong. I actually thought you were dead."

"Then what are you doing here?"

"None of your business."

"Don't you feel a little bit guilty for what you did?" Lola demanded. "Sasha probably hates me because of the things you've done as me."

Riley sneered. "True. That was nasty."

Lola could have stuck a cotton swab in both ears, yanking out the earwax. Her sister couldn't have conceded the point—sociopaths weren't capable of seeing the world through another person's perspective. Or maybe, just maybe, Riley hadn't cared enough to argue with her. Especially when Riley had no problem with what transpired in the woods that night all those years ago.

"I could still kill you," Lola said.

"Please. You wouldn't hurt a fly."

"Must be furious at Vincent now."

Riley's jaw lowered. "Don't you dare mention his name."

"I know Vincent died right before your nineteenth birthday," Lola said.

"How could you possibly know that."

"Grandma told me."

"She's probably a stuck-up brat like our father." Riley adjusted her coat. "Wait. Why did you mention Vincent?"

"Just a little suspicious he died of a heart attack at forty—he wasn't obese."

"What are you implying."

Lola cackled. "You're a smart person—figure it out yourself."

Lola wouldn't regret the accusation she just made—not directly saying what she thought Riley did was the best part. A little reminder how Riley wasn't as invincible as she thought she was. If there was one thing that Lola understood, then it was that information was power. And Riley wouldn't reveal she knew what really happened to Vincent. Especially without any concrete proof.

"It didn't have to be like this," Lola continued. You could've come to us."

"And say what?" Riley pressed. "How our father sold me on the black market because him and mom didn't plan on having a third child."

"Doctors make mistakes."

"I'm a person, not a wrong shoe size."

Lola would've rather been stabbed with a knife than have Riley make her comment. And her reasoning wasn't because of hoping Riley was a good person deep down—she didn't. Lola just couldn't forget her entire life being stolen from her. Said event was the type of horror story people watch unfold on the news, not in real life, because the truth wasn't supposed to be stranger than fiction.

"I'm a person too!" Lola exclaimed.

Riley shrieked at her sister. "I know."

"Doesn't seem like it. You had Vincent kill me without giving the matter a second thought."

"But you're alive," Riley said.

"You didn't answer my question about what you're doing in Los Angeles."

"I'm not going to."

Lola swallowed. "I hope you're proud of yourself."

"Run," Riley said.

"Excuse me?"

Riley lunged forward. "I'm gonna give you the consideration I never had."

"What are you talking about?" Lola asked.

Riley leaned on the ground, then picked up the pocket knife—the one Lola hadn't picked up. Lola's pulse hammered in her ears. Damn. She couldn't have been clueless enough to forget about picking up the pocket knife.

"I'm giving you time to flee before killing you," Riley said, waving the knife.

"Seriously?"

Riley inched closer, breath prickling Lola's skin. "I'm not kidding."

Lola did the only thing she could. She scurried out of the alley faster than someone running away from a venomous snake, because she didn't have to understand why Riley gave her this kindness. Not when there was no telling what her sister would do to her next. The kind of rage inside Riley couldn't be ignored, and Lola understood that idea better than anyone. The type of anger that festered over years was the most dangerous type of anger. It was the same anguish she would always carry from how Katrina assumed her life.

***

Lola slammed her apartment door shut sometime later.

Her panting continued for another few moments before the lock clinked and she looked Vanessa—who was seated at the dining room table, sipping coffee—in the eye.

"What's wrong?" Vanessa asked.

"I ran into Katrina." Lola tossed her coat on the table in front of the apartment door, then shuffled towards Vanessa.

"What?"

"I'm not kidding."

Vanessa pushed her mug aside. "That means we saw her at The Falcon the other night."

"And I was dumb."

"What do you mean?"

"I just tried to kill her," Lola revealed.

"Have you lost your mind?"

A pang of disappointment jolted Lola. And the size of the issue didn't matter. Whether she was 4, 24, and 104 didn't matter. Her grandmother was the closest parental figure she had, so she couldn't have let Vanessa down. Even if Lola would have thrown her better judgement aside for bashing in Riley's face with a hammer. There was still no forgiving what her sister did to her. Not now. Not ever. Took Lola a lot of time for realizing the point, yet some betrayals were labeled unforgivable for a reason.

Lola put her hands in her jean pockets. "I just used my pocket knife—it wasn't like I tried that hard."

"Doesn't matter. What if she finished the job?"

"She didn't come here to kill me," Lola blurted. "At least not until the end of our conversation."

"If she didn't visit LA for you, then it must be for your father."

"Come again."

Vanessa looked away. "Your father lives in LA."

"And you're only telling me this now?"

"He's a piece of shit for leaving you, Sasha, and your mother."

Lola craned her neck. A photograph on the kitchen counter stole her attention from the corner of her eye. Even if cobwebs coated both the golden frame and the upper part of the photograph. The photo was of her, Sasha, and their mother at Disney Land. AKA one of the last times the three of them were happy. Before Vincent. Before Mom's cancer. Before almost being killed. Before going to her grandmother and fleeing Connecticut. Damn. Now she was the walking, talking nostalgia cliché. Because she would have criticized anyone else for being so sentimental. Life was supposed to be easier, not harder. And she didn't even wanna speculate if life would get worse now that Riley aka Katrina knew she was alive. In retrospect, Lola almost sighed in relief. Her grandmother could have been a lot harsher with her about how confronting Riley wasn't the smart move.

"He's still my father," Lola said after a while.

Vanessa snatched a cookie from the tray in front of her on the table. She bit down on the cookie, crunching noises echoing.

"Wait. Do you think she came to LA for revenge against our father since he sold her on the black market?" Lola asked.

Vanessa shrugged. "Maybe."

A fly buzzed near Lola's face. She then swatted the bug, crushing it in one swift motion. Perhaps if her reflexes were strong enough for dealing with a nuisance then she might have stood a chance against Riley. It wasn't like Lola told Riley her address. No amount of resentment would make Lola do something so dumb. And if she survived the last eight years, then Lola might have been able to survive the rest of her life. It was a thought—just something to hold onto. She would never stop believing in how people needed comfort any place they could. No explanation necessary for how the universe's cruelty could never be underestimated.

"The whole thing was just so awful—I can't believe Sasha and I are related to Katrina," Lola said. "She didn't even care about ruining my life."

"No surprise there."

"I'm not afraid of her," Lola said.

Vanessa snorted. "You should be. She could resume focus on you after finishing your dad."

"Whatever."

"Enough." Vanessa wrapped her pearl necklace around her fingers. In fact, Lola almost giggled from the possibility of her grandmother breaking her necklace. Grandmas were supposed to be prim and proper, not on the verge of a nervous breakdown. "We're going to go back Connecticut—you'll be safer there."

CHAPTER 13

SASHA

Sasha was about to go for a jog a week after Dylan's impromptu call, yet her heart fluttered upon opening the front door. She must have been dreaming, because the guy standing in front of her couldn't have been there. However, Dylan remained on the front porch after Sasha blinked several times.

"What are you doing here?" Sasha asked.

"We need to talk."

Sasha couldn't swallow the lump in her throat. "How'd you find me?"

"You aren't as good at fleeing as you thought." Dylan adjusted his argyle tie, then tugged at the sides of his blazer.

"I'm serious. I want an answer."

"I put a tracking app on your iPhone," Dylan said.

"Excuse me?" Sasha's eyes bulged, worse than a deer's facial expression when a nighttime driver almost ran it over. But as much as Sasha prided herself in being a feminist, she couldn't reduce life to binaries. Sasha never recoiled in Dylan's presence like she had more times than she could count with Ivan. So, maybe, just maybe, Dylan had a good reason for doing what he did—even if Sasha might not have smiled from being monitored so closely, she wasn't some piece of cattle.

"Don't give me that look." Dylan paused for a second. "My intentions weren't sinister—I was trying to help."

Sasha folded her arms. "Stalking me isn't helping."

"I only did it because of Ivan."

"He's my problem, not yours."

"I couldn't take a chance." Dylan's face turned white. "Anyway, one of Ivan's associates showed up at my work."

Sasha shuddered. Dylan's comment was the only thing necessary for her being that trembling girl she was in prison despite her being twenty-four years old. If Ivan was willing to cross boundaries, then there was no telling what he would do. Like that time Ivan lit a cigarette after they had sex, only to ask her if she enjoyed it. She nodded in agreement, yet Ivan screamed and cursed her out in Russian. He then pressed the cigarette's hot embers against her back and she yelled so loud people on the opposite side of the world might have heard her. Something about expecting complete honesty from her—even if her response would've angered him. So, Sasha was thankful the scar was on her back.

Not having the wound on a visible part of her body meant inventing an outrageous lie wasn't required.

"I'm sorry he did that," Sasha said.

"I wanna know what's going on. Aren't we supposed to tell each other everything? Or maybe I was wrong about you developing real feelings for me."

Sasha chewed the inside of her lip—Dylan had a point. In a perfect world, she would have confided in him about she had one dark circle under her eye too many. There were only so many times she could close her eyes while with a customer or prayed life would get better at some point when Ivan threw her onto his bed and yanked her panties off, only for him to ask her if she enjoyed herself sometime later. Please. As if she would ever enjoy being with Ivan.

So, Sasha couldn't refuse Riley's offer when she got her letter almost two months ago. Having Dylan help her wouldn't have been enough no matter how appealing him playing the hero would've been. It'd take more than a guy like Dylan for defeating Ivan. Only a miracle would vanquish Ivan from her life.

"Why didn't you to come me?" Dylan asked. "I would've helped you."

Sasha's glare intensified. If she were a violent person, then she would have smacked Dylan. The situation wasn't about how Dylan felt, it was about her. Like with how being one of Ivan's girls was the only thing Sasha could do because she didn't have her GED let alone a college degree. No matter how many chills tingled her spine, Sasha would take the two-hundred-dollar hourly rate over a minimum wage job. Even if she should've gotten the full four hundred dollars as oppose to only half the money.

"You wasted your time by coming here," Sasha said.

"Who are you living with? Some contact you met in your travels?"

"Not exactly." Sasha tilted her head. Just because a neighbor might not have been watching didn't mean someone couldn't spy on her five minutes from now. And she couldn't forget about Tyler—he'd be back from classes in a couple of hours. So, Sasha shoved Dylan inside the mansion while a few raindrops pattered against the ground. She locked the door behind her, stomach still in her throat. There was no having it both ways—either Sasha would tell Dylan the truth or not—with the man who let her cry on his shoulder when Ivan broke her jaw.

"What's with the secrecy?" Dylan asked.

"I assumed my sister's life," Sasha said.

"Aren't you and Riley estranged?"

"We reconciled."

"Then what happened to Riley?"

Sasha looked away. "She killed herself."

He sighed. "I'm sorry—that couldn't have been easy for you."

"And now Riley's wife and stepson think I'm her."

Dylan laughed. "Are you joking? You've gotta know this con can't last forever."

Sasha made a clucking noise with her tongue. No reason for suggesting her arrangement would implode—Sasha might not have been perfect, but she wasn't a clown. Cece and Tyler believed her so far.

"It's not a joke. We could be a real family someday," Sasha said.

Dylan gripped Sasha's shoulders, making direct eye contact. "You don't actually believe that, do you? You can't be happy sharing a bed with someone you don't love."

Sasha didn't cringe from sharing a bed with Cece. It wasn't like Cece demanded sex. The several times they had kissed also hadn't made her take an hour-long shower and scrub and scrub till Cece's touch was no longer palpable like she did after her trysts with Ivan. Sasha just had to be honest with herself—the number of showers she took wouldn't change what Ivan did. She would still scratch her skin. Almost as if bugs covered her entire body no matter how many hours passed since Ivan slept with her.

"Cece is nice," Sasha said.

Dylan heaved out a louder sigh. "That doesn't matter. We've got a big problem."

"What are you babbling about?"

"Ivan threatened to kill my parents if I don't bring you back to Manhattan one week from today."

Sasha didn't need to hear anything else from Dylan. Appearing at Dylan's work was one thing, yet threatening violence was another. Following through with the threat was the only remaining step after that.

Sasha gasped. "And you're just telling me this now?"

"I couldn't lead with that."

"Are you gonna return me to Manhattan even if it's against my will?"

"No, but we've gotta figure something out soon. We both know Ivan always gets what he wants."

Sasha furrowed her eyebrows. "Wait. Does Ivan know where I am? Tell me you aren't stupid enough to reveal I'm in Connecticut?"

"How little faith do you have in me?" Dylan asked.

"Can you blame me? You just showed up, not even thinking about how your arrival might cause trouble for me."

"I'm trying to help. Besides, you hung up on me and ignored my subsequent texts and calls."

Sasha didn't respond. She couldn't argue with Dylan no matter how tempting doing so might have been—he hadn't lied. He had contacted her multiple times during the last week—she simply ignored him. And now she'd have to live with the consequences of her decision—almost as if Sasha chastised herself for blowing off Dylan.

"You're right. Let's not fight," Sasha said.

"I'm not trying to scare you, but if I could find you, then Ivan could too. Being in the Russian Mafia has its benefits."

Sasha grunted. "Fine. Got any bright ideas about how I can escape Ivan for good?"

"Not at the moment. But I'm sure we can figure something out."

"I'm sorry," Sasha said after drawing in a breath.

"For what?"

"I shouldn't be so harsh. You didn't have to find me, yet you did."

Dylan pushed a lock of her hair out of the way. "You know I'd do anything for you, right?"

"I know, I know." Sasha flashed Dylan a small smile. How ironic. She wouldn't have expected to fall in love with one of her clients. Perhaps the reason was because Dylan was her only client who she hadn't slept with—at least not until she initiated the tryst. And Sasha giggled from that truth. Dylan was still a man, so she needed pinching from how

Dylan just wanted to company while at dinner and later watching television.

Sasha's lips brushed up against Dylan's, yet he pulled back.

"Was I wrong? Weren't we having a moment?" Sasha asked.

"We should return to the Ivan issue."

"Right."

Dylan rocked his hands back and forth. "I just wish we knew where to begin."

"Yeah, me too."

"Wait. You aren't I stopped the kiss, are you?" Dylan asked.

Sasha had two options—she could lie or tell the truth. Yet maybe lying was okay. Truthfulness sometimes caused more problems than it started. And Sasha also maybe should have only focused on Cece. No matter how alluring having a happily ever after with Dylan was, she couldn't walk into a problem didn't anticipate. Like someone catching her cheating on Cece with Dylan.

"No, I'm fine," Sasha said.

"Good. Now please tell me that you might have a way for dealing with Ivan?"

"I don't know. Ivan could still kill me even if I returned."

"Don't even think it," Dylan said.

Sasha rolled her eyes. "If only Ivan could move onto a new obsession."

"Life isn't that simple."

"It'd be nice if it were."

"Come here." Dylan opened his arms, and Sasha didn't hesitate about hugging him. Not kissing him didn't mean they had to be ten feet apart at all times. So, maybe, just maybe, not having to deal with Ivan alone was enough for the moment.

***

Sasha sat on the living room couch hours later.

Dylan was long gone, and Cece just texted her about not being home for dinner because of an unexpected meeting. So, Sasha did the only thing she could—drink bourbon. In fact, she was on her third glass.

Footsteps echoed, then a guy coughed.

"Do you wanna talk about what's wrong?" Tyler asked.

"What makes you think something is bothering me?"

"You're drinking before dinner."

"I could be celebrating."

Tyler sat next to Sasha on the couch. "If something is bothering you, then you can be honest. Let me be there for you like you were for me."

The hallway clock chimed and Sasha's pulse soared. Hell, the room might as well have been spinning. Dylan and her hadn't reached a solution before he left and checked into his hotel room. And thought after thought popped into Sasha's head. Like with how the universe couldn't have been cruel for her giving her a second chance, only to yank it away. Life should have been getting easier with age, not harder.

Whether she could be honest with Tyler was a separate issue, though. Even if she hadn't thought twice about being there for him. A difference existed between venting to someone about a hectic day and revealing a double life.

"It's complicated," Sasha mumbled.

"Do you hate me that much? Because I'd never judge you."

"This has nothing to do with how our dynamic was in the past."

"Then what?" Tyler asked.

"You wouldn't understand."

"Try me." Tyler wiped a tear from Sasha's right cheek, yet Sasha didn't push him away. She could tell the difference between a friendly gesture—like with a parenting ruffling their child's hair—and Ivan groping her below the waist.

"You'd despise me if I were honest."

Tyler snickered. "Don't be ridiculous—I'm sure your revelation can't be that bad."

"Fine. You wanna know the truth?" Sasha finished her bourbon. "I've been lying to you, because I'm not Riley."

"Okay. I'm cutting you off."

"This has nothing to do with being tipsy," Sasha said. "I'm Riley's twin sister, Sasha."

"Riley has a twin sister?"

Sasha couldn't say Tyler's question shocked her. If roles were reversed, then Sasha wouldn't have mentioned her delinquent, prostitute sister to her family. That kind of life wasn't exactly "Keeping up with the Joneses" material.

"There's a very good reason for what I did," Sasha said.

"And what's that?"

"I assumed Riley's life so I could escape human trafficking."

"If you're living Riley's life, then where's Riley?"

"Riley committed suicide," Sasha whispered, almost not getting the words out.

"How?"

Sasha wiped a bead of sweat from her forehead. "By jumping off the bridge down the road and into the lake."

"That's awful," Tyler said.

Sasha grabbed Tyler's arm. "You can't tell your mother the truth—you just can't."

Tyler didn't even blink. "Relax. Your secret is safe with me."

Sasha's breathing slowed. Whether she believed Tyler or not didn't matter. Something went her way for once, and that was enough for the moment. Besides, she could either fight Ivan or fight Tyler, but she didn't have the tenacity for battling both of them. Not when a solution to the Ivan problem escaped her.

CHAPTER 14

TYLER

Tyler stumbled out of a motel room the following day after Sasha's revelation. Then, his jaw quaked. Jake stood by the window overlooking the courtyard, which was a few feet to the left of the room Tyler just exited.

"What are you doing here?" Tyler asked.

"I followed you."

"I can see that."

Jake crossed his arms. "I saw you tailing Mr. Parker after class."

"And you couldn't have minded your own business?"

"Nope." Jake pointed to Tyler's collar. "You might wanna fix your shirt."

Tyler grimaced after checking his shirt. Jake might have been a lot of things since he told Tyler to drop dead, yet he wasn't a liar. Tyler's tag was on the front of the tee-shirt, and he would be more discreet in the future. Doing so was the least he could do—Tyler wouldn't speculate about what his life would have been like if other people besides Tyler and Sasha uncovered his arrangement with Mr. Parker. Like if his entire campus became privy to his concrete. One false impression was the only thing necessary for providing fodder for gossip.

"Cheating on me with our professor is a new low, Ty," Jake said.

Tyler took his shirt off, then put it on the right way. "You've got no idea what is going on. But, hey. No secret you've got no problem judging me."

"I wouldn't have played detective if I didn't care about you."

Tyler pressed the elevator button to the right of him. "I'm not doing this."

"You owe me an explanation." Jake placed his hand over Tyler's right hand when Tyler was about to pull it away from the DOWN arrow.

"I don't have to give you anything."

"I'm sorry for what I said. That was insensitive of me in light of what happened to your first stepmother." Jake's breath tickled Tyler's skin.

And now Tyler might as well have been reliving the night he first slept with Jake. Something about his close proximity just electrified every cell in his body. Like with how Jake lingered in front of Tyler, hands wrapped around each other while they tilted their heads before kissing.

"If you're in trouble, then I wanna know," Jake said.

Tyler hissed. "Not here."

"I can't believe you're exchanging sex for grades," Jake said a few minutes later while him and Tyler sat in the front of Jake's car.

"Do you hate me?" Tyler asked.

"No. But I wished you'd come to me before agreeing to this indecent proposal."

"I didn't go all the way with Mr. Parker until after I broke up with you."

"I'm not concerned about that."

"You aren't?"

"Anything less than going all the way isn't a big deal," Jake said.

Tyler grinned. "Thanks."

"We've gotta figure a way out of this arrangement for you," Jake said.

Tyler whipped his head back and forth. Please. He knew better than for wishing a solution into existence. Real life wasn't like Disney cartoons when a magical solution appeared out of nowhere when all hope seemed lost.

"I need to pass math," Tyler said.

"You can't keep hooking up with Mr. Parker till the semester is over."

"I don't have a choice."

"You always have a choice," Jake said.

Tyler frowned. "No offense, but I don't have time for a lecture."

"I'm not scolding you—I'm only being honest."

"I didn't ask for your opinion," Tyler said.

"You decided to confess the truth to me."

"One thing doesn't make sense." Tyler fought back the tears—crying wasn't an option. Jake knowing the truth about what him and Mr. Parker were doing already created the allusion how he might as well have streaked across campus.

"I'm listening."

"Mr. Parker insisting on me no longer seeing you, yet he's still with his wife."

"You don't think he has real feelings for you, do you?"

Tyler shrugged. "Anything is possible."

A car alarm echoed through the motel parking lot, and Tyler almost jumped out of the front passenger seat. Nothing like an unexpected noise for ruining the mood. And the time of day didn't help either—the only lighting was from the stars and full moon glowing overhead in the night sky.

"Thanks for your honesty," Jake said.

"You've gotta promise me something."

"Okay."

"Please don't meddle. Doing so would make this whole thing even worse."

"Fine. But there's one thing I want." Jake's smirk widened. "Kiss me like it's just and you me and nothing else matters."

"Done." Tyler leaned towards Jake without another word, then pressed his hands against Jake's cheeks. Tyler closed his eyes, inhaling the sweet scent of whatever deodorant Jake wore. Tyler might not have had forever with Jake, yet he had this moment, and he'd make it count. Tyler—like everyone else—deserved getting caught up in picturesque kiss once in his life.

Jake knowing the truth might have also meant Tyler's life could only improve going forward. Admitting a problem was sometimes the only logical first step—Tyler's dynamic with Jake would never improve if Tyler never told Jake the truth.

***

Tyler walked through his front door sometime later.

Sasha happened to be sitting on the living room couch, sipping bourbon. So, Tyler's constricted throat was only natural. Nothing bad could happen to Sasha—even if most people wouldn't have approved of her con—because Sasha listened more than his own mother had. And said fact filled Tyler with more happiness than he ever knew was possible. The situation should've been reversed, because his fake stepmother wasn't supposed to care about him more than his own mom.

"Everything okay?" Tyler asked after stepping into the living room.

"I felt like having a drink."

"Is Mom home?"

"No. Another late night at the office."

"Wonderful."

"You can join me for a drink—I won't tell your mother," Sasha said. "And we could order a pizza for dinner if you want."

Tyler snorted. "Relax. My mother already knows I drink. As for the pizza, that'd be great. I didn't have time to eat today on campus"

Sasha giggled. "Hold on. Your mother knows about your drinking?"

Tyler plopped onto the couch. "Yeah, and she doesn't care as long as I don't drink and drive."

"Fair enough. Not like I'm in the mood for an afterschool special." Sasha chugged more bourbon. She grabbed the extra glass on table in front of her and poured a more than generous serving before handing Tyler the cup. "How was your day? Did you figure out what you're gonna do about your professor?"

"We don't have to talk about my problems."

"I'd rather discuss you."

Tyler had to acknowledge something—at least to himself, that was. If he got his way, then Sasha would always be Riley. Didn't matter if the idea was unfair for his mother. This was his chance for reclaiming a family. A family that had been stolen from him when his first stepmother, Janice died. A family that existed in name only once his mother married Riley. And a family that was now in reach. So, Tyler wouldn't let anyone or anything stop him from achieving this smaller goal. And he wouldn't even contemplate what would've happened if his mother ever unraveled Sasha's con.

"You'd be doing me a favor," Sasha continued.

"I want you to know I wasn't lying," Tyler said. "I've got no intention of snitching on you—I'd never stoop so low."

"I'm serious. I wanna know what you're going do about your situation. Pretending a problem doesn't exist only works for so long—just look at me and my predicament with Ivan."

"Jake discovered the truth." Tyler chugged half of his drink, ignoring the burning sensation in his throat. Maybe, just, maybe he'd trick himself into believing he had the perfect life one day. No harm in an occasional delusional—it wasn't like he thought he was Santa Claus.

"Is that a bad thing?" Sasha asked.

"No. I've just gotta figure out how to handle Mr. Parker," Tyler said.

"I propose a toast."

"To what?" Tyler asked.

"To being miserable together—at least we've got each other."

"Sure." Tyler's glass clinked against Sasha's, then he devoured his remaining bourbon. In a morbid way, Sasha had a point. The only thing worse than their respective situations was if they didn't have each other to confide in. Like that saying about misery loving company, because as Tyler realized long ago, corny sentiments often contained the most profound truth.

CHAPTER 15

RILEY

Riley's head remained on Josh's chest.

Josh stroked her hair while she continued cuddling with her "boyfriend." A week had passed since her encounter with Lola, Riley didn't regret letting Lola go away. The real Riley being alive wasn't her biggest problem—Adam was. She wouldn't stop until he lost everything—there was no forgiving selling her on the black market because she was born last and him and her mother hadn't anticipated identical triplets.

"Something wrong?" Josh asked.

"I want tomorrow night to go well."

"It will."

"How can you be so sure?" Riley asked.

"He'd be crazy not to care about you." Josh drank from the glass of water on the bedside table next to me. "Being your father also still means something even if he didn't live up to that role. He's gotta feel something even if the feeling is innate."

"Makes sense."

"Promise not to worry anymore about the dinner?"

"Fine," Riley said.

"There's one more promise I need."

Riley feigned a smile. "Anything."

"Promise me that your plan doesn't involve murder?"

Riley scooted away from Josh. "You should know better than asking a question like that."

"I'm serious, Riley."

Riley cackled. "Relax. There are plenty of ways for getting revenge without killing someone. I also have no desire to go to jail."

"Good."

"You believe me, right?" Riley asked.

Josh nodded. "Absolutely. We both know how you know better than to lie to me again."

"True."

Josh gave Riley a quick kiss on the lips, then rolled out of bed. "Wanna join me in the shower?"

"Maybe next time."

"No problem." Josh walked to the bathroom, lock clicking a moment later.

Riley breathed a sigh of relief once the gushing of shower water reverberated through the motel room. She didn't know what she would have done if Josh hadn't believed her. It wasn't that sleeping with Josh repulsed her—it didn't. There were worse guys she could be with. Yet Riley still wanted to take a moment for herself.

Not killing Lola in the alley was one thing, yet she'd be more conscious of her actions going forward. It was a thought, at least. If Lola survived all this time, then she couldn't underestimate Lola or anyone else. Like Adam, for example. Him caring about her at some point in the future couldn't stop her from completing her plan. Although what her plan actually entailed remained to be seen.

Another thought soon formed in her mind. More specifically, the question Josh asked about whether her plan involved murder. There was no denying how ambiguous her plan might have been. She had gone back and forth about whether she'd kill Adam. Providing joy and then ripping it away didn't mean she had to kill. Yet she couldn't deny the euphoria that gutting him like a fish would create. If she killed Adam, then that was it.

The bathroom door opened, revealing Josh. A towel remained wrapped around his waist while he grabbed a shirt and pair of shorts from one of the drawers.

"How was the shower?" Riley asked.

Josh shuffled towards Riley, shirt and shorts tucked under his right armpit. "Great. But it would've been better with you."

Riley couldn't have criticized Josh's neediness no matter much doing so tempted her. Counting to ten in her head was the only thing worth doing. Couldn't alienate until Josh until she was done with him.

Josh's face drooped. "Sorry. I shouldn't have come on so strong."

Riley tugged Josh's hands, pulling his body against hers. Their lips were now only a couple of inches away from her.

"I wouldn't have slept with you if I didn't want to," Riley said.

"Really?" Josh asked.

Riley cupped Josh's chin. "When was the last time I did something that I didn't want to?"

"Good point."

"Anyway, we can shower tomorrow night before the dinner."

Riley hadn't so much as sneezed during her offer, so she was getting better and better with this whole con thing with each passing day. Some people wouldn't have known how to manipulate while still distancing themselves from a person, yet that was one issue Riley wasn't preoccupied with. A simple push and pull she mastered a long time ago.

"Sounds good," Josh said.

"Would you wanna go out for Mexican food?" Riley asked. "I'm craving tequila."

"Sure."

"I still can't believe Adam manages an art gallery." Riley threw the covers off her, then got out of bed.

"What'd you expect?" Josh asked.

"I don't know. Drug dealer seemed like a likelier profession."

***

"Thank you for bringing the wine." Adam shifted his seat at the dining room table.

Riley's elbows slid onto the table. "Don't worry about it."

"It's fantastic. Moscato will be my new go to wine." Adam brought the glass up to his nose, then swirled the wine. After that, he sniffed the aroma

113

before finishing his glass and pouring himself another.

"Riley has great taste in wine," Josh said.

Adam chucked. "I can tell."

"And the best part was how the bottle was only eleven dollars with tax," Riley said.

"That's fantastic. You'll have to tell me the name of the store."

"No problem." Riley took another bite of ziti before having more wine. The mixture of the sweat and tart flavors electrified her taste buds while she let the wine linger in her mouth before swallowing it.

"I'm serious," Adam said, raising his voice.

Riley didn't know if she would have laughed or been embarrassed. Her father might have sported a buttoned-down shirt, khaki pants, and blazer, yet she couldn't shake the image of her father from her first conversation with him after she arrived in LA.

And Adam expanding his repertoire of good wine provided some amusement, and Riley bit her lip, suppressing her amusement. To Riley, Adam's idea of being a good host would have been providing Coors Light to guests.

Josh turned to Riley. "What are you thinking about?"

"Nothing important," Riley said.

"Don't be coy," Josh said.

"Josh is right. If you've got something to say, then tell us." Adam grabbed his napkin, wiping tomato bits from his lips.

Riley's gaze moved to the flame flickering from the candle on the middle of the table. Adam might have been a lot of things, yet she couldn't accuse him of not trying. Her plan couldn't have gone better if she tried.

"I'm just so thankful we're sharing a meal together," Riley said.

"Me too," Adam replied.

Riley's eyes widened. "Really?"

"Yeah." Adam grabbed his wine glass, then took a large swig. "I don't know what I would've done if you hadn't given me a second chance."

"Even though you were reluctant at first?" Riley asked.

"Yeah. Your persistence is a sign that you're meant to be in my life," Adam said.

Now, Riley couldn't stop herself from giggling. Her father was too young for corny speeches. His comment was the type of thing she would have expected from an elderly person.

"It's just a shame how Sasha can't be here with us," Adam said.

Riley almost spat at the wine in her mouth after exchanging a look with Josh. Sasha was the last thing they needed to discuss. Sasha was in Connecticut, and that was where she'd stay—if Riley had her way, that was. Adding Sasha to the situation was a variable Riley couldn't afford. No telling what Sasha might say or do. Just because Sasha didn't know Riley was really Katrina didn't mean she didn't know incriminating things about her. Like with Riley went into hiding with Vincent after framing Sasha for the fire that caused her stint in prison.

"Do you like sports?" Josh asked.

Riley's heart would have lurched if she was a good person. A part of her couldn't deny how she didn't deserve Josh. He just came to her aid despite Riley not asking him to do so, because that was husband material.

"Not really. The gallery takes up a lot of time," Adam said. "But I watch a lot of Netflix."

"That's cool," Josh said.

"I'd love to show you my gallery at some point," Adam said.

"That's be fun." Riley drank her remaining wine.

"We could make an afternoon of it and then go out for dinner. The gallery is closed on Sundays, so that might be the perfect time. You wouldn't want a tour during peak hours," Adam said.

Riley grabbed the wine bottle, which was a couple of inches away from the candle. She shook her head—the bottle was empty. Not even one drop of wine left at the bottom.

Deep breaths for her, though. The dinner going her way was what she needed to focus on. Anything else was a distraction. Besides, the abstract painting on the wall confirmed her initial impression of Adam. Noble people didn't have paintings of topless women in their dining room. So, in Riley's mind, she might have been more justified with her revenge scheme. Her father could have been a pervert, and she might have been doing the world a favor.

"I definitely wanna see the gallery," Riley said.

"Great," Adam said. "I've got a feeling this is gonna be the beginning of a whole new chapter in my life."

If only Riley had been drinking something when Adam made his comment—she would've spat out the beverage. Even the Hallmark Channel wouldn't have been so corny, further proving how different Riley was from her father. Riley was anything but cliché, because she refused to let anyone label her. Being a chameleon was necessary for psychopathic tendencies—she adapted on a moment's notice to suit whatever environment she was in. Life was also more enjoyable when played like a game. The only question was how soon she'd be victorious over Adam.

CHAPTER 16

LOLA

A little over a week had passed since Vanessa suggested leaving LA and returning to Connecticut. But Lola somehow succeeded with stalling, and they were currently seated on a park bench while a few clouds dotted the otherwise bare, blue sky.

Vanessa grunted. "You can't stall forever, Lola."

"I'm not stalling." Lola tied the knot in her headscarf tighter. Then, she pushed her Aviator sunglasses up the bridge of her nose. "We just don't need to return back in Connecticut."

"I can't be in LA indefinitely."

"Nobody is forcing you to stay."

"It's not like I have a choice."

"What are you talking about?" Lola asked.

Laughter roared, and Lola's attention drifted from Vanessa to the woman, man, girl, and boy playing Frisbee in the distance. Yet Lola couldn't fight back the burning sensation in her stomach. Lola would have given anything to have a carefree life, because her existence should have involved more than surviving. Like with how her life was stolen from her that night a couple of weeks before her seventeenth birthday. One evening shouldn't have had such an enormous impact on her life, yet it had. Lola shook her head in a vigorous fashion. Someday, that bitch, Katrina, would pay for everything she did.

"I can't leave you alone," Vanessa said.

"I'm twenty-four years old." Lola sipped her coffee. "It's not like I haven't taken care of myself these last seven years."

"You don't even have a job."

"What? Does sending me money every month make you angry?" Lola asked.

"It's not about the money, and you know it."

"Then what?" Lola demanded

"Tell me something. What do you wanna accomplish by staying here?" Vanessa nibbled on the last part of her croissant. "No offense, but you aren't with Preston anymore."

Preston. He was the one thing Lola wanted more than a real family. However, she could never have him. Not when his inquisition ensured her life imploding. No telling how he would react to how Lola wasn't her real name. The paradox was beyond cruel, though. Preston gave her an opportunity for confessing her problem, yet Lola just couldn't be honest.

"That's harsh," Lola said.

"It's the truth."

"He's dumped me, not the other way around." Lola finished her coffee, then tossed it into an adjacent garbage can. "I can't make him be in a relationship he doesn't wanna be in."

"That proves my point." Vanessa grunted. "And it'd be nice if you stopped arguing with me."

"I don't think Katrina is gonna kill me—you were right. She must be in LA because of our father."

"That doesn't mean she won't come for you one day."

A Golden Retriever barked, and Lola would have smiled if she hadn't been filled with more rage than a child after eating vegetables because of her conversation with her grandmother. A lady with gray hair—who sported a fur coat—was the dog's owner, and said fact was kind of ironic. A smaller dog would have been a more manageable pet than something as large as a Golden Retriever. And for once, the universe hadn't disagreed with Lola. A squirrel darted across the grass, and the Golden Retriever darted forehead, almost sending the owner flying.

"Don't invent a problem that doesn't exist," Lola said.

"You were the one who ran into Katrina."

"But she didn't kill me."

"She could have," Vanessa interrupted.

"There's one point you're missing." Lola played with a loose strand of her hair. "I don't have a life in Connecticut."

"But you would have me."

"That's not enough."

"I have bills to pay!" Vanessa exclaimed.

"You can pay them online." Lola giggled. "Or maybe your too much of a dinosaur for doing that."

Vanessa's lips twisted. "Don't insult me—I'm the only friend you've got."

"I'm not trying to be rude. I'm just telling you how I feel." Lola sucked in a deep breath. "Doesn't living in Connecticut while not spending anytime with Sasha kill you?"

"It's for the best. I can't be in her life if I've gotta keep you a secret."

"That's the real reason you resent me, isn't it?" Lola asked. "You're pissed for choosing me over Sasha?"

Vanessa didn't respond.

"Here's something you've might have missed," Lola continued. "I never asked you to choose between Sasha and me."

Sunlight glared in Lola's face while she tapped her feet against the ground. Lola almost never acknowledge that fact, yet a small part of her sympathized with Sasha despite her problems being more than enough to deal with. Abandoning her life was one thing, yet Lola hadn't been framed for a crime she didn't commit in addition to how she hadn't resorted to prostitution.

"Put yourself in my position," Vanessa said. "Could you associate with Sasha if you were me and knew what I did?"

"That's not the point."

Vanessa got up. "You're too much, Lola. You think you can go around playing games, but you're wrong. This is real life, and there are consequences."

Lola pouted. "I'm not playing games."

"It's a figure of speech." Vanessa clutched her purse strap. "Wanna be your own person? Fine.

Well, return to your apartment by yourself. I'm sure you'll have no problem getting an UBER or a LYFT." Vanessa marched away, drifting out of sight after another beat.

Lola kicked her foot against the garbage can, then wailed. Yet the physical pain didn't compare to her current increased heartbeat. Her grandmother was right no matter how harsh she sounded— Vanessa was her only friend. And maybe, just maybe, Lola would have to be smarter in the future.

A guy hollered. It was Preston.

"Is that you, Lola?" Preston asked, approaching Lola.

"Hi," Lola mumbled.

"What are you doing?"

"Just enjoying the day."

"The breakup left a bad taste in my mouth," Preston said.

"What's your point?"

"It doesn't have to be this way."

"I'm sorry Preston, but I can't be honest with you, and I don't wanna have to lie," Lola said.

If Lola was several years younger, then she would've cared how what she said sounded ridiculous. But she was beyond giving a fuck. Not ignoring just how complicated life could be was the one advantage she had over everyone else.

Preston sighed. "I shouldn't have been so demanding about you telling me your secret."

"No shit."

Preston wiped sweat from his face instead of responding to Lola's question.

"I hope you're doing okay," Lola said.

Preston pressed his hands together. "I'm not gonna force you to be honest with me if you don't want to, but feel free to call me if you ever need anything."

"Thanks."

"I'm serious. Don't be a stranger." Preston jogged away, then approached one of the park's snack vendors.

Lola licked her lips. Her life could have been worse. In a way, the universe handed her a gift. Whether she'd be honest with Preston was another question, though. Once she told Preston the truth, she couldn't undo her bombshell.

But maybe, just maybe, telling Preston the truth was best. Not rushing exposing Katrina was fair, yet the definition of insanity kept ringing in her mind. If she always lived in the shadows, then her life would never change. Besides, Lola would never have a real relationship with anyone unless she was honest about who she was. Her grandmother's money was one thing, yet no check stopped the emptiness from falling asleep way later than she should have each time a relationship failed.

CHAPTER 17

SASHA

Sasha sighed while remaining in her seat at the outdoor café.

Dylan was over half an hour late, and hadn't responded to her text about what caused his delay. And Sasha loved that fact. She didn't need one more bad thing—like the possibility of Dylan having a real emergency—happening.

Someone whistled at her. "Nice to see you, babe."

That voice. Her back hairs rose in a matter of seconds, because she had a pretty good idea about who stood in front of her even without making eye contact.

Sasha lifted her gaze off the table. "How the hell did you find me, Ivan?"

"This seat taken?" Ivan asked.

Sasha froze. Leaving wasn't an option no matter how much she would have loved to put a million miles between her and Ivan. Sasha didn't know if Ivan had a weapon on him, and wouldn't risk her life. Not until she understood the situation better.

Ivan sat in the chair across next to Sasha. He removed a pack of cigarettes and lighter from his leather jacket pocket. Ivan yanked the cigarette out from the pack, placed the filter in his mouth, and lit it in a swift motion.

"Disgusting," Sasha said.

"What did I tell you about showing me respect?" Ivan took a long drag. A plume of smoke fell from his mouth, and the vile stench stung Sasha's nostrils.

"Did you hurt Dylan?"

"That's for me to know and you to find out."

Sasha leaned forward. "I'm not playing a game, Ivan. If you harm one hair on Dylan's head, then I'll chop your balls off."

"I'd love to see you try." Ivan inhaled, then exhaled a thick, cloud of smoke. "We both know you don't have the guts to try."

"Don't underestimate me."

"I doubt you'd kill a fly."

A bee buzzed in front of Sasha's face and she crushed it, stinger digging into her palm. Thank goodness that she wasn't allergic to bees, because Sasha wouldn't have risked an allergic reaction just for proving a point.

Not being on drugs didn't mean her surroundings weren't spinning—they were. Sasha was nowhere closer to discovering what did or didn't happen to Dylan. And that fact more than sucked. Sasha didn't know what she would have done if she never saw Dylan again. Her almost kiss with Dylan wasn't how their dynamic could end. After everything she had been through, Sasha had no misgivings about her entitlement to a happily ever after with Dylan.

"What did you do to Dylan?" Sasha asked.

"I didn't do anything to him, but maybe you'd understood that if you weren't a dumb bitch."

There it was. The thing Sasha despised most about Ivan. Being a pimp was bad enough, yet she didn't have a word for someone who had zero respect for women.

"Cut the bullshit." Sasha sipped her coffee. "Dylan told me how you threatened to kill his parents if he didn't bring me back to Manhattan."

"We're beyond that."

"Excuse me."

"Dylan isn't my focus anymore—you are. People don't leave me."

Sasha slammed her fist against the table, ignoring the other patrons. "Where is he?"

"Relax. He's probably enjoying hotel room service."

"You didn't hurt him?"

"The plan was just to lure you to breakfast. After that, you're my problem."

"Let me guess. You're gonna kill me?"

"Quit being so dramatic."

"I'm not stupid, so please don't insult my intelligence," Sasha said.

"Fleeing and assuming Riley's life is clever—I'll give you that." Ivan tossed the cigarette onto the ground after taking his final drag. He grabbed something from his shirt pocket, concealing it in his hand before shoving his arm under the table.

The blade caressed Sasha's leg while she winced. The knife hadn't dug into her skin, drawing blood, yet Sasha wouldn't be fooled. Anyone could have inferred how she only had a matter of seconds before Ivan finished her.

"Just do it, you coward. Kill me," Sasha said.

"I'm not gonna kill you." Ivan removed his hand from under the table, clicked a button, and put the pocketknife back into his shirt pocket after the blade rescinded back inside the knife.

"You've gotta be joking."

"I'm not."

"Don't you want me to return to Manhattan with you?"

"Yes." Ivan lit another cigarette before blowing out smoke. "But I'm not lying—I'm not gonna hurt. Not this time."

"Then what?" Sasha asked.

"If you don't return to Manhattan with me in the next 72 hours, then I'll kill Cece and Tyler."

Sasha's teeth jabbed her lip. She shouldn't have been shocked by Ivan's latest threat. Not harming her didn't mean Ivan wouldn't harm other people. And using people that meant nothing to him as pawns was the gangster thing to do.

"Lovely," Sasha mumbled.

"You still have my cellphone number, so text me when you've made you're ready to leave."

"What makes you think I'll agree?"

Ivan cackled. "Have you forgotten how well I know you? There's no way you'd let other people pay for your mistake."

"I hope you know how much of a piece of shit you are."

"No need to state the obvious." Ivan got up, then stood behind Sasha, cigarette still in his right hand. The people at the table next to Sasha's had left a few minutes ago, so Sasha and Ivan had the entire outdoor portion of the café to themselves. He jerked her head backward with his left hand before shoving the cigarette's end in front of Sasha's right cheek. "Just because I'm not gonna hurt you for your disobedience doesn't mean I won't in the future. So, remember that when you're unable to fall asleep tonight. Be a shame to give you a scar like I did on your back."

Sasha cried after Ivan dashed down the block and was out of sight. Damn. She couldn't believe how naïve she had been. A smarter person would have anticipated the plan imploding, because she couldn't argue with Ivan. He was right even if Cece and Tyler were strangers to her. Sasha would have rather died than let someone else suffer for a mistake she made. Her stint in prison was all anyone needed for understanding that fact.

***

Sasha finished her bourbon hours later while sitting in the mansion's living room. But she didn't give herself a refill. Instead, tears lingered in her eyes. Cece was working late yet again and she had no idea when Tyler would be home.

Only Sasha just realized she hadn't been honest with herself. The situation stunk because of other reasons besides Ivan threatening Cece and Tyler. Dylan betrayed her, and that wasn't something that could be shaken off. He was the one person she should have been able to count on most.

Sasha rested her hands on her lap. How funny for her. The guy who had been a gentleman with her ended up hurting her the most. What irony.

Tyler shuffled into the living room. "Everything okay?"

"No, but I don't wanna discuss the problem."

"Might make you feel better."

"No. Not this time."

"What are you getting at?" Tyler asked.

"Ivan knows I'm in Connecticut and if I don't return with him to Manhattan within the next seventy-two hours, then he's gonna kill you and your mother."

Tyler's jaw trembled. "You've gotta be kidding me."

"I wish."

Tyler snickered after an awkward silence ensued between Sasha and him. And maybe, just maybe Sasha might smile again. If she had it her way, then Tyler would have come up with the perfect plan for dealing with Ivan. At least in the parallel universe where wishing what she wanted into existence was enough.

"What is it?" Sasha asked.

"I know how to deal with Ivan."

"How? Kill him?"

"No. However, the plan is kind of sneaky."

"I don't care. Tell me."

"If you recorded Ivan confessing to criminal activity and then emailed it to me for backup and threatened to release said recording if anything happened to you, then he'd have to leave you alone."

"That's brilliant—you should be a writer."

Tyler chuckled. "I'm actually a Creative Writing major."

"Cool. Anyway, I'm definitely gonna do blackmail Ivan no matter how risky doing so is. I'm nobody's bitch anymore."

"That's the spirit." Tyler patted Sasha's knee. "Remember I'm always here for you no matter what."

Sasha returned Tyler's pat with a shoulder clap. Sometimes, the best friend was the least obvious person. Tyler just saved Sasha's life, and she would be forever thankful for his suggestion. Even if the solution involved blackmail—it was a price she'd willingly pay.

CHAPTER 18

TYLER

Tyler entered the car parked by his curb the following morning after suggesting blackmail to Sasha. Then, he kissed the guy sitting in the driver's seat. Having a complicated life didn't Tyler couldn't take a moment for himself, and spend time with Jake before his morning class. Tyler wasn't a complete fool—he and Jake would arrive in separate cars.

They pulled back after a moment, and Jake handed Tyler the Venti Caramel Macchiato in his cup holder. "Here," Jake said.

"Thanks." Tyler smiled after taking the drink from Jake. Wow. He couldn't believe how idiotic he'd been. He didn't deserve Jake going out of his way when Tyler's brilliant thinking, yet here Tyler was, getting both Starbucks and Jake.

"Don't mention it, Ty."

"I didn't get you anything."

"Hanging out with you is gift enough." Jake scratched the top of his head. "But there's something we should discuss."

The empty feeling in Tyler's stomach expanded. Informing him they needed to chat was just what he wanted. Having his mother use that expression was bad enough.

Jake elbowed Tyler. "I'm not looking to fight with you—I actually have a plan for dealing with Mr. Parker."

"I'm listening."

Tyler hadn't thought twice about his response. He might have been a lot of things, yet he wasn't stubborn enough for refusing help. If Jake had a solution for the professor problem, then he'd listen. It wasn't like his life could get worse.

"End your relationship with Mr. Parker," Jake said.

A school bus's squeaked lingered after pulling up to the driveway across the street. The neighbor's kid—who couldn't have been more than chest level—scurried to the end of the driveway, then got on the bus. Tyler soon exhaled a breath. What he would have given to be in elementary school. Adults were wrong—ignorance wasn't bliss, it was protection. At least then Tyler wouldn't have juggled multiple blackmail plots. Tyler stroked his chin. He hadn't even known what blackmail entailed when he was in elementary school.

"Well?" Jake continued.

Tyler's eyebrows shot up. "That's not an option. I'd fail the class if I didn't continue sleeping with him."

"Not exactly."

"You're gonna have to be more specific."

"You've got all the power in the situation."

"I was the one who offered to do anything he wanted for a passing grade." Tyler looked away, shame burning through him. "What I didn't know was how sex was on his brain."

Jake laughed. "He has a wife."

"So?"

"Use that fact to your advantage. Tell him if he doesn't accept your fling is over in addition to continue changing your grades, then you'll expose him to his wife."

Tyler didn't know if he should be ashamed or proud of his boyfriend—he underestimated Jake. In the past, he would have never suspected Jake of suggesting an underhanded solution. Even if Tyler gave Sasha a similar answer yesterday afternoon. Jake was so paranoid about being accused of cheating that Tyler couldn't even do his homework with him. But maybe, just maybe, Tyler might have appreciated morality too much. The socially unacceptable thing was sometimes the right action, yet one fact hadn't escaped him.

"I don't know," Tyler stammered.

"What's to think about? It's the perfect solution."

"I don't wanna out someone who isn't ready to be out."

"Mr. Parker made you end our relationship," Jake said.

"True. I can't argue with that."

"What did you say?" Jake asked. "Are you gonna crush him so we can move on with our lives?"

"What about you?"

Jake's pupils dilated. "I don't know what you're getting at."

"What if he won't leave you alone. Not toying with me doesn't mean you won't become his next victim."

His smirk expanded. "Then make leaving me alone one of your conditions."

"God. You don't know how much I love you." Tyler placed his drink back in the cup holder, then kissed Jake. Except he used tongue this time, and Jake dug his fingers into Tyler's cheeks. More obstacles might arise in the future, yet Tyler ignored that fact for the moment. This was his second chance with Jake, and he wouldn't let anything or anyone ruin it.

***

Tyler was the last one left in his math class several hours later, yet he wouldn't have it any other way.

His pulse drumming in his ears wasn't even a big deal. If Sasha could face Ivan, then he could chat with Mr. Parker one last time. The campus was neutral territory and his life would be fine—eventually, that was.

Mr. Parker snickered from his chair behind the wooden desk at the front of the classroom. "Shouldn't you have left?"

"Would you mind locking the door?" Tyler asked. "I'd like to talk, and we can't have anyone interrupting us."

Mr. Parker gave a small frown. "I thought we weren't meeting till tomorrow night?"

"I promise I won't take up much of your time."

Mr. Parker walked over to Tyler, then cupped his chin. "Don't be ridiculous. You're never a bother."

An icy sensation tickled Tyler's back, but he just took several deep breaths. He'd be done with Mr. Parker in several minutes, and then him and Jake could celebrate later.

"The door," Tyler said.

"Right." Mr. Parker wobbled over to the door before returning to Tyler's desk.

Tyler didn't remain in his seat, though. Instead, he grabbed his backpack and stood on the tips of his toes. If he really wanted to have the power in the situation, then bravado was required. Mr. Parker couldn't irk him—not even for a second.

"Something wrong?" Mr. Parker asked.

"For you maybe."

"I'm not following. Did I upset you?"

"I'm breaking up with you," Tyler blurted.

"Then you'll fail math even if you pass one of the quizzes or tests."

Tyler would need a warm shower when he got home. He couldn't believe he'd ever been intimate with Mr. Parker—like yesterday after math class when they locked the door and Mr. Parker bent him over the desk. Being so close and vulnerable wasn't even the worst part. It was Mr. Parker wreaking of cigarette smoke. Any hotness his professor had vanished because of Mr. Parker not trying to hide the odor—that was what a decent person would have done. And in a way, sleeping with him Mr. Parker despite his smell being less than desirable resembled someone pointing a gun at Tyler, forcing him to make a decision.

"Nope," Tyler said.

"Do you have amnesia or something? You know our arrangement, and you need to accept the consequences of sleeping with me."

"I'm not afraid of you."

"Then you might wanna speak with more inflection in your voice," Mr. Parker said.

"If you don't accept our breakup, and continue giving me passing grades, then I'll tell your wife everything. I've still got your text messages."

"You aren't that cruel."

Tyler stared his professor. "Try me."

"Have you forgotten about Jake—I could fail him."

"Nice try, but that's one of the conditions."

"What the fuck are you talking about?"

"Making a move against him means making a move against me and I'd also drop your closeted status on your wife."

Mr. Parker snarled. "Tell me something. Are you enjoying this? Because the time we spent together was special."

"It's simple." Tyler gripped Mr. Parker's chin, clawing his fingernails into his professor's skin much harder than Jake had earlier in the day. "I've got no problem blackmailing you because sleeping with you meant nothing to me."

"You don't mean that," Mr. Parker said.

Tyler let out a loud chuckle. "Yeah, I do. At best, the sex was fleeting between us."

"Don't be impulsive—we had a good thing going, and I might be open to you also seeing Jake if you continue sleeping with me."

"Nice try. We're done."

Mr. Parker rubbed his eye. "You've got a lot of nerve doing this to me. I was the best thing that ever happened to you."

"If you believe that, then you need professional help." Tyler released Mr. Parker's jaw, then shoved his professor backwards.

One fact remained clear while Tyler waited for Mr. Parker's attempt at a witty comment. The euphoria from dominating Mr. Parker—even in a not so blatantly sexual way like touching Mr. Parker's chin—was palpable. It was about time for Mr. Parker to understand what not being in control was like.

Mr. Parker clenched a fist. "This ends when I say it does."

"Nope."

"You're making a big mistake, and you won't get away with this."

"Watch me." Tyler strutted towards the door, but turned around when he was about to unlock it. "One more thing."

Mr. Parker grunted. "What?"

"You might wanna join Grindr if you're looking for a man to get you off."

"Leave; I can't stand the sight of you."

"Gladly." Tyler exited the classroom and continued laughing while strolling down the hallway. He was free, and nothing would stop him for pursuing a second chance with Jake. Not even the lump in his throat from Mr. Parker's "big mistake" comment.

Any antics Mr. Parker might have been capable of were tomorrow's problem. Tyler defended himself for once in his life, and he could get used to doing so again in the future. If he didn't respect himself by insisting on a certain standard, then nobody else would do so for him. And there was the fact something went right for him. It might have only been mid-October, but it might as well have been Christmas morning, because the victory over Mr. Parker was just that sweet. And that fact was why Tyler texted Jake before getting in his car—they wouldn't forget about this victory anytime soon. Not if Tyler had something to say about it.

CHAPTER 19

RILEY

Riley mixed the shampoo through her hair while the shower water rattled against the bathtub, drowning out the sports game Josh was watching on the motel TV. She brought her head under the shower head, then rinsed her hair. Her red shampoo dripped into the tub before disappearing into the drain.

Her life couldn't have gone more perfectly if Riley tried. Adam was right where she wanted him—pursuing a genuine father and daughter relationship with her—and she would have felt sorry for him if she cared about being a good person. But no. Adam would be disposed of soon enough. And Riley couldn't forget about Josh—he hadn't so much as raised an eyebrow at her, so he remained clueless about her intentions.

The only other issue was Lola. And Riley wasn't even trying to complicate her life—getting revenge against Adam and stringing Josh along had to be her top priority. Riley just couldn't help imagining the anger coursing through her veins if roles were reversed and someone assumed her like she had with Lola. The emotion wasn't farfetched—nothing worse than someone stealing something that didn't belong to them.

Riley shook her head. Her first instinct was right. Lola could wait till later—if Lola wanted to kill her, then she would have done so that afternoon in the alley.

"What's going on?" Riley asked, towel wrapped around her when she exited the bathroom sometime later.

Josh stood in front of the bed, except his menacing glare hadn't caused Riley's pursed lips. The suitcase next to Josh's right leg was why Riley's mouth gaped. And she couldn't forget about Josh's clench left hand—she could only wonder what he was holding.

Josh didn't blink. "I'm leaving you."

"Why? I thought things were good between us?"

"I think this belongs to you." Josh uncurled his left hand, then through the ring at Riley. It fell on the floor in front of her and she kneeled, picking the gem up.

If only Riley anticipated her luck ending. Riley just couldn't imagine how Josh found her wedding ring—she had it buried in one of her bags.

"Did you go through my stuff?" Riley asked.

"Don't change the subject—this isn't about invading your privacy. But no. To answer your question, I wasn't snooping. I was looking for a Benadryl, and thought you might have one in one of your bags."

"Okay. Let me have it."

Josh locked his arms together. "Why would you have your wedding ring?"

"A lot of people keep old trinkets."

"This isn't your mother's wedding ring, it's the one Cece gave you."

"You're making too much of a big deal out of this."

"You aren't even gonna try spinning the situation?" Josh asked.

Riley couldn't believe what Josh just said—she shouldn't have had to correct him. She never did anything she didn't want to, and this was no exception.

Riley scoffed. "There's no point in defending myself when you already decided your opinion."

"You really don't get this?"

Riley shrugged. "I stand by what I said. You just wanna witness my eternal damnation."

"Hardly. This isn't about punishing you—it's about what this ring represents. It's your insurance policy when you dump me. Let me guess. You were gonna sell it at a pawn shop when we broke up."

"Do you realize how dumb that sounds? I've got no reason to dump you," Riley said.

"We both know that isn't true."

Riley shuffled over to Josh, then she stroked his hair, only for him to step back. "Don't be like this, babe. Don't you know how good I can make you feel?"

"Sex isn't gonna distract me—not this time."

"Then what?"

"I'm going back to Connecticut, and we're done here," Josh said. "Although the room is paid for till the end of the month."

"Fantastic," Riley said.

"I hope you're pleased with yourself, because now you don't have to invent a reason for ending our relationship."

Riley remained silent.

"Goodbye, Riley. If that's even your real name." Josh yanked the handle out, then wheeled his suitcase to the door. He cocked his head. "You better pray I don't tell Sasha that you're still alive."

Someone should have pinched Riley. She didn't think Josh was a complete idiot, yet she never expected him to be so cold. But maybe that was the problem. She underestimated him, and now she would suffer. Someone could only be treated like a doll for so long.

"You wouldn't," Riley said.

"Watch me." Josh opened the door with his free hand before it slammed behind him.

Riley didn't cry while she continued standing in front of the bed. No matter how she felt about Josh, he wasn't completely wrong. Breaking up with her meant Riley didn't have to invent some reason for dumping him. In a way, he did her a favor. Josh hadn't only freed her—he also gave her something for manipulating Adam with. Comforting his "upset" daughter was the type of thing a father wouldn't have thought twice about.

***

Adam snapped the top off the cap off the beer bottle hours later before handing Riley one while she sat in front of the bar and food counter at Adam's art gallery.

"Thanks." Riley took a sip, yet she wouldn't bitch about how drinking beer was comparable to drinking urine. Maybe having a bitter drink would take her mind off Josh leaving her, because pretending to be okay was something the distraught daughter would have done.

Josh took a more than generous swig of his drink. "How about a toast?"

"To what?"

"New beginnings. Great things sometimes happen in the most terrible situations."

Riley's self-control was the only thing stopping her her from laughing. Her father couldn't have been so naïve, yet here she was. Pretending to dream about a better future with a man who wouldn't even be a fleeting thought two months from now.

Riley nodded. "Sure. Having a little extra good luck never hurts."

Riley clanked her beer bottle against Adam's. Hell, she even smiled at him. The best was yet to come for her, because Adam would be her only focus now that she didn't have to continue stringing Adam along. The only question was what her final game of revenge would be. Killing him was the simplest—the ultimate ending. Ending the cycle of violence that began when he sold her on the black market all those years ago.

CHAPTER 20

LOLA

Lola sat at the same outdoor café she went to with her grandmother when Vanessa first arrived in LA. Her heart hadn't pounded as much then, though. And her heart's increased thumping wasn't because of her cappuccino. The reason why her life resembled a child on their first day of school was because Preston just took a seat at her table.

Being honest with Preston, and reconciling with him didn't make her naïve. He was her longest relationship she ever had—almost two years. And if there was a chance they could mend their dynamic, then Lola couldn't ignore the opportunity. Not when she would have always wondered what could have been.

"Thanks for joining me," Lola said.

"No problem. I'm always happy to see you."

The waitress walked up to Lola's table, then glanced at Preston. "Can I get you anything?"

Preston surveyed the menu for a beat. "I'll take a croissant and caramel coffee."

"Coming right up," said the waitress.

Preston flashed a smile. "Thanks."

The waitress left in a matter of seconds and Lola sipped her cappuccino. Wow. She was really gonna be honest with Preston and could only wonder how he'd react. Deep breaths, though. He had never given a reason for doubting him, so she would always believe the best in him until he gave her a reason to do otherwise.

"You were right—I haven't been honest with you," Lola said.

Preston chuckled. "Tell me something I don't know."

"But you've gotta know my deception has nothing to do with hurting you—I was only looking after myself."

Deception. Perhaps she should have chosen a better word. Lola needed all of five seconds for determining the word's negative connation, so Preston might have only thought she was gonna tell an even more outrageous lie.

"Relax." Preston extended his hand and stroked Lola's forehead. However, she didn't recoil from Preston's touch. If anything, Preston should have done more than rub her forehead. Like maybe that reconciliation kiss she dreamed of the second they broke up. "I'd never think you wanted to hurt me."

"Good."

The waitress returned, placing the cup and plate with the croissant on it in front of Preston. "Enjoy," she said.

"Thanks." Preston reached for his coffee, yet steam seeped from the top, so he placed the mug back down on the table.

"Please let me know if you need anything." The waitress once again left as fast as she appeared.

"Just tell me what's going on," Preston said. "We both know you'll feel better after doing so. And I promise I won't judge no matter how awful your bombshell is."

Lola let Preston's words linger in her mind. On a superficial level, she couldn't fault him for what he said. He played the role of supportive boyfriend to a T. But she couldn't help worrying about how outrageous the whole Katrina situation sounded.

So, Lola took another sip of her beverage— bitter and sweet flavors illuminating her taste buds— before speaking.

"Do you hate me?" Lola asked after she finished telling her story sometime later.

"Please don't put words in my mouth."

Lola rested her hand under her chin. "I'd understand if you didn't believe me—almost sounds like something from a soap opera."

"I have one question." Preston gulped more coffee before scarfing down the last bite of his croissant.

"Ask me anything. I've got nothing to hide."

"Why didn't you go to the police?" Preston placed his hand over his neck. "Couldn't your grandmother have gone with you?"

"Weren't you paying attention?" Lola took off her cardigan, then tucked it on the back of her chair. "I was scared. And all I had was my grandmother's word about our father selling Katrina on the black market."

"I'm so sorry you went through this. I can't imagine what your life has been like the last seven years," Preston said.

"You're right—you've got no idea what my life has been like—wondering if Katrina would find me one day."

"At least now I understand why you don't have any friends in LA." Preston chugged his remaining coffee.

"What do you wanna do about us?" Lola asked.

To hell with waiting. Lola was gonna get an answer about her relationship status with Preston, and there was nothing anyone could do about it. Closure was the least she deserved—it wasn't like she demanded diamonds and a mansion on a 100-acre estate.

Preston snickered. "Right to the point—I like it."

"I'm serious, Preston. Either you wanna be with me or you don't, but there's no in between," Lola said.

A cat from the nearby alley purred, and Lola whipped her body around. Hopefully, the black cat wasn't a bad omen. An extra negative force against her just wasn't something she wanted or needed.

"You should take up yoga—it might relieve your tension," Preston said. "But relax. I've already made up my mind."

"You have?"

"Yes. And if this won't convince you, then I don't know what will." Preston kissed Lola, fingers tracing her cheeks.

Lola couldn't be certain if she'd ever have another squabble with Katrina, yet she would forget about her troublesome life for a moment. Before she knew it, the kiss would be over, and she'd wonder if another obstacle might come between her and Preston. So, Lola didn't even fret when a steady patter of rain dripped onto the ground. The inner movie buff in her always wanted to experience a kiss in the rain.

***

"I know you're probably angry, but I don't care," Lola said.

Lola and her grandmother sat at her dining room table hours after Lola's chat with Preston, and she already anticipated the flack Vanessa would give her.

"I'm not mad," Vanessa said.

Lola choked on her wine, then coughed. "You aren't?"

"No. But I do have one request if you wanna stay in LA and be with Preston."

"What's that?"

"I wanna have Preston over for dinner and meet him." Vanessa played with her pearl necklace. "If you're gonna spend the rest of your life with him, then he must pass inspection."

Lola finished her wine. "Fine. I can live with that."

Cringing wasn't required for Lola.

Her grandmother's request was harmless—if she survived dropping her bombshell on Preston, then she could survive anything. A part of her also cherished the idea of a "meet and greet" dinner. The type of thing was something she never experienced before, so unlike other people, she'd take comfort in the mundanity of the dinner. The little things sometimes provided the most comfort.

CHAPTER 21

SASHA

Sasha stood by the mirror to the left of the front door, coating her lips a bright shade of purple. She stuffed the lipstick into her purse and tossed it onto the table next to her. Maybe, just maybe, she'd survive her meeting with Ivan. Stranger things happened all the time. Like patients waking up from a coma after a couple of decades. So, she'd be fine.

She could always kill him if the meeting didn't go her way, though. No remorse required for murdering Ivan—Sasha was only one person in a long list of people Ivan had no problem using.

The doorbell rang, and Sasha her jerked head towards the front door. Time to get the confession and move on with her life.

Sasha gazed one last time at the living room couch where her iPhone was. She turned on the recording app a couple of minutes ago, so inviting Ivan inside the mansion was the only thing left for her to do—her new home was the best place for giving Ivan his answer. This way, Sasha controlled her surroundings.

The doorbell beeped several more times, and Sasha opened the door.

Ivan grumbled. "What kept you so long?"

Sasha giggled. "I wanted to look nice for you."

"Why? You hate me?"

"My looks are the only thing I have to hold onto."

"Whatever."

Sasha gesticulated at Ivan. "Please come inside and make yourself at home."

Ivan's gaze narrowed. "Okay. What's up? You've never used please with me before."

"No reason for our dynamic to be unpleasant."

Ivan followed Sasha into the living room. Sasha sat on the couch next to her iPhone, and Ivan did a 180 of the living room.

Sasha's heart skipped several beats. Looking nice and appearing polite couldn't have meant Ivan suspected something was wrong. Surely, Ivan must have believed she valued her life and wouldn't pull some stunt.

"Something wrong?" Sasha asked.

"No. I was only admiring my surroundings. Seems like you've traded up since your life in Manhattan."

"Survival is the only thing that matters."

"Fair enough." Ivan plopped right next to Sasha on the couch. "Anyway, I want an answer. Are you gonna return to Manhattan with me or am I gonna kill your new family?"

"We've got plenty of time for that."

"Not really. Our flight back to Manhattan leaves in three hours."

Sasha would have snorted if she didn't wanna risk angering Ivan. She couldn't fathom how Ivan assumed she'd say yes. Ivan was a lot of things, yet he couldn't have been blind from the disgust radiating from Sasha's eyes when she was with him.

"There's something we're gonna talk about first," Sasha said.

Ivan wiggled his eyebrows. "And what's that?"

"I've always wondered something."

Ivan stroked a lock of Sasha's hair. "You're gonna have to be more specific, babe."

Sasha forced in a breath. Not the end of the world if Ivan called her, "babe." The feeling of wanting to run to the bathroom and take a shower could be ignored for the moment. Weakness wasn't an option with Ivan. Not when he would exploit it as a weapon against her, because failure just couldn't happen.

"Well?" Ivan demanded.

"Did you really kill Red Tooth?" Sasha asked.

"What's it to you?"

"Only curious to see if your reputation is as big as you claim it is. Most people can't get away with murder."

"Yes, I put a hit out on him," Ivan said. "Big Tree killed him for me, and I relished every second of it. I did what nobody in my family has ever accomplished. Kill the rival crime boss's son."

Sasha massaged her knee. Most people—even wicked ones—still had contradictions, which revealed a sliver of humanity. But not Ivan. Just when Ivan couldn't get worse, he had. Human life shouldn't have been worthless to Ivan. Yet Ivan wouldn't have hesitated with kicking a puppy or throwing a baby out a window.

"Are we done?" Ivan asked.

"There's one more thing I want from you."

"You're awfully bossy—I hope this means you'll swap roles when I fuck the shit out of you later."

"Admit you raped me," Sasha snapped, breathing becoming more intense with each passing breath. "Just this once—it's only you and me."

Ivan blinked. "Rape?"

"We both know I never willingly shared a bed with you. Sleeping with you was only about my self-preservation."

Ivan huffed. "Fine. If it means less attitude from you later, then I'll admit it. Coercing you into sleeping with me was what got me off. Nothing like raping a defenseless blonde. Although it'd be nice if you were honest with me."

"What are you getting at?"

"Admit a tiny part of you enjoyed it when I pounded the shit out of you."

So much for needing a shower being her only visceral reaction. A tinge of nausea overcame her, because Sasha wouldn't have slept with Ivan if he was the last man on Earth. Hell, hooking up with a troll instead of Ivan would have been preferable.

"Not even for a second," Sasha said.

"Whatever," Ivan said. "But let's go, bitch."

"I'm not leaving with you."

"Excuse me?" Ivan asked. "You must not have been paying attention because I won't hesitate with killing Cece and Tyler."

"Do whatever you want, but let me check Twitter for a second." Sasha grabbed her iPhone before pressing STOP on the recording app. Then, she emailed the recording to both her and Tyler.

"You're even dumber than I thought you were," Ivan said. "I'm threatening your family, yet you're checking your social media."

"I'm not going anywhere with you. Game over." Sasha played back the recording. Hell, her lips formed a devilish grin. Ivan would get what was coming to him for once in his miserable life.

"What the fuck?" Ivan knocked over the living room table. "Don't tell me you're dumb enough to think blackmailing me will work?"

If only Sasha preserved Ivan's pinched facial expression. That moment was something she would have replayed over again for the rest of her life if she had her way. A small amount of arrogance made Sasha human, because for the longest time, she never thought this day would come. People like her didn't escape their abusers and get a happily ever after since the concept was a pipedream at best.

"I got the best of you, and you're gonna leave me alone. If you don't, then I'll go to the police." Sasha paused for a second. "Because you didn't just confess to rape. You also confessed to murder."

Ivan hissed. "Nobody would believe a slut like you."

"That's why I got two confessions from you. So much for you always anticipating someone's next move," Sasha said.

"You bitch!" Ivan exclaimed.

"That's smart bitch to you."

"I could kill you right here and now and then dissolve your body in acid. Tyler and Cece would never know where you were."

Sasha cackled. "You've got no leverage. I emailed the recording to both Tyler and myself when I said I was checking Twitter."

"Damn you!"

"Congrats, Ivan!" Sasha said. "And I can only hope you have a long, miserable life ahead of you."

To hell with people who always insisted on being positive. Sasha just didn't get those people. Doing bad was sometimes the only thing a person could do, because the saying "two wrongs don't make a right" was bullshit. Some people deserved every bad thing that happened to them. It wasn't like her Ivan problem could have been solved with tea and cookies.

Ivan's nostrils flared. "People don't leave me."

"Watch me." Sasha tossed her hair over her shoulders with one flick of her neck. "Anyway, this is the last time we're gonna chat."

"I'm not this monster you think I am," Ivan said. "I know something about your family that you don't know—something that would change your perception of your entire life. And you're gonna wanna hear what I have to say."

"You're blowing smoke up my ass."

"Not this time," Ivan said.

"I'm not an idiot, so please leave before I call 911 on you and report an intruder."

"I'm serious, so you might wanna put aside your hatred of me."

"Save your breath for someone who pretends to give a fuck," Sasha said.

"It's about Riley. Correction, it's about the person you think is Riley."

Ivan could have offered Sasha a billion dollars and she wouldn't have batted an eye. There was nothing left to discuss with Ivan. People sometimes needed to be taken out like trash, and he was no exception. Sasha could also finally leave the past behind her, because that was worth more than a pint of ice cream during a heatwave. The old her—the scared little girl who let Ivan smack her around or have his way with her—was dead.

Sasha pointed to the front door. "I don't care. Now go, because the cops showing up won't be your biggest problem if you don't leave in the next five seconds."

"Huh?"

"I'll skip 911, grab a knife from the kitchen, and slit your carotid artery."

"Fine. Although don't say I didn't warn you," Ivan spat.

"Newsflash. You mean nothing to me."

"Remember one thing."

"And what's that?" Sasha asked.

"Now that I'm leaving your life, you're cemented into your con forever."

"What's your point?"

Ivan put his hands in his jacket pockets. "You'll grow tired of living a lie one day, and that emptiness will be my ultimate revenge against you."

"Please. You're gonna have to try harder if you wanna get a rise out of me."

***

Sash clinked her glass against Tyler's. "Cheers."

"Cheers," Tyler said.

Several hours passed since Sasha's final conversation with Ivan, and she now sat on the living room couch, having a drink with Tyler. Cece's one millionth night out with a client hadn't even made Sasha fret. And the reason wasn't even because of her dilated pupils. Nothing mattered since Ivan was gone.

"Now let's just hope Mr. Parker leaves you alone." Sasha took another swig of her bourbon.

Flames crackled in the fireplace. Perfect night for a fire since a distinct chill filled the air because of Connecticut's current cold spell. Although Sasha didn't only enjoy the warmth from the fireplace because it provided heat. Making a fire provided another picturesque moment—a moment that convinced her that her new life was where she belonged.

"True," Tyler said. "But we've got bigger issues to worry about than Mr. Parker. My mother's birthday is coming up, and we should plan a dinner—to preserve your cover and all."

"Maybe you're the one who should relax more," Sasha said.

"I guess."

"A party sounds like what we need."

Tyler grinned. "Okay. You might have a point."

CHAPTER 22

TYLER

Tyler and Jake sat on Tyler's bedroom floor, backs pressed against the bed. Tyler just closed the laptop lid, and Jake chuckled.

Tyler scrunched his eyebrows. "What's so funny?"

"You were right—I enjoyed *Pan's Labyrinth* much more than I thought I would."

Tyler elbowed Jake. "Maybe you should trust my opinion more."

"I have no problem deferring to you plenty of times," Jake said.

"I know; I was only teasing."

"What do you wanna do now?" Jake asked.

Maybe, just maybe, Jake would like the idea that popped into Tyler's head. Even if having sex might have seemed random. If they were gonna have a fresh start, then they needed to embrace said opportunity. At least according to Tyler, that was. Nothing like making new memories for forgetting about the old ones.

"I'm not sure." Tyler scooted closer, left leg brushing up against Jake's. Then, Tyler winked. "Did you have something in mind?"

"We could order pizza."

"I had something in mind." Tyler paused for a minute. "Hopefully, you'll like it."

"Another movie?" Jake asked.

"It's better than a movie."

"Now I'm intrigued and you've gotta tell me."

Tyler's lips grazed Jake's right ear. His stomach sank, and he might as well have been inside a tornado. He never thought him and Jake would get a chance. "We could have sex," Tyler said.

"Your mom and Riley are downstairs watching a movie."

"Doesn't matter. We can lock the door."

"I don't think sex is a good idea—at least not right now," Jake said.

"Are you still angry about the Mr. Parker situation?"

Jake exhaled a breath. "It's not about being annoyed—it's about my concern for you."

"What do you mean?" Tyler asked.

"We haven't really discussed the situation and how that did or didn't make you feel."

"You've lost me." Tyler scooped up a handful of chips from the bowl on the floor. After that, he chugged his remaining Diet Coke. He belched in a matter of seconds, yet Jake hadn't given him a disapproving look. If anything, a blank facial expression remained plastered on Jake's face. So,

Tyler's stomach sank a little. The most intense comments and situations didn't always cause the most dramatic reactions. Sometimes, the calmness in people's demeanor was why Tyler's back hairs jumped up. Almost like when the eye of the Hurricane passed by a town—there was still more bad weather left.

"You slept with your professor for a better grade."

Tyler scowled. "I didn't go all the way with him until you and I broke up."

"Fine." Jake slid the sleeves up of his button down, plaid shirt. "Maybe this is more about me than you."

"I'm gonna need more specificity."

"You don't consider yourself a victim?" Jake mumbled.

Tyler might as well have been an antelope in Africa that had a lion surprise attack it. He never once considered whether Mr. Parker was a predator. Although he had to be honest with himself about one thing. A part of Tyler wondered if he wasn't the first student Mr. Parker slept with. Something about Mr. Parker's comfort with the arrangement—like someone knowing exactly what to do after a drought in their sex life.

"No," Tyler said after the longest time. "I agreed to sleep with him, and he never made me do anything I didn't want to."

"It's still dubious consent." Jake grabbed a few chips from the bowl on the floor in front of him. He scarfed down the chips, crunching noises echoing through the bedroom while his sour cream and onion breath tickled Tyler's skin.

"I'm an adult and made a choice."

"If you say so." Jake snatched another handful of chips and ate them faster than the previous serving.

Tyler fought back the confusion. Nothing like counting to twenty in his head for a slower pulse. Jake wasn't him, and might not have understood the headspace that was required for agreeing to Tyler's arrangement. So, Tyler would be patient with Jake just this once. No need for an argument ruining their relationship before it began.

"What? You think what Mr. Parker did is wrong?" Tyler asked.

"It's kind of an abuse of power."

"I'm nineteen years old."

"If you say so."

"Let's drop the subject." Tyler extended his hand, then rubbed Jake's forehead. "We're finally together and I don't want anything to ruin that."

"Fine. Have it your way."

Tyler couldn't have been more thankful about Jake's response if he was a famine victim finally enjoying a gourmet meal. Nothing good would come from focusing on Mr. Parker. He was the past, and he'd remain there. Making superficial conversation was the only thing he and Jake had to do, and Tyler could live with that. It wasn't like he had to live in the same house as Mr. Parker.

"Anyway, do you wanna order a pizza?" Tyler asked after his stomach grumbled. "The waffles I had for brunch aren't enough to hold me till breakfast tomorrow."

Jake placed his hands on his lap. "Sure. I only had cereal and a yogurt today."

"I'll to the kitchen and get the menu. You'll never believe this, but the pizza place doesn't have a website."

Jake grinned. "I bet the place won't stay in business long."

"You're probably right."

***

Tyler sat next to Sasha in the dining room the following evening. Balloons hovered in the air and a **HAPPY BIRTHDAY** banner covered part of the wall.

Time for Tyler to finally have a little fun. If his mother arrived home in the next century, that was.

"I'm sorry my mother had to stay an hour longer at work," Tyler said.

"You've got nothing to apologize for."

"She'd rather be at the office than here."

"On her birthday?" Sasha asked.

"You can't tell me how you haven't noticed how I'm closer to you than Cece?"

Sasha played with a strand of her hair. "You've got a point."

"I just wish she'd stop punishing for what I did. What happened was a one-time indiscretion," Tyler said.

"I don't know if I like the sound of this."

"It involves Riley," Tyler murmured.

"Come again?"

"Summer before freshman year of college—the night of my eighteenth birthday." Tyler finished his Champagne, not appreciating the mixture of carbonation, sweet, and tart flavors exciting his taste buds. If he was gonna tell Sasha the truth, then he needed as much booze as possible.

"You don't have to tell me if you don't want to."

"It's fine."

"Are you sure?" Sasha asked.

"You'll never believe this, but your sister was actually nicer to me," Tyler said. "My mother blew off my birthday to go out with friends—it was the only day she had off from work and ages. Anyway, Riley took me out clubbing. We got drunk and then slept together when he came home."

"Hopefully, you took an UBER or a LFYT?"

Tyler nodded. "We did."

"So, what? Did your mother catch you in bed with Riley?"

"It's worse."

Sasha glared at Tyler. "How can the situation get worse?"

"Riley and I were still pretty exhausted from our partying so we fell asleep after having sex. But I woke up sometime later, discovering Mom peeking into my bedroom. However, she never mentioned the issue." Tyler wavered for a beat, banging his fingers against the table. Over a year might have passed since the tryst, yet the soft texture of Riley's skin and tangerine scented shampoo remained tangible. No matter how devious Riley might have been, Tyler couldn't get over her being there for him when his mother wasn't. Nothing like two people becoming one, because what Tyler hadn't told Sasha was that he didn't only sleep with Riley. She was the first person he ever had sex with. And he'd have to live with his stepmother taking his virginity for the rest of his life, hoping the regret would eventually become fainter.

"And you're convinced she's punishing you?" Sasha asked.

"Exactly."

"Don't take this the wrong way, but is there any chance you might have been dreaming and thought you were awake?" Sasha asked.

No. Sasha was wrong. The dread filling his insides certainly felt real that night.

"I'm positive Mom saw me in bed with Riley." Tyler grabbed the Champagne bottle, then refilled his flute. "Now you know why I helped you preserve your cover by planning this dinner. Riley can never return."

"Riley is dead, Tyler."

"That's the thing. I don't think she killed herself."

"What are you getting at?" Sasha asked.

If Tyler spilled his tryst to Sasha, then he might have continued with his next thought. Then, he might not have been so burdened. A person could only deal with so many things at once before snapping under pressure.

"What if she staged her suicide?" Tyler asked. "You can't tell me it's not convenient that you have Riley's driver license, keys, credit cards, etc. The only thing that's missing is her wedding ring. If she really wanted to end her life, then she would've left you the wedding ring too. Just think about it. It's like Riley needed the ring for an insurance policy in case whatever scheme she planned backfired."

"I don't know…"

"Her body never turned up," Tyler said.

"Lake Solomon is a big lake."

Tyler locked his fingers together. "Not gonna change my mind about Riley still being alive and how she must be plotting something big."

"Why did you sleep with her if you hate her that much?"

"I was lonely."

Sasha patted Tyler's shoulder. "You don't have to worry about me going anywhere."

"Good."

"It's easier said than done, but I hope you'll forgive yourself, Tyler," Sasha said. "Nobody is perfect. Just like Riley and your mother. Riley wanted an unlimited supply of money and your mom wanted a trophy wife—no offense or anything."

"None taken."

"I know no thanks is necessary, but I appreciate our friendship," Sasha said.

"Me too. Although I've got another problem," Tyler said. "Jake didn't wanna sleep with me last night."

Sasha jabbed her fist through the air. "Shit. I forgot to ask you about the situation with your professor."

"It's over, but that's not my problem. Jake thinks I'm dirty and probably will never touch me again. In fact, he didn't kiss me goodbye or hello yesterday."

"Just calmly tell him how you feel," Sasha said. "Problems only become unmanageable when they fester over time."

Tyler couldn't disagree with Sasha's advice. If something bothered him, then he would say something. He dealt with Mr. Parker, and his intimacy issue with Jake would be fixed sooner rather than later.

Footsteps grew louder and louder, and then someone hollered at them upon entering the dining room. It was his mother.

"What's all this?" Cece asked.

"Riley wanted to do something special for your birthday, so she got Champagne, party decorations, and Chinese food," Tyler said, pointing to the takeout containers on the middle of the table.

Cece clapped her hands together. "That's just what I need after a long day. And thank goodness for my family, because I might quit my job."

Tyler drank more Champagne, then licked his lips. Thank goodness for small favors, because Tyler didn't know what he would've done if his mother criticized the birthday celebration. So maybe, just maybe, this family dinner would cement their perfect image. Tyler could hope, after all. Nothing wrong with trying to regain that special magic him, his mother, and first stepmother, Janice, had. Everyone deserved one safe place in the world.

CHAPTER 23

RILEY

Riley took the wads of cash from the cashier—who stood behind the glass counter in front of the cash register—in back of the store, then stuffed the bills into her purse. Sometimes, the most drastic steps were the right ones. It wasn't like Riley had another choice now that Josh was gone—she needed to secure her future.

The cashier chuckled. "No offense, but I'm surprised a pretty lady like yourself would give away such a pretty wedding ring."

"You and me both."

"Hopefully, you aren't in some kind of trouble," the man said.

Riley shook her head. "Just need a nest egg—that's all."

He rubbed his black mustache. "I know the feeling—I'd love to retire."

Riley leaned closer. "Do you mind if I ask you a question."

"Sure. I'm always happy to help a beautiful woman."

Riley wasn't sure if she should have blushed or recoiled. On a superficial level, the man's compliment resembled a best friend's praise. Yet the man would have been crazy for thinking he had a chance with Riley. Not on her life. Riley had standers, and would never sleep with a man pushing sixty.

"I need your discretion," Riley said.

"Then you came to the right place."

"Perfect."

"I can't help you until you tell me what's wrong," he said.

"You wouldn't know where to get a gun, would you?" Riley asked. "It has to be a place that doesn't ask questions."

"Today's your lucky day. I know exactly where you should go."

"Great!" Riley exclaimed. "You have no idea how much this means to me. Sometimes a woman doesn't have a choice with defending herself."

He coughed. "As in fleeing a domestic violence situation?"

"Something like that."

Another lie wouldn't hurt Riley. It wasn't like she wanted to be a good person. Nope. She passed that point a long time ago when she swapped "Katrina" for "Riley." And no big deal if she lied more than people breathed. Riley had the guts to do what other people—hone a skill no matter how malicious the talent was.

"Here." The man slipped her a piece of paper.

"Thanks. I'll never forget this."

"I hope your situation resolves itself," he said.

She smiled. "It will. Anyway, have a great day."

The placard on the door jingled and a bald man strutted into the shop while Riley headed towards the exit. Wow. She was so close to getting the revenge against Adam she always wanted, and nothing would stop her.

***

Riley peered into the art gallery window hours later. Nobody was inside except Adam—who stood behind the counter unpacking cases of beer.

Perfect. Surprise was something she could use to her advantage.

She opened the gallery door, then flipped the lock. After that, she closed the blinds. And Adam remained behind the counter even when the clicking of her high heels against the tiled floor grew louder with each passing second.

"Don't do that again!" Adam smacked his hand over his chest. "Didn't anyone teach you not to sneak up on a person? What if I had a heart condition?"

"Sorry."

Adam peaked at the front of the gallery. More specifically, the closed blinds and locked door. "What's going on?" he asked.

"We've got something to discuss." Riley groped the gun from the outside, purse strap around her right shoulder.

"I thought things were going well with us?"

"They were, but that's because I wanted you to think that."

"Am I missing something?" Adam asked.

Riley cackled. "I'm not Riley; I'm Katrina. I've been impersonating her for the last seven years."

His jaw shook. "I don't know what to say."

"Spare me the fake contrition. We both know what you did."

"I don't know what you're referring to."

"I might be a lot of things, but I'm not oblivious," Riley said. "I'm an identical triplet. Sasha and the real Riley were born first, yet you and your wife were expecting identical twins, not triplets. I guess doctors still have trouble reading sonograms."

Adam crossed his arms. "This is quite the story."

"It's not a story; it's the truth," Riley said. "My only crime was being born last."

"What? Do you want reparations or something?" Adam demanded.

"I want my life back. The one that was stolen from me."

"Huh?"

Riley's gaze narrowed. "I missed out on having a real estate heiress as a grandmother."

"I can give you money—the gallery has been pretty successful."

"Beats me." Riley finished taking in her surroundings. "All of the paintings are crap."

Adam put his hands up. "We don't have to fight."

"A little late for that. You weren't the one whose mother was addicted to pain pills," Riley said.

For once, Riley hadn't thought about staging a reaction. She wasn't lying about her mother's drug problem. The only issue was her honesty was too little too late. She already became the person she was a long time ago, and nothing would chip away at her darkness. The ugliness that enable her flipping on Vincent—the only man she ever loved—and taking the money and fleeing after killing Vincent.

"That was Ivan's fault—he should've found a better person to raise you," Adam said.

"Impressive. Admitting to what you've done," Riley said.

"I really am glad you're in my life."

"You just don't want me to hurt you."

"I'm sorry for what I did."

Sweat drenched her back. "You're such a bastard. First you sell your baby on the black market and then you abandoned your wife a few years later. Real humanitarian behavior right there. Somebody should nominate you for the Nobel Peace Prize."

"I don't expect you to forgive me."

"How big of you," Riley spat.

"How'd you discover the truth?"

Riley pulled her purse strap further up her shoulder once it started slipping. "My mother told me everything on her deathbed. Then, I ran away."

"Obviously, you've had a tough life."

"No shit," Riley said.

"I'm sure we can arrive at a reasonable solution."

Riley let out a breath. "You're right. It doesn't have to be this way. Would you mind if I went into the bathroom and splashed some cold water on my face?"

"Do you need me to show you where it is?"

"No. I remember where it is from the other day."

"Great."

Riley walked out of the art gallery's bathroom several minutes later, leather gloves gripping the gun. To hell with playing the long game. Getting close to Adam only to kill him was good enough. No need for professional humiliation before destroying his life—this way was better for her. Simpler, really.

Adam cocked his head from his spot in front of the counter. "What are you gonna do? Kill me?"

"I don't know—you tell me. Give me one good reason to let you live."

CHAPTER 24

LOLA

Lola sat at the dining room table in her apartment next to Preston and her grandmother. Somehow, this dinner was actually happening, and she could have almost squealed in excitement. If she could do something normal like having her boyfriend meet her a family member, then there might have been hope for a better life someday. Even if she would never be healed until Katrina was vanquished, and she could be "Riley" again.

Preston glanced at Lola. "Something wrong, babe?"

"Nope. Everything is fine," Lola said.

The smell of warm cheese, tomato, and other herbs rubbed against Lola's nostrils. The pizza might not have been New York pizza, yet it was good enough. Ordering takeout took the pressure off this evening.

"Preston is right. You've looked like you seen a ghost," Vanessa said.

"Grandma, please!" Lola exclaimed.

Vanessa sipped her red wine. "I'm sorry, but the comment couldn't be helped."

"Let's just get to the point of this dinner," Preston said. "What will it take for convincing you Lola will be okay?"

"It's not just about your relationship," Vanessa. "Katrina could still be in LA for all we knew. Nothing worse than a false sense of security."

Preston refilled his wine glass. "I could move in with Lola or she could move in with me. Either way, this relationship is meant to last."

Lola didn't need someone to pinch her from Preston's comment despite how they never discussed moving in before. Not every terrifying thing would keep Lola up at night. No matter how many challenges she had in the past, she needed to build a new life for herself, and nobody would stop her. Not even that bitch Katrina.

Vanessa threw her napkin onto the table. "Fine. I won't protest."

"Really?" Lola asked.

"You've got my blessing, and I couldn't be happier for the two of you," Vanessa said.

"Thank you, Grandma." Lola finished the rest of her red wine before flinching. The bitter and dry flavors lingered on her tongue too long, proving her grandmother should have let her pick the wine for the meal.

"One thing." Preston wet his right index finger, then wiped Lola's upper lip. "Sorry. You had so tomato sauce there."

"No worries," Lola said.

"You were saying?" Vanessa asked.

"Right," Preston said. "I'm not gonna let anything happen to Lola—it's a promise."

***

Lola and Vanessa stood in the airport parking lot the following morning.

Gray clouds remained clustered together in the sky, yet the impending rain wasn't why Lola fought back the tears. When the universe gave her something—like a fresh start with Preston—then it also took something from her—Vanessa.

"Isn't this what you wanted?" Vanessa asked.

Lola grabbed a tissue from her pocket. "Yeah. It's just a shame you live in Connecticut."

"You could visit. Or maybe I can visit you again in a couple of months."

"Sounds like a plan," Lola said.

A silence ensued between Lola and her grandmother. The sadness would pass soon enough. Lola didn't think she was perfect, yet goodbye was simple enough in light of everything Katrina did to her.

"There's something I want you to do," Vanessa said.

"And what's that?" Lola asked.

"Check on your father." Vanessa took her hand off her suitcase handle, then took out a piece of paper from her purse. After that, she handed it to Lola.

Lola gave Vanessa a blank look "What's this?"

"The address of Adam's art gallery—that'd be the best place to see him."

Lola might have had to bring Vanessa to a doctor and check for dementia. No good reason existed for visiting Adam. Yeah. She couldn't even bring herself to call Adam her father—some wounds couldn't be healed by time.

"Give me one good reason why I should do this?" Lola asked. "Everything that happened to me is his fault."

"Forgiveness is a wonderful thing," Grandma squealed.

"Seriously? Do you need a diagram for explaining how he set everything into motion when he sold Katrina on the black market?"

"Then do it for yourself."

"You're too much."

"You need to find out if Katrina has gotten to him. If she hasn't, then you're still safe for now," Vanessa said.

Lola sneered. "Give me one good reason."

"You'd want someone to reach out to you if you might be in trouble."

Lola could have shrieked while Vanessa's words lingered in her mind while a steady drizzle fell onto the ground. Vanessa's remark was logical enough, because Lola never speculated about what she would have done if she didn't have her grandmother helping her.

"Fine," Lola said. "But then you've gotta consider doing something for me. I'm not the only one who has had a tough life. You should give serious consideration to being in Sasha's life, especially if you don't know what came of her train station encounter with Katrina."

"I'll consider it."

"Fair enough." Lola rubbed Vanessa's shoulder. "I love you so much."

"You don't have worry about the money—I'll keep sending you it every month."

"Thanks."

***

Whether her reason for visiting Adam the following morning was because of getting good karma, having nothing to do since Preston was at work, or Vanessa being right didn't matter. Lola currently stood in front of the art gallery.

There was one problem, though. The door was locked.

Lola's pulse echoed in her ears. Leaving would have been easiest—she showed up, and couldn't force Adam to talk with her if the gallery was locked, the blinds were drawn, and there wasn't a CLOSED sign. But no. Something about the situation bugged her more than someone not liking a person upon a first meeting despite not having a logical reason.

So, Lola took out the bobby pin in her hair and fiddled with lock. It clicked after several tries, and Lola shut the door behind her after entering the art gallery.

"Adam?" Lola called out.

No answer.

Lola was just about to leave a moment later when something caught her attention. More specifically, the body on the ground in front of the bar counter. The person's head was lying in a thick pool of blood.

One quick glance at the man's face was all she needed.

The cheeks might have been heavier and there might have been wrinkles. Yet the face was otherwise the same as the man who abandoned her and Sasha when they were kids. The man who hadn't even blinked when her and Sasha stood in the living room while their mother kneeled, sobbing for Adam to say that fateful afternoon.

Lola wouldn't play amateur detective, though. One step closer, and she might get a finger print or loose strand of hair on something.

No amount of denial changed Lola's sudden realization. Her happy ending with Preston would have to wait. If Katrina really killed Adam, then she might have been coming for her next. And she couldn't risk Preston's life. If Katrina killed Adam, then she could kill again.

She had one option. Run.

CHAPTER 25

SASHA

Sasha opened the front door, about to go for a jog. Except she shuddered from the person standing on the front porch. Someone who was worse than Riley or Ivan—there was just no forgiving Dylan.

"I'm not doing this." Sasha closed the door, yet Dylan grabbed it just before it slammed, forcing himself into the mansion.

"We need to chat," Dylan said.

"I've got nothing to say to you after what you did to me. How could you sell me out to Ivan? Maybe I was wrong about you being the love of my life."

Dylan lifted his brow. "What did you just say?"

What a great start to her morning. Sasha would have to be more mindful about her feelings in the future. For a moment, she forgot how they hadn't said, "I love you" to each other.

"Doesn't matter. The point is you need to leave," Sasha said.

"Not until we talk."

"Forcing yourself into this house isn't a good look."

"I would never hurt you—at least not physically."

Sasha paused for a beat. Once again, finer details revealed the truth. Dylan never getting violent with her didn't matter. Risking her life wasn't something that could be forgotten about, because he wouldn't have done that if he loved her. If Dylan was so concerned about his parents, then he should've came to Sasha—they could've figured something—because that was what she would've done if faced with Dylan's predicament.

Sasha grunted. "Leave before I call the police."

"Would you really call the cops?"

"What do you think?" Sasha asked. "There's nothing between us anymore."

"Don't be like this."

"You couldn't have thought coming here was smart?"

Dylan gripped the sides of his unbuttoned blazer. "You don't understand. He was threatening my parents and I didn't have a choice."

Sasha could have slapped Dylan. Making excuses for bad behavior was about one of the worst things someone could do. If the situation was different, then Sasha wouldn't have betrayed Dylan. She couldn't. Doing something so horrible to the person she loved most perplexed more her than a geometry problem. And that reason was why she couldn't forgive Dylan. Not even in a superficial way.

"And you betrayed me," Sasha barked.

"You're clearly okay."

"I'm the one Ivan repeatedly raped, not you."

Dylan rubbed the side of his lip while Sasha's menacing gaze didn't disappear. Harshness was better than being in a relationship with someone she couldn't trust or respect. If Dylan was so concerned about his parents, then he should have told her the truth upon their first interaction after he arrived in Connecticut.

"I'm not leaving," Dylan said.

Sasha didn't respond while the wind rattled against the mansion, creating a brief chill. Dylan might have been the last person she wanted to chat with, but she might not have had a choice, which was so great—she was supposed to be regaining control of her life, not losing control. Dylan's persistence might have been one of those times when it was better to give someone what they wanted. Sasha only hoped one thing, though. Dylan wouldn't take her folding as an invitation to visit her again.

Sasha wrinkled her nose. "Fine. But we aren't doing this here."

"Perfect. We can go to my hotel room."

"On one condition." Sasha felt her right pocket, then sighed in relief. Her house key was in it. "No funny business between us if I go to your hotel room."

Dylan smirked. "I can't make that promise."

"I'm serious, Dylan," Sasha said, raising her voice.

"Okay. I won't hit on you unless you want me to."

"That's more like it."

"I'm sorry." Dylan kneeled a few minutes after he and Sasha arrived at his motel room.

Except Sasha didn't give Dylan a sympathetic look while Dylan remained on his knees. Instead, she cackled. "You're gonna have to try harder," Sasha said.

"What more do you want me to do?" Dylan asked. "It's not like Ivan is a problem. You're obviously okay."

"That's not the point."

"Let's try this." Dylan stood, then inched towards Sasha who stood in front of the bed on the left side of the room. Then, Dylan fondled her shoulder.

Sasha didn't fall back onto the bed—she might as well have heard him out if she came all this way. Besides, she'd be rid of him soon enough.

"I don't expect you to forgive me right away, but I would appreciate a second chance," Dylan said. "Think of it as a probation period."

Sasha hesitated. "I don't know…"

"I already spoke to my boss. He's fine with me working out of the Connecticut office instead of the New York office."

Her pulse sped up while sweat even clung to her forehead. It was as if giving him a second chance might have been realistic. Giving Dylan a trial period would have been the logical thing to do. Yet the image of Ivan gripping her head while holding his lit cigarette also remained etched in her mind. He could have put the cigarette out on her cheek, and there wouldn't have been a damn thing she could do to stop him.

There was one remaining issue, though. Something she couldn't ignore.

"What about Cece?" Sasha asked. "Are you content with being my side piece?"

"Disappearing again is another option. I've got a lot of money saved up."

"I actually care about Cece and her son, Tyler."

Dylan put his arms around the back of her neck, then met her gaze. "We can do whatever you want, babe."

"You certainly know how to pitch an idea."

"That's why I get the big bucks at my advertising job."

"I'm not sold on a redo," Sasha said.

Sasha was being serious, because her reasoning had nothing to do with Dylan groveling for the sake of groveling. If Dylan wanted a second chance, then he was gonna have to say something Sasha hadn't already heard. Something that would've reminded Sasha of why she gravitated towards Dylan in the first place, because it'd take a major event for changing Sasha's opinion of Dylan. Almost as if why she should take Dylan couldn't be summed up in a neat phrase.

"I could say I'd do everything differently if I could, but there's no way of you knowing that for sure, so I'll just say this." Dylan remained silent for a minute. "We're all human and make mistakes, because I wouldn't think twice about giving you a second chance."

When Dylan was right, he was right. Sasha couldn't argue with him. Regardless of what happened, she had no doubt about him forgiving her. He hadn't even looked the tiniest bit alarmed after she told him everything when he first arrived in Connecticut.

"Something like this can never happen again," Sasha said. "If it does, then I'm leaving you for good."

"Understood." Dylan extended his hand, and Sasha shook it.

The gesture didn't stop at a handshake, though. Dylan pulled Sasha up against his body before kissing her. But Sasha didn't tell him to stop or pull away. She closed her eyes while the smooth, cotton-like texture of Dylan's lips brushed up against hers. He eventually gave her tongue, and his hands shifted to her cheeks. But Sasha didn't end the embrace. She even closed her eyes, savoring every moment. Life wouldn't always be a fairytale, but this moment was, and she'd let herself get swept up by the moment.

"That was amazing," Dylan said sometime later, arms wrapped around Sasha while the two of them remained in bed.

"It was."

"Since I'm working on earning back your trust, I'd appreciate if you considered doing something for me."

"What is it?" Sasha asked.

"Think about leaving this con behind and starting somewhere fresh. Somewhere you don't have to pretend to be someone you aren't or where Ivan isn't."

Dylan really knew how to talk to her, and Sasha was ecstatic about that fact. No matter how much she might have molded into "Riley," she couldn't deny how the arrangement was unfair to Cece. She didn't deserve to be married to a stranger.

"I'll think about it," Sasha said.

"Thanks. That's all I expect."

Sasha sat in bed the following evening reading a book just like Cece. Except her eyes remained on her book while Cece closed it, and tossed it aside. Cece then tilted her head towards Sasha.

"Do you mind chatting for a moment?" Cece asked.

"Sure." Sasha closed her book, then placed it on the bedside table while the faint glow of moonlight trickled through the bedroom window.

Cece giggled. "Relax. I'm not angry with you."

"Good to know."

"I wanted to thank you for the surprise birthday dinner the other night. I never knew you could be so thoughtful."

Sasha's teeth pricked her lip, almost drawing blood. "Don't worry about it."

"I'm serious. You've come a long way from the first time we met."

"I was happy to do it. Tyler also helped," Sasha said.

"No need to bolster his image, if he wants to make amends, then he can do so himself."

Sasha couldn't help having sympathy pangs for Tyler—he was right about his observation. She was closer to Tyler than Cece, and that was more than pathetic. Cece could have at least feigned interest in Tyler's life.

"What are you talking about?" Sasha asked.

Cece sighed. "I haven't forgotten about his eighteenth birthday."

"Yet you aren't disappointed in me?"

"I expect this from you, not him."

Sasha's eyes bulged. "Excuse me?"

"I'm serious."

"You're judging the situation too harshly."

"Give me one good reason I should forgive Tyler," Cece said.

"We were both drunk and it meant nothing to us. Go ask Tyler yourself if you don't believe me."

Cece pouted. "Alcohol doesn't make you a different person—it just makes you do things you wished you had the courage to do when you're sober."

"You should forgive Tyler—it'd mean a lot to me."

"Fat chance." Cece grabbed a bottle of lotion on the left bedside table, then squired some onto her arms, massaging it in good. "He made a choice, and now he's gotta to live with the consequences."

Sasha screamed. "Enough! Tyler made a mistake, and it's pathetic of you to hold onto this anger. Doing so never gets anyone anywhere. You never know what's gonna happen tomorrow, and you don't want your last thought of your son to be his eternal damnation."

Cece rolled her eyes. "Fine. I'll try."

"Are you serious?"

"Your bossiness turns me on." Cece moved towards Sasha. Then, she got so close to Sasha that their lips almost touched. "Fuck. You've got no idea how badly I want you. What do you say? We haven't been intimate in ages."

An itch shot up the back of her head, and Sasha rubbed it. At a first glance, she shouldn't have slept with someone who thought she was someone else. But she also couldn't forget about Dylan's proposition—the one about leaving Connecticut behind. If she kissed in addition to slept with Cece, then that would complicate her life more, possibly forcing her to stay—leaving Connecticut wasn't ideal when she didn't know if Cece would actually forgive Tyler. And that reasoning was why she knew what she had to do.

"Sure. I'd love to have sex," Sasha said.

"Really?"

"A little pleasure never hurt anyone."

"This is better than winning the lottery."

Sasha didn't laugh or make a witty joke. Instead, she initiated the kiss. Perhaps she could fall for Cece if she really wanted to. It was worth a try, at least. She had nothing to lose.

CHAPTER 26

TYLER

Tyler could only run from his past for so long. That idea was why Tyler couldn't act surprised when Mr. Parker accosted him in one of the academic buildings before his first class of the day. Even if Tyler would have rather smelled formaldehyde in a morgue than interact with Mr. Parker outside of his class. But Mr. Parker was about to have a big problem if he didn't get out of Tyler's way.

"Could you move?" Tyler asked.

Mr. Parker pressed his arms together. "We need to talk."

"We've got nothing to discuss."

"I disagree."

"You just don't know when to quit it. Tell me something, how's your wife doing?" Tyler didn't even hide his smile. No regret necessary for what he just said to Mr. Parker, because his professor needed to know who was in charge.

"She's fine," Mr. Parker croaked. "But I'm serious—We've gotta talk. It's important."

"Give me one good reason to believe you."

"It's a delicate matter." Mr. Parker scanned the hallway—nobody was within earshot at the moment. "I'd like your help with coming out."

"I don't owe you anything."

"I want to leave my wife," Mr. Parker said.

"It wouldn't be appropriate to socialize outside of class." Tyler loosened his backpack strap slightly. "I wouldn't wanna send the wrong message."

"I've got nobody else to turn to, and I meant what I said. I'm not taking no for an answer no matter how much you don't want be bothered with me."

Tyler dug his fingernails into his palms, yet not hard enough to draw blood. He couldn't believe his professor. If Mr. Parker's personal crisis was that serious, then he should have seen a counselor, priest, or called a crisis hotline. Mr. Parker might not have raped him, yet Tyler wouldn't extend any good will to his teacher. Mr. Parker meant nothing to him, and soon he'd less insignificant than when people's joints flared before a change in barometric pressure.

"I'm begging you, Tyler," Mr. Parker whimpered.

Maybe, just maybe, Tyler didn't have a choice regardless of everything he just thought still being true. If he didn't want Mr. Parker to be a problem, then he'd humor him. Although there would be clear boundaries. Tyler was savvier than Mr. Parker might have given him credit before. Something as innocent as patting someone's shoulder might be viewed as an invitation for something more sexual.

Tyler gritted his teeth. "I'll help you this one time, but that's it. Wanting to come out to your wife doesn't mean I lost my leverage. I could still go to the Dean and say you forced me into sleeping with you, so I'd pass your class."

Tyler's stomach tangled, yet he wouldn't budge. It wasn't that he disrespected real victims. He just had to give Mr. Parker one more reminder about who was in charge. Besides, the point wouldn't have been a complete lie. Mr. Parker suggested the arrangement, not him.

"Understood. But believe me when I say this— your grade is the least of your problems," Mr. Parker said.

A couple of students flocked down the hallway and a silence ensued between Tyler and Mr. Parker while Mr. Parker's tongue wet his lips. However, Tyler didn't so much as sneeze. Even if Mr. Parker might have been thinking of him in a sexual way. Emotions really were a sign of weakness, and Tyler wouldn't play weak. Not anymore.

"You can come over to my house at three o'clock this afternoon," Tyler said. "My mother will be at work and my stepmother has a hair appointment."

"Sounds good."

"I'll send you the address right now." Tyler took his iPhone out from his pocket, and his fingers clicked against the keyboard. Then, something beeped. "There."

"Thanks," Mr. Parker said.

Jake put his hands on his hips after marching over to Tyler and Mr. Parker. "What's going on, Ty?" Jake asked.

"I was just reminding Mr. Parker about what's at stake if he fucks with me, but he got the message," Tyler said.

Jake shot Mr. Parker a look. "You better not be harassing Tyler."

"It's fine, babe." Tyler gave Jake a quick kiss on the lips. "I've got the situation under control."

Mr. Parker's Adam's apple rose. "Absolutely."

Mr. Parker darted down the hallway and was soon goon. And Tyler couldn't have been happier if Christmas and his birthday fell on the same day. Even spending one extra second with Mr. Parker was one second too many.

***

Tyler's doorbell rang at exactly 3:00 P.M.

He waited several seconds—nothing wrong with yet another reminder of how Mr. Parker was at his mercy—before walking out of the kitchen and towards the front door.

"Hi," Tyler said after opening the front door.

Mr. Parker grinned. "Nice to see you."

Tyler gesticulated at Mr. Parker. "Let's get this over with."

Mr. Parker followed Tyler inside the mansion, except Tyler sucked on his teeth. But his reaction wasn't because of anything Mr. Parker said. The bag—which was the size of a bag a dentist would give after a teeth cleaning—was why Tyler's gaze hadn't moved.

"What's in the bag?" Tyler asked.

"My little secret."

191

"You said you wanted to come out to your wife?"

"That was only a ruse to spend more time with you," Mr. Parker said. "Whether you accept the truth or not, we've got some unfinished business."

"We're finished. Or maybe you just have amnesia."

Mr. Parker stepped closer to Tyler, then dug his right hand into the pocket of his khaki pants.

"What are you doing?" Tyler asked.

"Think fast." Mr. Parker injected Tyler's neck with a syringe faster than someone could count to three.

***

Moaning woke Tyler up sometime later.

The front of his body was pressed against his mahogany desk. His posture wasn't Tyler's biggest problem, though. His shorts and boxers and were at his ankles and his skin prickled from the cold texture of two hands gripping his waist. And Tyler couldn't forget about how he could almost couldn't keep his eyes open and how the room must've been spiraling around him. Something then clicked in his mind— Mr. Parker injected him with something before he passed out.

"Good. I'm glad you're awake," Mr. Parker said. "Maybe you'll enjoy yourself now—I'd hate for you to miss everything."

Tyler would have rubbed his eyes, yet the weight of Mr. Parker's body—he must have been a good thirty pounds heavier than him made that impossible.

"What's going on?" Tyler asked.

"I'm just finishing what I started—a good reminder of who is really in charge. But enough talking—you're ruining my concentration." Mr. Tyler continued panting, smoky cigarette smell once against stinging Tyler's nostrils.

"You've gotta stop," Tyler said.

"Not till I finish."

Tyler yelled. "Someone please help me!"

"No use. Nobody is home." Mr. Parker dug his fingernails deeper into Tyler's waist while his panting grew louder and louder.

What a fucking idiot. Tyler wanted to kill himself for how he agreed to Mr. Parker's proposition at the beginning of the semester. Nobody would believe Mr. Parker raped him since he willingly slept with his professor numerous times. So, Tyler closed his eyes. Doing so was the only thing he could do—he could pretend the situation wasn't happening. In fact, the only thing that would have made the situation better was if he dropped dead of a heart attack.

Footsteps echoed, then someone screamed before something thumped against the floor.

Tyler opened his eyes.

Mr. Parker was lying on his carpet, and Sasha stood in front of him, holding a bookend.

Tyler feigned a smile after sliding his boxers and shorts up his leg. "Thank you."

"What the hell happened?" Sasha asked.

"He lied to me," Tyler stammered.

Sasha placed the bookend on the desk, then wrapped an arm around Tyler. "Everything is gonna be okay."

Tyler let out a louder shrill, almost unable to catch a breath. "He arranged a meeting under false pretenses. And he injected me with something—a sedative, I guess."

Sasha's jaw twitched. "Wow. I can't believe this is Mr. Parker."

Tyler's sighing continued. "Nobody is gonna believed he raped me."

"I believe you," Sasha said.

"This isn't over yet," Mr. Tyler said, lunging towards Sasha. "You've got some nerve interrupting me before I finished, bitch."

Mr. Parker threw Sasha against the purple bedroom wall, one arm against Sasha's neck, the other against her stomach, pinning her.

The hell with violence never being an acceptable solution. Tyler did the only thing he could think of while Mr. Parker strangled Sasha. Tyler grabbed the bookend, then hit Mr. Parker in the head. Mr. Parker released Sasha before stumbling backwards onto the floor. Kneeling, Tyler swatted Mr. Parker's head over and over again, drawing blood while Sasha caught her breath.

"Die, asshole, die!" Tyler exclaimed, refusing to stop until the light went out in Mr. Parker's eyes.

Sasha remained silent.

"Shit!" Tyler mumbled after shifting his weight towards Sasha. The bookend thwacked against the floor while he gripped both sides of his head, smearing blood on his face. "I killed him."

Sasha petted Tyler's shoulder. "It's okay—I'm not gonna let you go to jail over this."

"I was so stupid," Tyler said.

"You had every right to kill him—he raped you."

"What are we gonna do?" Tyler asked. "We've gotta dispose of the body."

"We'll figure something out, but you gotta remain calm. I'm just glad my haircut appointment got canceled at the last minute even though they should have called to let me know that."

Footsteps echoed through the hallway, then the door creaked. It was Jake.

Tyler soon followed Jake's gaze, which went from the bag Mr. Parker brought, which was on the desk, and then to the bottle of lube on the bed, and to the ripped condom wrapper on the floor, before finally traveling to Mr. Parker. More specifically, his blood caked head.

"What the hell is going on?" Jake asked. "When you didn't text back about whether we'd hang, I knew something must've been up.

"He raped me, Sasha saved me, then he tried to kill Sasha for interrupting, and then I killed him," Tyler revealed. "But I refuse to go to prison for murdering him. He deserved to die—end of discussion."

"You won't go to prison," Sasha said.

"Your stepmother is right," Jake said. "You aren't gonna go to jail, Ty. Let's get a shovel and tarp, and bury him in the woods like the dog Mr. Parker is."

Tyler laughed. "Calling him a dog would be an insult."

"You're right. But let's get to it," Jake said.

"Your boyfriend is right," Sasha said.

***

Jake scooped the last bit of dirt onto the spot they buried Mr. Parker in the woods in back of Tyler's house. The shovel then clanked against the ground while wind cut through the air, nipping

Tyler's face. If he wanted a sign about whether his relationship with Jake would last, then he had one. Not every boyfriend would help cover up a murder, and Tyler would never be able to repay the kindness, but he'd spend the rest of his life trying.

Tyler cleared the phlegm from his throat. "You guys have gotta promise me something."

"Anything," Sasha said.

Jake winked at Tyler. "You know I'd do anything for you."

"We're never gonna discuss tonight again," Tyler said.

Jake and Sasha nodded at him.

"Good." Tyler's teeth chattered. "Fuck. There's only one problem."

Tyler heaved a sigh after tilting his head—Mr. Parker's actions weren't the evening's only issue. Tyler just couldn't get over the owl hooting from a nearby tree. More specifically, it's glowing yellow eyes. No wonder he'd never been a fan of the outdoors—never knew what would happen in nature. Almost as brutal as his spine tingling at the brutality of humans. At least indoors, Tyler could live in a bubble.

"What?" Sasha asked. "Is this about his cellphone? I said I'd dispose of it. Maybe in a pond in a neighboring town after I park his car somewhere."

"It's not the cellphone. It's what's on it," Tyler said. "What if his wife has the phone company look up his text messages once she realizes something is wrong?"

"What are you getting at?" Sasha asked.

"I texted him my address," Tyler said.

"Did you text anything else after? Like anything that would hint he might have wanted to sleep with you today?" Sasha asked.

Tyler rubbed his hands together, creating heat. Good question on Sasha's part.

"Nothing suggestive. But there's our previous text messages." Tears formed in Tyler's eyes, then dripped down his cheeks. "God. This was dumb. We're never gonna get away with this."

"Don't think like that," Jake said.

"Jake is right. Tell me exactly what your texting relationship was like with Mr. Parker?" Sasha asked.

"We were friendly, but we didn't text about the arrangement. He was paranoid about his wife finding out," Tyler said.

Sasha zipped up her jacket after more wind roared. "Then you're fine. Just say Mr. Parker was gonna meet with you for a tutoring session, because office hours aren't convenient."

"That's a good plan," Jake said. "I also have friends with professors who let them text if they're gonna be late to class, so it's not completely inappropriate for you to be texting Mr. Parker."

"Okay. Cool." Tyler stuffed his hands into his jacket pockets. So much for fall not being cold.

Jake put an arm around Tyler. "Don't worry. We're in this together, and will support you no matter what. Even if you feel like breaking your no discussing what happened tonight rule."

Tyler's breathing slowed for a beat. He couldn't deny his gratitude for both Sasha's and Jake's support. Some trauma victims didn't have that luxury.

"Absolutely," Sasha said.

"Thanks again for everything," Tyler said.

"It's done and that's all that matters," Jake said.

Tyler's breathing still hadn't slowed down despite how he wasn't alone. A part of him would never get over the evening's twistedness. And Tyler wasn't only referring to Mr. Parker raping him or killing him. Jake, Sasha, and him would be bonded together forever because of burying Mr. Parker in the woods. And that was a hell of a thing to have in common. Nothing like bonding over murder.

CHAPTER 27

RILEY

Riley drooped the F-bomb after returning from her Starbucks outing and checking the drawer and making sure the money she got in exchange for her wedding ring was still there. The money was gone, and for the first time in her life, she didn't know what she'd do.

Returning to Cece at some point seemed like the logical thing to do—she'd run out of money eventually—yet she couldn't fly back to Connecticut if she didn't have money for a plane ticket. And it wasn't like she had an emergency credit card—she didn't.

"Shit!" Riley said to herself.

A thought popped into Riley's head, and it might've worked. That was if luck was on her side.

The shop owner's interest in her could be exploited. Riley wouldn't sleep with him, but she would be foolish for ignoring his wandering eyes that afternoon. So, maybe, just maybe he'd give her money for a flight to Connecticut.

***

The placard bounced against the glass door while Riley entered the shop sometime later—it was in walking distance of the motel. The man stood behind the counter, wiping his glasses with a cloth. Then, he grinned after looking up.

"I need your help, Garret," Riley said after approaching the counter.

"Sure. Come to exchange another piece of jewelry?"

"Not exactly."

"Then what?" Garret asked.

"Someone stole the money from me. It might've been the maid or another hotel employee who had access to the room."

Riley had no problem with wanting a medal. Not directly blaming the stolen money on the maid was smart. She would have come across as more of a bitch, and she couldn't have that. And her current averted gaze helped too. Almost as if her shame created even more sympathy. In fact, someone might have mistaken her for an actress.

"I'm not sure how I can help you," Garret said.

Riley sobbed. "I need money for a flight back to Connecticut—I'm still running from the really bad man."

"I wish I could help, but I can't."

Riley resisted shouting at Garret. If she wanted him to bleed money, then she might have to work for it a little bit, and that was fine so long as she got her money.

"You don't have a spare eight hundred dollars lying around somewhere?" Riley asked.

"I have some of my money tucked away in a safe in the breakroom, but I'm not just gonna hand it over without any questions."

Riley flipped her hair over her shoulders. "You really think I'm conning you?"

"Do you want my honest opinion?"

"Absolutely," Riley said.

"You seem like a nice girl." Garret sipped his coffee from the mug left of the register. "I even have a daughter your age."

Riley would have to say a blessing later. The situation couldn't have been going any better if a suitcase full of money fell from the sky. Mentioning he had a daughter gave Riley even more to work with—almost as if Garret brought his gullibility on himself.

"Wouldn't you want someone to help your daughter if she was in trouble?" Riley asked.

"Yes," Garret mumbled.

"Then please help me."

"Okay. You've talked me into it." The man disappeared into the breakroom, leaving Riley alone.

Thank goodness for how most people believed the best in others—a fact Riley discovered a long time ago. Even if someone didn't know a stranger, making a positive assumption was still easier than thinking the worst in someone. Optimism occupied less headspace than always wondering when crossing paths with a bad person would happen.

Garret exited the breakroom, heading to the register.

"I'm sorry, but it's all in twenties." Garret handed Riley the money. "Although I'd appreciate you doing me one favor."

"What's that?" Riley stuffed the money into her purse. "Make sure the money doesn't leave my sight?"

Garret pointed his finger, smiling. "I knew I liked you for a reason."

The shop door opened, and a woman with neon green hair strutted inside, heading towards the counter.

"Take care of yourself," Garret said.

"You too." Riley left the place and didn't even fret from the downpour of rain falling onto the sidewalk. In fact, she hadn't jumped when purple tinged lightning zig-zagged across the sky and thunder roared after another beat.

Something did make her choke, though. And the reaction wasn't sudden remorse for conning the shop owner. A woman with yellow teeth, and a ripped shirt and jeans stood in front of the Subway next to Garret's shop. Almost as if Riley was positive the lady might have been homeless. A jar filled with a few bills by the lady's feet also provided a good enough clue in addition to how the person's hair fell a couple of inches below her knees.

Charity might have been an overrated concept to Riley in the past—nobody saved her from Adam selling her on the black market just because she was born last. But not today. She could afford to give the woman money since Garret gave all her twenty-dollar bills. And doing some good karma didn't hurt. Riley could never anticipate when she might need extra luck tackling a problem.

Knowing when she would need positive vibes also wasn't exactly physics class. She would have bet anything how Sasha was still "Riley," and might not give up the role without a fight, so she'd have to figure out how to deal with Sasha sooner rather than later.

Riley pulled out a twenty from her purse once she snapped out of her internal digression, then strutted over to the jar, not even cringing from how the woman wreaked of body odor. "I hope this makes a difference," Riley said.

"Bless you," said the lady.

Money. Check. Next stop: Clearing her stuff from the motel. Then: Connecticut.

Riley wouldn't let the Sasha issue bother her for now, though. She could invent a solution on the plane ride back to Connecticut. Accomplishing her biggest life goal—revenge against Adam for what he did to her—was the only thing that currently mattered. And if everyone else in the world knew what was best, then they wouldn't mess with her. If they did, they'd die just like Adam.

CHAPTER 28

LOLA

Déjà vu was the only word Lola would have used to describe standing on Vanessa's front porch while stars lit up the evening sky. She just rang the doorbell, and prayed her grandmother would open the door ASAP. Just because someone might not have currently pointed a gun at her, didn't mean her life wasn't in danger. The faint murmur of the wind was the only thing she needed for her head swaying from side to side. Almost as if she was in a horror movie, and the serial killer was seconds away from killing her. There was no forgetting her father lying on the floor, blood soaked holes in his head from his gunshot wounds.

Lola clutched her suitcase handle harder. Life shouldn't have repeated herself, but she couldn't undo what happened. Even if she could only run so many times—a person could only flee for so long.

Lola pressed the doorbell again.

The worst part about leaving LA was abandoning Preston—he'd probably never give her a second chance after playing games.

Lola would eventually find a way to live with the disappointment, though. No matter how hard her life was, she was still alive. And that fact counted for something. Katrina would have to try harder if she wanted to kill her.

The door opened.

Vanessa's jaw shook. "What the hell are you doing here?"

Lola sulked at Vanessa. "I'm in big trouble."

"I don't understand. I thought things were good between you and Preston. It was the whole reason I felt comfortable leaving you alone."

"May I please come inside?" Lola asked.

Vanessa gestured at Lola. "Sorry. My manners escaped me."

"Don't worry about it." Lola wheeled her suitcase into the house while Vanessa locked the front door behind her.

Vanessa cracked a smile. "Why don't you go into the living room? I'll go make some tea and bring out a tray of sugar cookies—I baked earlier."

"Sounds like a plan." Lola followed Vanessa's instructions—she left her suitcase by the front door and scurried towards the living room couch.

Lola kept rubbing her cheeks while sitting on the living room couch. Thank goodness for Vanessa—she didn't know what she would have done if her grandmother wasn't there for her. She deserved at least one person's unconditional support.

Vanessa walked into the living room, carrying a tray with teacups and a plate of cookies. Then, she placed it on the glass living room table before joining Lola on the couch.

"I added extra honey just like you like it," Vanessa said.

"Thank you." Lola grabbed her cup, then sipped her tea. The sweetness from the honey exhilarated her taste buds. Lola snatched two cookies from the plates, and the mixture of the buttery, floury, and vanilla flavors aroused her mouth even more than the sweetened tea had. Almost as if the cookies offered more comfort than retiring. And that was why she didn't pay attention when Vanessa frowned at her loud munching sounds—good food needed to be appreciated.

"Tell me what happened," Vanessa said.

"She killed him."

"You're gonna have to be more specific." Vanessa drank her tea, yet didn't take a cookie. Lola even snickered. Her grandmother must have been on a new diet, and would probably boast about her new eating habits anytime soon. Although Lola wondered who Vanessa baked the cookies for if she didn't plan on eating them.

"I'll have to bake more cookies tomorrow, but that's fine," Vanessa said. "They were supposed to be for a friend from my book club."

Lola's back hairs rose. It was if Lola was psychic, and she almost wailed for how her intuition didn't help her with her love life.

"Sorry," Lola said.

"Don't worry about it. Anyway, what were you saying?"

"Adam is dead, and I'm pretty sure Katrina killed him."

"What about your relationship with Preston?" Vanessa asked.

Lola lowered her head, placing her hands in front of her eye. "I broke up with him—I slid a letter under his apartment door before leaving LA."

"I'm so sorry," Vanessa said. "Nothing I say will make the situation better."

"Listening helps." Lola finished her tea before taking another cookie. If her heart ached, then she might as well have good treats. "I just can't believe how naïve I was—I should have seen this coming."

Vanessa patted Lola's knee. "Don't punish yourself. Nothing wrong with wanting to believe the best in the situation. But know one thing—I'm proud of you for how you tried making your relationship with Preston work. That's the only time I've seen you display vulnerability, and I hope you'll do so again when the time is right."

"Don't count on it."

Vanessa released her pearl necklace, then it smacked against her chest. "If you and Preston are meant to be, then you'll find your way back to each other."

"You don't have to tell me what I want to hear. Anyone with half a brain can tell my relationship with Preston is done for good."

"I wasn't humoring you," Vanessa said.

"You weren't?"

Vanessa giggled. "Nope. Love is like Santa Claus—the world would be a darker place without believing in it."

Lola sat up straighter on the couch. "That's an interesting way to look at romance."

"Trust me. I know what I'm talking about. Anyway, I presume you'll be staying with me for the foreseeable future?"

"You assumed right."

"I'm sorry for how the situation unfolded, but having company again will be great."

"You just need to date—there are plenty of apps you could use," Lola said, fighting back laughter.

"I'm too old for that," Vanessa said.

"Sixty isn't old."

"Tell that to my gardener," Vanessa said. "He stopped looking at my chest ages ago."

Lola's mind drifted back to Vanessa's comment about comparing love to Santa Claus. The idea comforted her in a small way. Yet Lola wasn't a little kid anymore, and accepted how some heroes got unhappy endings while some villains got their happy ending. If crime had no payoff, then nobody would do it. The only problem was knowing that fact did nothing for her. Lola's stomach just tightened more.

CHAPTER 29

SASHA

Steam trickled from the tea kettle spout's while Sasha stood in the kitchen. Cece already left for work, and Tyler was upstairs sleeping. Sasha closed her eyes, then her body shook. She couldn't believe the Mr. Parker situation. If Tyler hadn't killed him, then she'd be dead. But she hadn't wanted her life to resemble *I Know What You Did Last Summer*—there was no guarantee Mr. Parker's death would remain a secret forever.

The kettle rattled louder, snapping Sasha out of her digression.

Assuming the worst would've only wasted time. Meticulous planning was one thing, yet she didn't want her life to become a self-fulfilling prophecy. She just had to make it through the day, and wouldn't think about the following day until she had to.

Steam engulfed the kettle after it shrieked more, then Sasha flicked the switch. If she wasn't careful, then she'd burn down the mansion.

The universe had other plans for her, though. The doorbell rang when she started pouring water into the mug. Maybe, just maybe, the person would go away if she ignored the front door.

The doorbell rang three more times.

Sasha couldn't ignore the person any longer. If the doorbell rang four times, then the issue couldn't have been mundane.

Sasha walked out of the kitchen, then opened the front door. "What are you doing here, Dylan?"

Dylan bit his lip. "Bad time?"

Sasha remained silent for a moment. Inviting Dylan into the mansion was harmless despite how their recent tryst would remain burned in her mind for the foreseeable future. It wasn't like Tyler would snitch on her. That was the advantage of helping him cover up Mr. Parker's "murder."

Sasha threw a glance inside. "Please come in."

Dylan entered the home, then Sasha closed the door behind her. Sasha headed towards the kitchen, and Dylan followed behind her.

Dylan glanced at the cup half filled with water that had a teabag sticking out of it. "Oh. Maybe this wasn't a good time."

Sasha giggled. "Don't be silly—the tea can wait. What's up?"

"I was wondering if you thought anymore about my offer. You know. The one about leaving this life behind and living with me in Manhattan."

Sasha would've been lying if she said Dylan's offer hadn't tempted her. However, Tyler and Cece weren't dolls to be disposed of when she was bored. They were real people with real feelings, and they might've been devastated if she abandoned them. And she couldn't leave Tyler and Jake alone to deal with him the aftermath of Mr. Parker's death. They weren't even twenty years old, and couldn't be expected to process the ordeal by themselves. Especially if the police stopped by one day. Although if Sasha got her way, then she hoped Mr. Parker's wife would assume he was unhappy with their marriage and left her. It'd all come down to how much Mr. Parker's wife was invested in the marriage. No longer giving a fuck about the marriage would've ensured his wife accepting the simplest explanation.

Dylan crossed his arms. "Well?"

"I need more time."

"I don't understand what the problem is. Didn't you wanna sleep with me?" Dylan asked.

"The truth is more complicated than that."

Dylan pushed a lock of her hair out of the way. "I can't help you unless you tell me what's wrong."

"What makes you assume something is wrong?"

"Have you met yourself?"

"Good point."

"Don't tell me there's a threat worse than Ivan?" Dylan asked.

Sasha looked away. "Don't make me lie to you, because I don't want to."

His gaze constricted. "Are you protecting someone?"

"Dylan, please!" Sasha exclaimed.

"Okay. Okay." Dylan adjusted his blazer. "I get your point. But I can't wait around forever, so you have forty-eight hours to decide if you wanna be with me or not."

"Seriously?"

"I'd like an in person answer no matter what your decision is. We deserve closure after everything we've been through." Dylan clapped Sasha's shoulder before exiting the kitchen.

Sasha's stomach churned. Not once had she anticipated dealing with a romantic ultimatum. Even after the endless hours of pop culture she consumed.

Blaming Dylan would've been unfair, though. Everything he said was true—he had a life, and couldn't put it on hold forever. Doing so would've been unfair to him, because Sasha wanted him to be happy no matter what happened between them.

Footsteps shuffled, growing louder and louder. Sasha shifted her weight—Tyler stood in the kitchen's entrance.

"Can I make you anything for breakfast?" Sasha asked.

"That's sweet of you."

Sasha couldn't help disagreeing with him. Doing something for him didn't require much effort. Besides, the offer was the decent thing. A home cooked meal was the least he deserved after suffering so much. Her life might've been different if someone showed her kindness while she was in Ivan's clutches.

Tyler lifted his brow. "Who was at the door?"

"A friend."

Tyler snickered. "Are you really gonna lie to me after everything we've been through? Haven't I proven I'm trustworthy?"

Sasha couldn't argue with Tyler. He had numerous opportunities for informing Cece that she wasn't Riley, yet he hadn't. And that fact meant more to Sasha than it might've to someone else.

Loyalty was hard to come by in a world that got worse with each passing day—according to the news, at least.

"It was someone from my past life," Sasha said.

"Who?" Tyler asked.

"A client."

"Oh my."

Sasha played with a strand of her hair. "Calm down. This guy is one of the good ones."

Her response hadn't required flinching. Dylan was her only client who hadn't made the first move. He was a "talker," and wanted someone to hang with or watch a movie with. In fact, Sasha made the first move—not Dylan. Something exciting existed from Sasha initiating the sex for once—like when a high school senior ditched on senior skip day despite the possibility of suspension.

"If you say so," Tyler said.

"Fine," Sasha said. "I'll tell you the truth. I slept with him the other day, and he wants me to choose between him and my new life."

Tyler didn't respond.

"What?" Sasha demanded. "You don't hate me for cheating on your mother?"

"I'm not gonna judge you after you helped me. Besides, Cece isn't innocent."

Sasha waggled her eyebrows. "It'd be nice if you two got along."

"Don't count on it."

The doorbell rang, yet Sasha didn't ignore it. Dealing with the person proved best—she only needed to point to Dylan's earlier visit.

Except Sasha didn't count on finding a package on the ground by the front door, not a person.

Sasha grabbed the package before heading back inside.

Opening the package didn't mean risking her life because of how there was no return address. Ivan wouldn't mail her a bomb—doing so wasn't personal enough. If he wanted her dead, then he would've returned to Connecticut and slit her throat.

Only one way to find out what the package contained, so Sasha would just get the task over with. She tore through the package, discovering a leather journal and piece of paper.

Sasha perused through the diary first. Her heart then leapt out of her chest. There was just no believing what she was reading. She would've recognized the handwriting anywhere—it was Riley's.

But what she read couldn't be true.

The ramblings confirmed every terrible thought she had about Riley. Riley confessed to framing Sasha for the fire that "killed" Vincent, including how Vincent pulled one of his teeth out so Riley could plant it at their house. One tooth was the only thing the firemen found. Riley also copped to sneaking into their grandmother's place after the fire and planting the lighter and gasoline in Sasha's room in addition to how Vincent gave the police an anonymous tip about Sasha. Apparently, her and Riley's mother left family money from the real estate empire that they'd inherit on their eighteenth birthdays. And Riley hadn't felt like sharing.

The goosebumps didn't stop. Being sent to jail for a crime she didn't commit wasn't the worst part—the entries and photos before the confession was. Vincent never abused Riley—she was a willing participant in the affair. Riley only wanted Sasha to think abuse happened so she'd feel guilty.

Sasha's head ached. Her discovery didn't change Riley wanting a reconciliation with her. Perhaps killing herself was another way to make her feel guilty. Sasha wouldn't put anything past Riley now.

Sasha didn't fret after returning focus to the journal. The rips at the end of the diary didn't puzzle her. Missing entries was a blessing, because Sasha didn't wanna know much worse the situation could've gotten.

She couldn't forget how her package included a photo not in the diary. It was of Riley, and she was in a lobby. Except the picture's location and subject weren't the issue. The photo's time stamp was what caused her twitching jaw—it was a full twenty-four hours after Sasha assumed Riley killed herself.

Once again, her surprise might've been misplaced. Tyler mentioned the possibility of Riley being alive. Pretending to be dead was the type of sick thing Riley would've done.

Tyler rubbed Sasha's back. "Something wrong? You've been standing by the front door for a good ten minutes."

"Riley is alive," Sasha blurted.

Tyler's pupils enlarged. "Come again?"

"Riley just wanted me to think she killed herself," Sasha stammered. "And now the only question is what has she been planning, because it must be something big."

"I don't even know what to say."

Sasha gripped the photo and journal harder. "I don't mean to be rude, but there's something I've gotta do.

***

Sasha did something she thought she'd never do—visit her grandmother, or Vanessa, as she should've referred to her as. Vanessa hadn't done anything that fit the role of grandmother in a long time.

If there was a possibility that Vanessa knew something about Riley, then Sasha would risk dealing with suppressed emotions.

The only problem was Vanessa hadn't opened the door yet, so Sasha rang the doorbell two more times.

The door creaked after several more minutes.

"What are you doing here?" Vanessa asked.

Sasha coughed. "We need to put our past behind us and focus on the future. For the moment, at least."

"What are you babbling about?"

Sasha waved the diary and photo at Vanessa. "Riley recently faked her suicide in addition to how she was responsible for the fire I was framed for because she was having a consensual affair with Vincent."

Vanessa's face turned pale. "Oh my…"

"I need to know if you've heard from Riley."

"I'm sorry, but I can't help you." Vanessa slammed the door.

So much for Sasha hoping Vanessa would help her. It wasn't enough that Vanessa didn't support her through her prison sentence. Vanessa couldn't even be bothered with chatting, so Sasha kicked her feet against the ground. She wasn't asking for diamonds—she just wanted something to go her way for once.

Something caught Sasha's attention while she almost descended the front steps. A woman with wavy hair stood by the third story window of

Vanessa's home. Except the woman's hair was shorter and a darker shade of blonde than when Sasha saw Riley during their reconciliation.

Sasha wouldn't barge in and confront Vanessa and Riley. If her grandmother wanted to help the evil twin, then that was her business. She'd find another way to get answers. No matter how she spun then situation, something didn't add up.

***

Sasha sat next to Dylan on the mansion's front steps the following day.

Blue continued waning from the afternoon sky while Sasha waited for Dylan to speak. Hopefully, he'd accept what she said. Sasha couldn't have handled both Dylan having a meltdown and Riley and Vanessa scheming against her.

"It's admirable you don't wanna run away again," Dylan said.

"Do you hate me?"

He squeezed her hand. "I could never despise you."

"Really?"

"You're an amazing woman." Dylan sighed. "But I wish you weren't falling on the sword."

"What do you mean?"

"You seem too concerned with doing the right thing," Dylan said. "No offense, but you should be concerned with your own happiness."

"My reasoning isn't about being noble." Sasha inhaled a breath. "It's about how I'm a part of something with Tyler and I don't wanna lie to you."

"What if Tyler didn't have his crisis?" Dylan asked. "You can't tell me you've got real feelings for Cece."

"I could."

"I'm not gonna argue with you." Dylan stood. "But there's something I'd like you to oblige me about."

"And what's that?"

"One last kiss."

The offer seemed reasonable enough for Sasha. A difference existed between kissing Dylan and sleeping with him. Cece also had another late night at work planned, so she wouldn't catch them.

"Whenever you're ready," Sasha said.

Dylan pulled Sasha against his body, then kissed her. But Sasha didn't close her eyes this time. Their goodbye kiss was the opposite of pretending life was like a fairytale. This was the last time she'd see Dylan, and she wanted to remember what he looked like. Life might've been fleeting, yet Sasha deserved this small memento.

Sasha clasped her chest a couple of minutes later while she hadn't moved from her spot on the front steps. Riley stood at the edge of her driveway, yet her hair was longer and resembled the same light shade of blonde as Sasha's.

Blinking several times only made Sasha stroke her cheek. Riley was no longer at the edge of the driveway after opening her eyes. But said fact didn't change Sasha's current opinion—Riley was planning something, and the only question was what the collateral damage would be.

CHAPTER 30

TYLER

Tyler almost paused the movie playing on his laptop and asked Jake if something was wrong. His boyfriend kept giving him discreet looks every couple of minutes, and Tyler would've rather Jake mentioned what was going on. Doing so would've been the simpler option—even if Tyler could've guessed the various possible thoughts swirling in Jake's mind. Rape and burying a body in the woods wasn't something that happened every day.

Tyler closed his eyes for a beat while wind slammed against his house, creating a faint murmur. The events of that fateful night would stay with him for the rest of his life. No erasing how Mr. Parker bested him, because Tyler thought he was in control of the situation.

Perhaps Tyler ultimately won, though. He was alive whereas Mr. Parker wasn't.

Jake pressed the spacebar on Tyler's laptop. "We should talk."

Tyler shifted his posture while remaining seated on the floor in front of his bed. "Okay. What's up?"

"Shouldn't I be asking you that?"

"We don't have talk about that night. In fact, I'd prefer if we didn't."

"I'm sorry, but I can't do that," Jake said.

Tyler frowned. "Why not?"

"You were raped, Ty."

Tyler didn't know whether to sob or shriek. His trauma wasn't exactly polite conversation. Almost like when someone knew their friend's kid was ugly. The friend knew it, the parent knew it, and the rest of the world realized the fact too. But that didn't mean it'd be discuss. Although Tyler had to be honest with himself about one thing. He'd speak out of other side of his mouth if Jake didn't make a big deal about his rape and Mr. Parker's death.

"It's not like I can visit a counselor and discuss what happened," Tyler said. "Do you want everything to unravel?"

"I never said you had to speak with a therapist."

"Then what?"

"I'd be okay if you wanted to vent." Jake fixed his shirt collar. "That'd be the normal thing to do."

"What do you want me to say?"

"I can't imagine what being raped was like."

Tyler fought back the tears. Crying only accomplished so much, because he'd still have to live with what happened to him after his outburst was finished. So, any relief from his incident would be fleeting like everything else in life.

"What do you want me to say?" Tyler exclaimed. "I was stupid enough to think sleeping with my professor was okay, and now he's dead."

Yeah, Tyler blamed a part of himself for the situation. Not because he deserved to be raped—nobody did. But because of how naïve he had been. There was a reason why people left convoluted schemes to television shows. It was because real life had consequence. Like when Tyler closed his eyes, only to doze off for a moment. Mr. Parker's moaning remained audible in addition to him gripping his hips remained palpable, so Tyler would have dark circles under his eyes for the foreseeable future. And there wasn't a damn thing he could do about—it wasn't like he could get a lobotomy.

Jake cringed. "Sorry. I shouldn't have asked."

"Don't stop now."

"I wanna be here for you."

"Hanging out is good enough—you can't undo that night," Tyler said.

"I know," Jake mumbled.

"I can't imagine what his wife must be thinking."

Jake snorted. "If someone knew what we did, then we'd be in jail."

"I'm not so sure about that."

"I don't think someone is gonna blackmail us."

Tyler couldn't shake the feeling of doom. Life just wasn't that easy—Mr. Parker tricking him into a meeting at his house proved said fact. It'd be like the universe to make him suffer as much as possible.

"They already reassigned his classes," Tyler said.

Jake rolled up his sleeves. "What's your point?"

"What happens when he doesn't return?"

Jake's face sagged. "We'll deal with it then. But you've gotta promise me one thing."

"I'm listening."

"You can't sleep with his replacement in exchange for a better grade," Jake said. "But I will promise to stay up with you all night if you need help."

Tyler wasn't sure if he should lecture Jake. His boyfriend's joke was kind of in bad taste, yet getting angry wouldn't accomplish anything. Tyler would still be wondering if he had flashbacks of the incident every time he closed his eyes.

"Thanks," Tyler's forced out.

Jake squeezed Tyler's hand. "You don't have to thank me; I'm your boyfriend."

Tyler didn't blink from Jake's touch. He distinguished between a good touch and a bad touch. It wasn't like Jake would hurt him. At least not physically, that was. Although Tyler couldn't speak for every trauma victim, because he imagined some people might've been afraid of their own reflection.

"I bet you wish we weren't dating," Tyler said.

"Don't say that. I don't have any regrets because of knowing you."

"That's kind of you."

"It's the truth." Jake grabbed a handful of popcorn from the bowl to the left of him. "I don't know what I would've done if we never met."

"There's one thing I've always wanted to know."

"And what's that?" Jake asked.

"What made you talked to me at the party Freshman Year?" Tyler asked. "You didn't have to make an effort."

The outside wind roared even louder, and a chill filled the air. Tyler wondered if he said the wrong thing. If Jake didn't' have a problem with the question, then he would've responded already.

"Where is this coming from?" Jake asked.

Tyler shrugged. "Only curious. Most people at school just treated me worse than gum on the bottom of your shoe."

"That's not true."

"You can't pretend school isn't cliquey."

Jake didn't respond.

"There's something you should know, but I don't want you to be angry with me," Tyler said.

"Don't tell me you killed someone else?" Jake asked.

Tyler cackled. "Not exactly."

"Then what?"

Tyler ignored his pulse echoing in his ears. He was gonna be honest with Jake about who Sasha was. And Tyler's reasoning had nothing to do with causing trouble. Jake might as well have known what he got himself into, because he had been there in the woods that night, burying Mr. Parker. It wasn't like Jake couldn't be trusted—he could. Jake could've meddled in the Mr. Parker situation after following Tyler to the motel, yet he hadn't. And Tyler would hang onto that fact forever. Some people might not have been able to say they trusted their significant other with serious issues.

Tyler didn't look away—not this time. "Riley isn't Riley. She's really Riley's identical twin sister, Sasha."

"Come again?"

"I'm telling you this because Sasha and I discovered she's alive and might be planning something twisted."

"What does this have to do with me?" Jake asked.

"If you're interacting with Sasha and she's acting weird for no reason, then it's Riley."

"Why is Sasha living her sister's life?"

Tyler rested his free hand under his chin. "She wanted to escape sex trafficking. Riley most likely staged her suicide so Sasha would assume her life."

"Thanks for the warning." Jake smirked at Tyler. "There's one thing I've always wanted to know about you and Riley."

Tyler had a feeling of where the conversation was headed, yet he'd take a deep breath. No need to cause trouble until he had a reason for alarm. Perhaps he was wrong, and Jake's question would surprise him.

"And what's that?" Tyler asked.

"Why do you hate her so much?" Jake demanded. "It's gotta be more than her being selfish."

"Because I slept with her once."

Jake's jaw trembled. "Lovely."

"You asked." Tyler bit his nail. "My tryst with Riley was also before we met, so I didn't cheat on you."

"Fair enough," Jake said. "But you don't really think Riley would do something awful?"

Tyler averted his gaze. "I don't know what to think anymore."

Jake pursed his lips. "Thank you for your honesty. It couldn't have been easy for you."

"Don't mention it."

The heavy patter of outside rain grew louder while Tyler crossed his legs. He'd once again take his advice. There was no guarantee Riley would cause trouble for his relationship with Jake. She had months to do that before staging her suicide and Sasha assumed her life.

There was still something about treating life like a game of chess, though. Tyler never knew what person he was getting with Riley in the morning when he came downstairs and had breakfast. And that fact was what scared Tyler the most. Nothing comforting about the unknown.

GHAPTER 31

RILEY

Riley changed her mind about who to manipulate.

And that fact was why she stood on Josh's front porch while the full moon lit up the night sky. Taking her life back from Sasha would've been too complicated. Riley didn't only have to consider Sasha—she also had to consider Cece and Tyler. Josh was the simpler option, because he was only one person, not three. Although Riley's stomach burned from the possibility of how Sasha might not have appreciated her gift as much as she should've. Riley witnessed every second of the kiss between Sasha and the mystery guy. And that event was more than eye roll worthy. Fooling around with someone wasn't smart if Sasha hoped to remain Riley and escape sex trafficking.

Riley couldn't forget about the most important reason she showed up at Josh's place. She had no way of knowing if Sasha told Cece and Tyler the truth. There was a good chance that Cece and Tyler wouldn't have accepted Sasha after finding out she conned them for several months, yet Riley wouldn't fall victim to hubris. If there was one thing that she'd learn in her twenty-four years of living, then it was to expect the unexpected.

But she'd have to quit stalling and ring Josh's damn doorbell already. She couldn't angle her way back into his life unless she spoke to him. So, she sucked in a breath and counted to five in her head.

Riley pushed the doorbell, and the front door opened after another a beat.

Josh's jaw lowered. "Sasha?"

"It's Riley." Riley grunted. "Wait. Why'd you think I was my sister?"

"No reason."

Riley had to take Josh's statement at face value. Starting an argument for no reason wouldn't help her cause. Even if she suspected that she didn't know something major. Like when a college student returned back to their university after studying abroad for a year and hoped nothing would change with their friends. Except the returning student's life was anything but the same—almost like random puzzle pieces that didn't go together.

Josh folded his arm, wrinkling his suit. "I've got nothing to say to you."

"You can't win unless you know what the game is."

Josh snickered. "Good to see you haven't changed."

"You didn't expect to never to hear from me again, did you?" Riley flipped her hair over her shoulders. "You know I'm not leaving until you let me inside, so save yourself the trouble and invite me in already."

Someone should've given her a medal. The old her would've threatened to scream if Josh didn't let her in, but she hadn't resorted to such theatrics. Riley still had nothing to gain from alienating Josh. Nothing worse in life than being poor, because she had less than fifty dollars left from the money the pawn shop guy gave her. Apparently, flights from California to Connecticut costed more than she anticipated.

Josh huffed. "Fine. You can come inside."

Riley entered the home, then Josh locked the door behind her.

"You've got five minutes," Josh continued.

"I can live with that."

"What was so important that you had to bother me?" Josh asked, still standing by the front door.

"Shouldn't we go in the living room and sit down on the couch?"

"Weren't you paying attention? Your visit isn't gonna be that long. Just say whatever it is you came here to tell me, and then leave."

Riley would learn not to burn bridges later. She hadn't done herself any favors with Josh, because his current hostility was the last thing she needed. He shouldn't have been counting down the minutes till their conversation was over. Besides, Riley was supposed to be the main attraction, not the pit-stop.

"Fine." Riley played with a strand of her hair. "I wanted to apologize to you and see if you'd take me back. Keeping the wedding ring wasn't fair to you."

"I don't care about the wedding ring." Josh undid his tie, then threw it on the mahogany table by the front door.

"What are you talking about?" Riley demanded. "You were obviously upset, so don't deny it."

Josh laughed louder this time. "I know everything, Katrina."

"What are you talking about?"

"You're an above average schemer, but you aren't perfect." Josh paused. "You left one of your diaries here, and I mailed it to Sasha."

Riley's throat constricted. Josh couldn't have said what he just had. If it was the diary she thought it was, then she was in big trouble. There was no way Sasha could read the end of the journal. If she did, then everything she worked so hard for would be ruined.

Josh lunged closer, breath almost prickling Riley's skin. "Relax, babe. I tore out the last several pages, so she doesn't know you're really Katrina."

"But you hate me?"

"Those last few pages are my insurance policy in case you ever fuck with me," Josh said. "And no. Before you think about killing me, I don't have those last few pages here. I gave them to someone who has instructions to release them if something happens to me. You know. Like if you murder me like you killed Adam."

Riley hissed at him. "How do you know about Adam?"

"I watch the news."

"You can't prove I killed him," Riley said.

Yeah, Riley resorted to denial when all else failed her. Doing so was the only option she had, because what she said was technically true. Josh had no way of linking her to Adam's death regardless of the current contempt radiating from his eyes.

"I don't need to prove anything—this isn't a court of law." Josh sneered. "Your life is about to get even better."

Riley pushed her purse strap further up her shoulder. "Why? What else did you do?"

"I didn't just send Sasha your diary—I sent her a picture with a time stamp from one of the hotel lobby security cameras."

"So? We fucked at numerous hotels before leaving town?"

"You're missing my point," Josh said. "It was the hotel we stayed at the day after leaving town."

Riley just wasn't having a good day, and would've gone to church and pray for a better life. If she was a spiritual person, that was. There was just no comprehending all her recent bad luck. She deserved everything and anything, and would be damned if that didn't happen.

Riley let out a scream. "What are you saying?"

"Sasha knows your alive." Josh cracked his knuckles. "Anyway, you should go now. But good luck lying your way out of this one."

Riley couldn't believe Josh. It was like being with her hardened him and Riley would be more mindful of dealing with people in the future. Josh might not have wanted to harm her, but she might not be so lucky next time. Nothing worse than her becoming the victim of the monster she created.

Riley cackled. "I'll give you one thing—you aren't as dumb as I thought you were."

"Things could've been so different if you told me the truth."

"You wouldn't have understood," Riley said.

Josh's eyebrows inched up. "We'll never know what could've been."

"It wasn't all a lie with you—the sex was good."

Josh opened the door, then eyed Riley. "Get the hell out of my house."

Riley grabbed her suitcase's handle, then wheeled it out of the house. Then, she turned back to Josh. "I'm gonna come back for you one day. You're as bad as my parents for denying me the life I could've had," she said.

Riley wasn't 100 percent certain if she meant what she said, yet Josh didn't need to know that fact. If she really wanted to kill Josh, then she could've grabbed the gun from her suitcase—the one she got from a back-alley dealer before killing Adam—and give Josh three bullets in the head. But no. Just like with the waitress who flirted with Josh when bringing him wine, knowing she could kill was enough. She also didn't feel like cleaning up anymore messes at the moment.

"Looking forward to it," Josh said.

***

Riley stood by Cece's front door the following morning, only to be greeted by Sasha's frown.

Sasha sported a tee-shirt, and sweatpants, and her hair was in a ponytail. Sweat also hadn't stopped dripping down her face in addition to how Sasha hadn't taken the earbuds out of her ears.

"Surprise, Sasha!" Riley exclaimed.

"What the hell are you doing here?" Sasha asked after taking the earbuds out of her ears.

"You should be nicer to me considering how I saw you making out with that guy the other day."

"I'm not afraid of you." Sasha let out a breath. "I know everything, bitch. Like with framing me for the fire and how you lied about Vincent abusing you."

"Clever girl."

"The only thing I don't know is what you were doing when I was in prison and what you were up to after staging your suicide. Had to have been more than wanting me to feel guilty."

Riley would've giggled if doing so wouldn't give away everything. Sasha might've known Riley was alive, but she didn't know Riley was really Katrina. And Riley would never let that piece of information go. The truth was the one advantage she had over Sasha, and she would exploit the nugget for everything it was worth. And in a way, she was thankful for Josh. He could've spoiled everything, yet he hadn't. So, Riley would find a way to thank him someday—she just wasn't sure what that was.

"Wouldn't you like to know," Riley said.

Sasha wiped another bead of sweat from her forehead. "What do you want?"

"What makes you think I want something?"

"Please." Sasha snorted louder than a pig. "That innocent girl routine isn't gonna work with me. You're nothing but a manipulative psychotic bitch."

Riley clapped her hand over her chest. "Ouch."

"Save the theatrics, and get the hell out of my sight."

"I want my life back—the one I leant you."

"Not a chance. I might not be you, but I'm ten times the wife and stepmother you ever were."

"Have you slept with Cece?" Riley asked.

"Yeah, I have—not that it's any of your business."

"I'm impressed. I didn't know you had it in you to use sex to manipulate someone."

"It's not a con if I care about Cece and Tyler," Sasha said. "I also know you slept with Tyler. Should've known something was up when you made that offhanded comment about Tyler my first night back in Connecticut."

Riley rubbed her eyelid while a squirrel grabbed an acorn and darted up a nearby tree. She couldn't believe what her sister said was true, yet it was. Even if her tryst with Tyler felt like another lifetime ago. The important thing was just like Josh, the Tyler situation could've been worse. One night of drunken stupidity hadn't ruined her life, because there were worse guys to sleep with than Tyler.

Riley stared her sister down. "I'm serious, Sasha. I want my life back, I've got no money."

"That's not my problem, bitch."

"You can call me a bitch as many times as you want, but that isn't gonna change how Ivan is still out there."

Sasha put her hands on her hips. "Nice try, but you can't use Ivan against me. I blackmailed him to leave me alone."

Riley smirked. As much as she needed money and a place to say, Riley couldn't deny gawking over the challenge. No fun feuding with someone who was too weak to fight back, because Riley never once considered how Sasha would be more than willing to do whatever it took to get what she wanted.

"Perhaps you're no longer the innocent one," Riley said.

Sasha shook her shirt in her face. "I should kill you for what you did to me. Sending me to prison for a crime I didn't commit is beyond despicable."

"You're still alive."

"I was beaten several times while in prison."

Riley licked her lips. "What a sad story. Maybe you should tell Oprah, and she can have someone write about it in her magazine."

"There's something I wanna know," Sasha said. "You have longer and blonder hair then when you did at Vanessa's in addition to how you're slightly tanner."

"You've officially lost it."

Riley once again suppressed her glee. If she had to guess, then Lola—the real Riley—must've been the one staying with their grandmother. And said fact was great. Sasha might lose her mind trying to figure out what was going on.

"Has our grandmother been helping you?" Sasha demanded.

"It's not my fault if Vanessa took in stranger who looks like us."

Sasha didn't speak.

"You aren't gonna let me have my life back, are you?" Riley asked.

"Not a chance."

"I'll go, but you haven't seen the last of me." Riley wheeled her suitcase down the front steps without looking back at Sasha. Leaving didn't make her weak—it made her practical. No use in starting trouble if she didn't have a plan.

And no regret existed for not taking out her gun and killing Sasha just like with giving Josh a temporary reprieve. Riley couldn't kill Sasha in broad daylight in addition to how she wasn't prepared for cleaning up a messy crime scene inside the mansion.

This way was better, really. Murdering Sasha might happen one day, yet no rush in killing her.

Savoring her victory would let Riley revel in the win even more. Like an alligator lurking in a swamp, stalking a bird for hours before leaping out of the water and killing the animal. The only question was how much bloodshed there'd be.

CHAPTER 32

LOLA

Lola sat on the living room couch, having tea and cookies with Vanessa.

Her grandmother hadn't said ten words to her since sitting down next to her fifteen minutes ago, though. And Lola had a pretty good idea for what caused Vanessa's next Botox bill. But whether she should say anything remained a mystery. No matter how awful Vincent hitting her with the rock and Riley assuming her life was, Lola couldn't deny how she wasn't the only one suffering.

Vanessa jabbed her fists. "I hate this!"

"Let me have it."

"It's not about you, it's about that bitch Katrina."

Lola giggled. Her grandmother had only used bad language a handful of times, and Lola could only imagine the various thoughts swirling in Vanessa's mind. Favoring one grandchild over the other couldn't have been easy.

"Just refer to her as Riley since I'm Lola." Lola grabbed a cookie from the metal tray in front of her on the living room table. Except she hadn't anticipated her tooth almost cracking. So much for hoping for soft, buttery, and sweat sugar cookies. Biting into a rock wouldn't have been nearly as scary.

"It doesn't matter what we call her—she's still a bitch," Vanessa said.

"At least Sasha knows part of the truth."

"It's not enough."

Lola straightened her blouse. "Say it already. You hate how I didn't go to the police the night they tried to kill me."

Lola kept a secret for the last seven years, and she wasn't about to tell Vanessa the truth. But this type of deception wasn't something that imploded lives. It was only a quiet detail, something Lola dealt with while staring at her bedroom ceiling in the evening when she should've been asleep. She sometimes wondered what life would've been like if she never went into hiding. Maybe then Sasha wouldn't have gone to jail for Vincent's death and she would've been able to make a relationship.

Lola nibbled on the inside of her lip. She'd come so close to having a happily ever after with Preston work, only for the universe to snatch her life from her. Fleeing didn't make her a coward—running was the right thing to do. Vanessa hadn't been there when she gasped at Adam's lifeless body. In a way, she did Preston a favor. Although she would've been lying if she hadn't hoped Preston saw the news. Adam's death was something ripe for a juicy headline since he was the former husband of someone connected to a real estate empire. Perhaps Preston might locate her. Vanessa's address was something that could be looked up on the internet. Lola could dream, after all. Her temporary delusion of grandeur of reuniting with Preston was harmless. She had plenty of time to deal with reality later. There was no shortage of cruelty in the world, and life would be unfair again soon enough.

Vanessa's eyes widened. "You think?"

"Living life in the shadows was the safer option."

"Your mother didn't raise you to be a coward," Vanessa said.

"We'll never know what Mom would've thought," Lola said. "Unless you're gonna blame me for her cancer as well."

"Don't be ridiculous. I would never be so cruel."

Lola patted Vanessa's hand. "I never wanted life to be like this."

"I know, I know."

"There has to be a way out of this without risking our lives."

Vanessa pointed a finger at Lola. "You should never have been by your bedroom window—Sasha could've seen you."

"It wasn't like I put on a show for the neighbors."

Vanessa spat out her tea. "I should hope not."

Lola could've elbowed Vanessa. It wasn't like she stood by her bedroom window on purpose. She just happened to be at the location at the time of Sasha's visit. But it wasn't like Sasha confronted Vanessa about her presence, so perhaps she hadn't seen Lola. Adding another wishful thought to the list was harmless at this point. Wasn't like she had terminal cancer and thought she'd make a miraculous recovery. Please. Even Lola wasn't that clueless, because delusions only got people so far.

"How did Sasha seem?" Lola asked.

Vanessa pushed her sleeves up. "How do you think she was?"

"Must've been a lawyer in another life. Nothing like answering a question with another question."

"This isn't a game," Vanessa snapped, face turning whiter than snow. "People's lives have been affected."

"If there was a way for Sasha to know the truth without endangering ourselves, then I would've done so already. I'm not heartless like Riley."

The doorbell rang before Vanessa could respond.

"I'll get it." Lola stood, then exited the living room. Except Vanessa grabbed her arm when she approached the front door.

"I can't believe you!" Vanessa exclaimed. "Have you learned nothing? You're supposed to be keeping a low profile, so go hide in the kitchen.

Lola pouted, then did as Vanessa said. No point in arguing with her grandmother even if life shouldn't have resembled that of a caged animal's. It wasn't a special occasion, and Lola had no reason for pushing the limits of what she could get away with.

Shaking her head while standing in the kitchen was the only thing Lola could do. There was no denying she recognized the voice of the man chatting with Vanessa by the front door—it was Preston.

Lola would do what she fucking pleased for once in her life, so she hadn't blinked at Vanessa's scowling after shuffling out of the kitchen.

"I really don't know why I bother with you!" Vanessa said.

"We can trust Preston." Lola craned her neck. "What are you doing here?"

Preston waved the note at Lola. "Did you seriously think this would be okay? You were supposed to trust me."

Lola's mouth gaped. "There's something you don't know."

"Save it," Preston said, raising his voice. "I saw the news about Adam."

"I didn't wanna put you in danger," Lola said.

"I'm gonna go make more tea." Vanessa darted away without another word, and Lola and Preston were soon alone.

"You aren't supposed to make decisions for me," Preston said.

"I wasn't trying to hurt you."

"Doesn't matter. There are two people in a relationship, and I'm not gonna lose you—not again."

Lola kicked her feet against the tile floor. "What do you want from me? If my sister conspired to murder me once, then she could do it again."

"I just wanna be with you." Preston leaned forward, hands caressing Lola's cheeks. Then, he kissed her.

Lola didn't push Preston off her. Nothing wrong with the kiss, because the embrace was like greeting a friend after a long time apart. Might not have seen each other much, yet that connection still lurked, begging to be explored.

"I'm not going anywhere," Preston said after the kiss.

Something peaked at Lola from the corner of her eye. Preston hadn't come empty handed.

"Is that why you brought a duffle bag?" Lola asked.

Preston nodded. "Yeah, because we're gonna end the game once and for all. I don't know how, but you've gotta take your life back."

Maybe, just maybe, Lola's luck would change. She and Vanessa might've been unable to handle Riley themselves, but there was strength in numbers. And Preston might've been just what they needed. The only question left was how soon Riley would be exposed.

CHAPTER 33

SASHA

Sasha exited Starbucks after treating herself to a cup of coffee while small swaths of sunlight poked through the cloudy sky.

Fear might've been weakness, yet Sasha couldn't deny her pulse roaring in both ears during her confrontation with Riley the other day. So, Sasha wouldn't regret doing something for herself even if she could've made coffee at home. Except she didn't count on bumping into Riley a second time while shuffling down the sidewalk.

"Surprise, bitch!" Riley exclaimed.

"You're gonna have to find a more creative insult."

"Bitch works fine for me."

"What do you want from me?" Sasha demanded. "I already told you I'm not giving up my newfound life for you."

"I don't want anything from you."

Sasha swallowed. "Come again?"

"You heard me." Riley pushed her sunglasses further up the bridge of her nose. "After this conversation, we'll have nothing more to discuss."

"Just like that?"

"Yup," Riley said. "I've got more important things than you being consumed with jealousy."

Sasha might as well have been dreaming. Riley would never leave her alone—doing so wasn't in the nature of a psychopath. Yet Sasha only had her intuition to go off of. It wasn't like she could accuse Riley of doing something wrong without proof. If Sasha had, then she would've just driven herself crazy.

"I've never been envious of you," Sasha said.

Riley clapped her hands. "Yeah, you have, and it's okay. Anyone would wanna be me."

"You've got quite the opinion of yourself."

"If I don't believe in myself, then nobody else will," Riley said.

"Where's your suitcase?" Sasha asked. "Don't tell me you found someone gullible enough to take you in."

"There was a spare room at one of the local churches."

Riley must've been stoned. Sasha couldn't picture Riley being in a church even if she had nowhere else to go. Riley would've burst into flames upon entering the church, and Sasha would've loved every moment of the event. Riley's downfall was the least Sasha deserved after everything her sister put her through.

Sasha cackled. "You're beyond God's help at this point."

"It's only temporary." Riley remained silent for a moment. "Tell me something. Does Cece know you kissed someone that wasn't her?"

"I thought you weren't gonna cause trouble for me?"

"Doesn't mean I can't have fun," Riley said.

"It's your turn to tell me something," Sasha said. "Having nobody care about you must feel pretty good."

Sasha wouldn't regret matching Riley jab for jab. Morality was overrated, because being a good person wouldn't change everything Riley did to her. Sasha would've even gone as far as to say that nobleness was emptier than a donut's calories. It wasn't like she wanted to be a serial killer—Riley just needed to know Sasha wasn't the same weak girl she was in prison.

Riley stuffed her hands into her jacket pockets. "Plenty of people care about me."

Sasha couldn't resist cackling again. "The local church doesn't count."

Riley grabbed a strand of Sasha's hair. "I sent you to prison once, and I could do it again."

"Let's get something straight." Sasha shoved Riley's hand off her hair, then squeezed Riley's arm.

"No need to hurt me."

Sasha leaned into Riley's right ear. "I could kill you for what you did to me, bitch."

"Go ahead. Do it."

"I'm not gonna murder you in broad daylight."

"Playing it safe only gets you so far."

"For all I know, you killed Vincent because you didn't wanna share the inheritance with him."

"Conjecture won't get you anywhere."

"It's not conjecture if you're flinching," Sasha said.

A woman holding a child's hand with each arm just strutted by Sasha and Riley. And Sasha couldn't help taking her attention off Riley. Sasha's life would've been so much simpler if two young children were her biggest problem. No tantrum would've compared to all of Riley's antics—it couldn't. Riley was in a category all of her own, because she was just that evil. In fact, Riley could save Sasha from a burning building, and Sasha's opinion wouldn't change. At least this way, Sasha could protect herself if she didn't have any misgivings about who her sister was.

"I'm not wavering, I'm just annoyed," Riley said.

Sasha released Riley. "You're the one who spoke to me, because you could've just kept walking."

"I'll give you that."

"You owe me one thing."

"And what's that?" Riley asked.

A steady drizzle splattered onto the sidewalk, and Sasha could've whipped herself. She couldn't have been stupid enough to forget her umbrella. Tyler mentioned something about rain at breakfast several hours ago.

"What the hell happened to you?" Sasha demanded. "It's like you became a different person after your seventeenth birthday."

"You wouldn't believe me even if I was honest."

Sasha glared at her sister. "Try me."

"Nah. I'll leaving you wanting more—nothing like being in control."

What a surprise that Riley hadn't been honest with her. She'd probably keep spinning her lies for the rest of her life, and Sasha couldn't do anything about that. Nope. Getting on with the rest of her life was the only thing Sasha controlled. And said fact was okay, because only a fool would've thought her and Riley could be real sisters.

"See if I care." Sasha shifted her weight, fixing the ache in her back. Her jaw then trembled. The girl who looked just like her except for shorter hair and a darker shade of blonde stood across the street. Yet the person couldn't have been Riley—her sister remained next to her.

Sasha blinked several times. The person was gone after Sasha opened her eyes.

"What? You've got nothing to say?" Riley asked.

Sasha wouldn't mention the person who looked like her and Riley to Riley. Not after Riley would only make a joke. Sasha also wouldn't get an honest answer from Riley, so no point in wasting her energy.

Sasha forced a smile. "Have a great life, Riley. I hope you get everything that's coming to you."

***

Sasha sat next to Cece in bed, yet they weren't doing anything to adventures. They both just happened to be reading—Cece a gardening magazine, and Sasha an Agatha Christie books she bought for ninety-nine cents after running into Riley earlier in the day.

Cece closed her magazine. "Can we chat for a second?"

"Sure. Everything is okay?"

Sasha didn't wanna go looking for problems that didn't exist, yet she still had to be mindful about the universe's sick sense of humor. Riley could've lied and found some way of informing Cece about her kiss with Dylan.

Cece's face lit up. "Everything is fine."

"Good to know." Sasha placed the bookmark in her book, then put it on the bedside table next to her. "But don't leave me in suspense."

"We've become much closer and you've even been getting along with Tyler."

"Isn't that a good thing?"

Cece raised her palm at Sasha. "Please let me finish."

"Sorry."

"I wanna renew our wedding vows," Cece blurted.

"What brought this on?"

"No time like the present for embracing our renewed relationship." Cece tucked a lock of Sasha's hair out of the way. "But you don't have to give me an answer this second—just promise you'll think about it. Could be fun."

"I'll definitely consider it," Sasha mumbled.

"Fantastic."

Sasha couldn't have said she was surprised—she wasn't. Her relationship with Cece was one thing she'd have to address at some point. Ivan and Riley being out of her life didn't mean the universe wouldn't keep throwing problems at her—it would.

Embracing her new life over a future with Dylan hadn't didn't mean she wanted to do have a vow renewal ceremony. Playing house was one thing, yet Cece deserved to be married to a real person, not an illusion of a person.

And Sasha was gonna have to do something she never once imagined since assuming Riley's life— tell Cece the truth about who she really was. Doing so was the last remaining step if she wanted to create a real family with Cece and Tyler. The only question was how Cece would react to the news, because some people might not have appreciated how life was ambiguous like she did.

CHAPTER 34

TYLER

Tyler discovered Sasha drinking bourbon in the living room after returning home from his classes.

Tyler furrowed his eyebrows. "Something wrong?"

Sasha looked up from her glass. "I didn't hear you."

"I wasn't exactly quiet."

"Why don't you join me for a drink?" Sasha asked. "Some perspective would help."

Tyler walked over to the bar cart a few yards away from the living room couch. He poured himself a more than generous serving of bourbon without adding ice to his drink. Then, Tyler sat down on the couch next to Sasha.

"Don't tell Ivan is back?" Tyler asked.

"Worse." Sasha chugged the rest of her beverage before sighing and placing the glass on the table.

"Is Riley back?"

Sasha wiped her lip. "We had two run-ins, but Riley isn't the reason for afternoon drinking."

Tyler chuckled. "No offense, but you're gonna have to give me a clue. I'm not psychic."

"Cece wants to renew our weddings."

"What's the problem? Haven't you two gotten closer?" Tyler brought the glass up to his nose, sniffing it. He waited a beat before taking a swig. And he didn't wince when the liquid trickled down his throat, pricking it. A drink was the least he deserved if he was gonna listen to someone's problems. Not having a nervous breakdown didn't mean his rape and Mr. Parker's death didn't still weigh on his mind. It did, and Tyler would just have to pray he'd be okay one day.

"She doesn't know I'm not really Riley."

"Oh." Tyler finished his bourbon. "That might be a problem."

"And I don't know what to do," Sasha said. "Your mother doesn't deserve to renew her wedding vows to her fake spouse."

"You care about her, right?" Tyler asked.

Sasha ran her fingers through her hair. "Absolutely. And I can't deny how we've become quite the family unit."

Tyler couldn't argue with what Sasha said. He would've chosen Sasha over Riley any day. Aside from the night of his eighteenth birthday, Tyler couldn't recall one kind thing Riley ever did for him or his mother. Not even something simple with taking out the trash or unloading the dishwasher.

And that fact was so great. If Riley couldn't make an effort with even a small task, then him and his mother were in trouble. It wasn't like he or Cece ever asked Riley for a kidney, because they'd probably have better luck with a stranger.

Tyler scratched his chest. "She's gonna want an answer at some point."

"I know," Sasha spat.

"I wasn't saying that to hurt you—I was just being honest."

"You know your mother better than I do," Sasha said. "Would she be angry if I told her the truth?"

Tyler shrugged. "I guess."

"I'm gonna need more than that—my entire life is at stake."

"Don't be so dramatic," Tyler said. "It's not like someone has a gun to your head."

"Not helping!" Sasha exclaimed. "The point is, I have a decision to make."

"There's one thing I'd like to know."

"Go ahead."

"Why stay? Do you really feel obligated not to leave because of what happened to me?"

"I don't know what to think at this point."

"You can't tell me Dylan wouldn't have taken care of you?" Tyler got up and poured him and Sasha a refill. "Here."

"Thanks." Sasha took the glass from Tyler, then took a small sip. "Ivan might not have been able to do anything to me, but I still might've ran into him if I went back to Manhattan with Dylan."

"Fair enough. Anyway, I can't tell you what to do—only you can decide that," Tyler said. "But I can remind you about the importance of trusting your intuition."

Tyler's teeth chattered, then he rubbed his hands together. Sporting a sweater didn't mean there wasn't a chill in the air—there was. The calendar was getting closer and closer to the official start of winter, and there wasn't anything Tyler could've done about it. Although Tyler could've made a fire. Nothing like the embers crackling in the fireplace while having a few drinks with a friend, because that was the word he would've used to describe Sasha. His previous point about being closer to Sasha then Cece remained true.

"Enough about me." Sasha took another sip, then put the glass on the table. "Tell me about yourself."

"Excuse me?"

"You don't have to put on a façade for me. I'm a rape victim in case you've forgotten that," Sasha said.

Tyler's Adam apple throbbed. "I'm not trying to fool anyone."

"It's okay not to be okay."

"Do you wanna know the truth?" Tyler asked.

Sasha motioned her head.

"I wrote a letter detailing all my feelings about Mr. Parker," Tyler continued. "I then threw it in the fireplace."

Tyler hadn't expected to chat about the letter, but it was just him and Sasha in the living room as opposed to his life being dissected in front of a room full of strangers. Sasha would never judge him, she couldn't—not everything they'd been through. Most people would've already exposed Sasha if they were in Tyler's position.

"I hope you didn't hold back—that man is a monster for what he did to you."

Tyler grinned. "Yeah, I might've used some profanity. It's not like anyone is gonna read the letter."

"You didn't want Jake to read what you wrote?"

"It was something I did for myself," Tyler said.

"Good enough." Sasha put her hands in her lap. "I made my decision—I'm gonna tell Cece the truth. It's the least I can do after all the bravery you've shown."

"You just gotta fake it until you make it."

Tyler meant every word of what he just said. No harm in a little bravado. Nothing would ever get done if people never made bold decisions. It wasn't like he jumped off a building, thinking he was Superman and would be able to fly.

"Don't say that," Sasha said. "The strength you've shown since that night is admirable. I'm sure Janice would be proud of you."

Tyler lowered his gaze. "Nice someone said her name. I can't even remember the last time Mom mentioned her."

Sasha clapped Tyler's knee. "She might still be struggling with the loss."

***

"That was amazing, Ty," Jake said sometime later.

Tyler continued having his head on Jake's chest while his boyfriend stroked his hair. They were lying in bed with the covers wrapped around both of them, but Tyler wouldn't have traded this afternoon with Jake for anything in the world. Not even for one more conversation with Janice.

An earlier point remained true—every trauma victim was different. Some people might've waited longer before being intimate again. But not Tyler. He wanted nothing more than Jake to have his way with him from the second his boyfriend walked into his bedroom.

To Tyler, the mundanity of how sex was comparable to a routine with all the steps between the first kiss and cuddling in bed provided more comfort than getting unexpected good news. Jake was the one person who'd never hurt him.

"You're awfully quiet," Jake said.

Tyler smiled. "Relax. I'm fine."

"Tell me something—anything. It doesn't have to be serious."

Tyler caught his breath. "Sasha is gonna tell my mother the truth about how she's not really Riley."

"Wow. I don't have to tell you how that's a big step."

"No, you don't." Tyler coughed. "Hopefully, it goes okay."

"You care about Sasha that much?"

Jake should've known better than to ask that question, because Tyler didn't have to contemplate his answer. Sasha was the only other person besides Jake that he could depend on, and he also wouldn't have traded that fact for anything in the world. There'd be times he'd need something and Jake wouldn't be there, but Sasha would.

"She was there for me that night," Tyler said.

"You're right, and that's something I'll always be thankful for. I wouldn't have been able to help you by myself."

"Don't sell yourself short."

"It's the truth," Jake said.

"If you say so." Tyler closed his eyes, and Jake resumed running his fingers through Tyler's hair. Jake wrapped his free arm around Tyler, snuggling them together. For the moment, nothing else mattered to Tyler, including when and where Sasha would tell Cece the truth. Everything other than Jake could wait till the following day. If Tyler didn't take time for self-care, then nobody else would do it for him. In fact, that sentiment was one of the only guarantees in life.

CHAPTER 35

RILEY

Riley stood on Josh's front porch.

Her hand remained on her suitcase handle while waiting for Josh's arrival. But her heart hadn't skipped several beats from the possibility of Josh being unhappy with seeing her. Riley was doing what needed to be done. She also didn't have any other options, because she couldn't do what she planned alone. A part of her also couldn't deny how Josh wasn't ugly even if they'd never have a real relationship.

The door opened, then Josh glared—not even so much as forcing a smile. "What the hell do you want?" he asked. "I told you to leave me alone."

"I'm not done with you."

"I have nothing else to say, not even if Sasha doesn't wanna have anything to do with you because of what you did to her."

"I don't think you wanna have this conversation outside," Riley said "You wouldn't want one of your neighbors to overhear us, would you?"

"Are you threatening me?"

Riley giggled. "Trust me. You'd know if I was threatening you—it's not like I don't have a gun."

Josh's eyes bulged, accentuating their black color. "You have a gun?"

"I'm not gonna shoot you, because you're more useful to me alive." Riley twirled a strand of hair around her finger. "I also paid attention to when you warned about how you'd arrange for the diary pages to be leaked if something happened to you."

Josh didn't respond. Instead, he continued eyeing Riley.

"If you're gonna believe one thing, then believe I don't wanna have those diary pages leaked." Riley cleared her throat. "May I please come inside?"

"Why should I do you any favors?"

"It's the same reason why you talked to me the other day. You wouldn't chat with me if you weren't curious about what I was up to."

Riley might not have attended an Ivy League school, yet she had no doubts about how she wasn't a complete idiot. What she lacked in academic skills, she made up for with reading people. Josh might not admit the truth, but a part of him had to have been intrigued by Riley. And person would've been intoxicated by her—she was the perfect combination of sexy and dangerous.

"You disgust me," Josh spat, fingers playing with his argyle tie.

A crow screeched after landing on Josh's front lawn. Riley's spine even tingled despite how she avoided displaying weakness whenever possible. Riley wondered if the crow might've been a bad omen. Something to consider, at least. She could never be too careful—one wrong move and her plans would be over.

"You'll wanna have a little more conviction next time you live," Riley said. "Maybe then I'd believe what you said."

Josh grimaced. "You can come in. But I wouldn't make yourself too comfortable if I were you."

"I can live with that." Riley wheeled her suitcase into Josh's home, then he locked the door behind them.

Josh titled his head. "What do you want?"

"I wanna finish what I started all those years ago—revenge for what happened to me."

"I read those diary pages before handing them to my friend for safekeeping."

"What's your point?" Riley demanded.

"I know what you did to Vincent," Josh said. "You confessed to killing him a couple of years after you staged his death with the fire, and you might do the same to me."

"Vincent got greedy, but you'd never be stupid like him."

"What you did to Sasha was despicable—it wasn't her fault that Adam sold you because him and your mother didn't anticipate identical triplets."

"Life isn't fair," Riley touted. "And you've got no right to judge me—you don't know what it's like having a mother as a drug addict. Especially between fixes."

"Sasha went to prison for a crime she didn't commit."

"It's in the past."

Josh took his blazer off then tucked it under his right armpit. "You still haven't told me why you need me."

As much as Riley almost gave Josh a dirty look, she couldn't. What Josh just said was true. She hadn't gotten to her point.

"I wanna kidnap my grandmother and Cece," Riley said.

His gaze narrowed. "Are you gonna kill them?"

"I haven't decided that—but I'll let you when I reach a decision."

Josh grabbed Riley's wrist. "This isn't a game, Riley. This is real life."

Josh once again should've known better than to say what he just mentioned. Anyone who spent even several minutes with Riley could've inferred her that she loved games. Nothing better than the euphoria from being in control because of people depending on her mercy. Not that she'd be benevolent. If she had a shitty life, then everyone else deserved the same. Only fair.

"I don't plan on killing you." Riley took a dramatic pause—Josh needed to understand how important the next bit was. "But you still don't want me as an enemy, because I'd turn your life into a nightmare."

Yeah, Josh didn't hold all the leverage in the situation. Riley could still prove her seriousness when she needed to, because she couldn't let Josh misbehave. Not when he didn't have a choice with helping her.

Josh's lips quivered. "Fine."

"You'll help me?"

"Yeah, but we'll be sleeping in separate bedrooms."

"Until you change your mind," Riley said.

"I wouldn't count on that," Josh said. "Now go take your suitcase and purse to the guest bedroom, because I'm not gonna do it for you."

Riley didn't know if she should be happy or alarmed by her lip licking. Josh hadn't just grabbed her he also had no problem with bossing her around, and her arousal hadn't stopped. Nothing like a man who asserted himself, because Riley would've had no respect for Josh if acted like a wimp.

Riley gave Josh a mock frown. "And here I thought you were a gentleman."

"Get out of my sight."

"Gladly."

CHAPTER 36

LOLA

Lola hadn't lifted her gaze off the menu since opening it several minutes ago. She and Preston were sitting at a table at Madame Helena's—one of the most prestigious restaurants Lola knew of—yet Lola couldn't help thinking about her conversation with Vanessa the other day. The one involving her grandmother scolding her how she treated herself to an impromptu outing in town. What she hadn't told Vanessa was that she spotted Sasha and Riley. Lola couldn't imagine what Vanessa's reaction would've been if she knew that. Lola hadn't forgotten Vanessa's frown lines when had the alley encounter in LA—the one where they both tried to kill each other.

Preston squeezed Lola's hand. "Still thinking about your fight from the other day?"

"I don't wanna discuss it," Lola said.

"Your grandmother let us have a date, so that's something." Preston closed his menu, then shoved it aside. "No point in knowing what I want if the waitress hasn't even gotten our drink orders yet."

"Sorry."

"You've got nothing to be sorry about—it's the waitress's fault, not yours." Preston glanced at the table. "She hasn't even brought us bread yet."

"I'm sure it'll arrive soon." Lola met Preston's gaze. "No thanks might be necessary, but I'll say it anyway. Thanks for never giving up on me."

"No problem, babe." Preston leaned forward, giving Lola a quick kiss. "But perhaps we should've gone to a different restaurant."

Lola did a 180 around the restaurant—Preston might've had a point. And Lola's reasoning wasn't even about the echoing of various chatter. There wasn't one free table in the restaurant, and it wasn't even seven o'clock.

The overhead lights weren't flickering and a questionable odor didn't fill the air, so that was something. Her and Preston deserved the best—no telling when they'd get another outing. Vanessa would probably never let them have another outing if she had her way. In fact, Lola was surprised her grandmother hadn't locked her away in a tower.

Someone giggled, then Lola adjusted her posture. A woman in a white uniform and a black apron stood in front of her and Preston. "Apologies for the delay," she said. "We're short staffed. Although it's nice to see a couple in love. Anyway, can I get you two started with a drink?"

"I'll have a gin and tonic," Preston said.

"I'll have a margarita, but no salt," Lola said.

The waitress scribbled the orders down on her mini notepad. "No problem. I'll also bring out some bread and butter."

Preston cracked a smile. "Much appreciated."

The waitress was gone as fast as she arrived, yet Lola wouldn't complain. The more time she and Preston had to themselves, the better.

Lola flipped her hair over her shoulders. "When did you start drinking gin and tonics? I thought cosmos were your go to drink?"

"I'm trying something new," Preston said.

"I like it."

"And it's great how you're predicable about your drink order," Preston said. "Even with not wanting salt on your margarita."

Lola shivered. "It's a drink, not a sauce."

"Fair enough. I don't even like bloody mary's"

"You probably know this already, but get whatever you want."

"Good to know," Lola said. "Although I'll be glad when our drinks and bread arrive. Do you know what you wanna order?"

"I'll probably get a pork chop," Preston said. "What about you?"

"No idea." Lola returned her attention back to the menu. "The lobster and fillet mignon both sound good. The lasagna too."

"Get all of it."

"Seriously? Do you want my stomach to explode?" Lola asked.

Preston sipped his water. "I was joking."

"I know—I was only giving you a hard time."

Their banter was why they made the perfect— at least in Lola's mind. Some couples might not have been able to joke, yet that wasn't a problem for them. And said fact was great. Life couldn't always be serious, because she deserved a break after all the terrible things that happened since Vincent smacked her in the head with a rock that damn night in the woods.

Preston winked. "What are you thinking about?"

"Nothing important—I'd tell you if you needed to know."

"Fine. Keep your secrets."

"Here you go." The waitress placed the bread and drinks on the table. "I'll give you several more minutes to decide what you wanna order."

"Sounds good." Lola sipped her margarita. The combination of lime juice and the distinct flavors of the tequila and triple sec jolted her taste buds. At least the bartender hadn't been stingy with the tequila.

***

Lola and Preston returned from the restaurant hours later, except Lola's pulse soared upon entering the house. The lights were off, so Lola flicked them on.

"I'm sure everything is fine," Preston said. "No need to panic."

Lola didn't need Preston to humor her. Doing so would only make more sweat cling to her brow. If something happened to Vanessa, then they'd need to deal with it. Her grandmother was the only family she had, and Lola would've rather died then let anything terrible happen to Vanessa.

"Grandma?" Lola called out.

No response.

"Grandma?" Lola bellowed for the second time.

No response or shuffling of footsteps.

"Vanessa?" Preston asked, raising his voice.

Still no response or scraping of shoes against the floor and carpet.

"Shit." Lola kneeled, then picked something up before standing. She flashed the diamond earring at Preston. "Something happened to my grandmother—she'd never be careless with her jewelry."

Preston rubbed Lola's shoulder. "We'll find her. It's a promise."

CHAPTER 37

SASHA

Sasha couldn't keep running from her past.

That sentiment was why she was gonna tell Cece the truth while they sipped bourbon in the living room while embers sizzled in the fireplace. The truth always came out eventually, so that was why it didn't matter if Ivan or Riley would cause problems for her or if Sasha had no doubt that Tyler wouldn't out her secret. Honesty would be no trip to Starbucks, yet she was in control this way. Sasha of all people appreciated the irony of power, because that was the one thing she hadn't had when she was one of Ivan's girls.

"Something wrong?" Cece asked.

Sasha sipped more bourbon. The sharp taste stung her throat, yet she hadn't wavered. Knowing the right thing to do didn't mean she couldn't have liquid courage, because she couldn't tell Cece the truth without the boost.

Sasha coughed. "I have to tell you something, and you aren't gonna like it."

"Don't tell me you don't wanna renew our wedding vows." Cece finished her bourbon, then pushed the glass to the side on the living room table. "I was looking forward to it—from sending out the invitations to the actual ceremony."

"I'm not Riley."

"What are you talking about?" Cece asked. "Who do you think you are? The Queen of England?"

"This isn't a joke." Sasha paused for the longest time—these next few seconds were last moments of normalcy, and she'd savor them while she could. "I'm Sasha, Riley's identical twin sister."

"Riley doesn't have any siblings—she's an only child."

A knot formed in her stomach, and Sasha didn't speak. Surprise somehow always found her even if she should've known better. Telling Cece she was an only child was the type of thing Riley would've done—less variables that way.

"I'm really not lying." Sasha took another swig of bourbon. "My name is Sasha, and I assumed Riley's several months ago."

"Fine. I'll play along." Cece picked one of her nails. "What happened to Riley? She couldn't have disappeared into thin air."

"Do you remember the weekend you and Tyler went to Savannah?"

"Yes, but what does that have to do with anything?"

"I visited Riley here that weekend. She reached out and wanted to help me escape sex trafficking. Except she staged her suicide, hoping I'd assume her life."

"Why would she wanna play dead?" Cece demanded.

Sasha shrugged. "I don't know what she did during her absence, but it couldn't have been good. She framed me for a fire when I was a teenager. Little did I know she was both in cahoots and sleeping with our stepfather the entire time. Although I'm pretty sure she later killed him because she got greedy."

"Why would she do that?" Cece asked, massaging her chin. "That's not my Riley."

"Don't pretend like Riley was some noble person—she wasn't. She only wanted your money and you wanted a trophy wife."

"That's not true! You also don't know a damn thing about my marriage with Riley, so you should shut up."

"I'm not telling you this to upset you." Sasha drank more of her beverage. "But you deserve the truth—I couldn't go through with the vow renewal ceremony until you knew the truth about me."

Cece rose. "How kind of you. You're a real Mother Teresa."

"Please don't hate me," Sasha whimpered.

"Don't grovel—it's pathetic."

"Don't you understand? I really care about you and Tyler. In fact, I probably care about him more than you do."

Cece pointed a finger at Sasha. "Don't ever speak to me about Tyler again—you've got no place in this home after lying to me all these months."

Sasha's cackling reverberated against the living room walls. "Someone had to look out for Tyler, because you didn't. Did you know he was sleeping with his math professor in exchange for a better grade?"

"I had no idea," Cece murmured.

"That's because Tyler couldn't trust you, but don't worry," Sasha said. "I was there for him when he broke the affair off and his professor raped him."

"What did you just say?"

"That's right—Tyler's professor drugged and sexually assaulted him." Sasha inhaled a breath, yet the pause had nothing to do with emphasizing her role in Tyler's life. Sasha's skin always tingled from that fateful night. A professor harming one of their students was about as slimy as life. "I know Tyler was raped because I walked in on the incident and stopped it. But that pissed Mr. Parker off so much that he tried to kill me. Fortunately, Tyler killed him first. We then buried his body in the woods his house."

Cece screamed so loud the figurines on one of the table should've broke. "I don't want to listen to this. No amount of supporting Tyler changes how everything was a lie between us. Shit. You don't know how violated I feel."

"I never lied about my feelings for you—I even chose you over my ex-boyfriend."

"What?" Cece asked. "That's supposed to make me feel better for you conning me? No thanks. I've never been played for a fool before, and I certainly won't be with you."

"I wanted to sleep with you," Sasha pleaded.

"I don't wanna hear this." Cece didn't respond for the longest time. But she opened her mouth, she yelled even louder than before. "You have ten minutes to clear your shit out of the house before I call the cops on you."

"Don't be like this—we can work this out."

"I'm serious. I want you out of my house," Cece said.

Sasha couldn't believe Cece's current demeanor. Expecting forgiveness so soon might've been naïve, but what she said remained true. Sasha had been there for Tyler when Cece hadn't, and that should've counted for something. If she was really this terrible person Cece thought she was, then Sasha would've used what she knew about Tyler against him.

"I'm not going anywhere." Tears pricked her eyes, and Sasha wouldn't fight them any longer. And her reasoning wasn't about manipulating Cece. There were dozens of things she could've said if she wanted to play games. Sasha just couldn't get over how Tyler and Cece were the only family she'd ever known, and wasn't about to lose that. Not after she fought so hard to have a good life.

"If you won't go, then I will." Cece snatched her purse from the living room table. "I'm gonna stay at one of the local motels, and you better not follow me."

Cece stormed out of the living room without another, yet Sasha didn't resist Cece's exit. Cece must've needed time for herself, and the situation would sort itself out.

***

Sasha remained in her spot on the living room couch hours later.

Cece had been serious about staying at a motel, because she hadn't returned. Although Sasha might've had a more urgent problem—Tyler. He'd return from the party he and Jake were attending, and she'd have to tell him what happened with Cece.

Counting to thirty in her head slowed her breathing down, and she grabbed her iPhone from her pocket. Life might not have been ideal, but she didn't have to be alone. She would call Dylan, and he'd console her like he always did.

What an idiotic idea for her to consider. Contacting Dylan would be unfair—she embraced her new life with Tyler and Cece, and had to live with the consequences. Nostalgia pangs would disappear, and she'd have her family life with Cece and Tyler back even if she had no idea how that would happen.

The lock snicked.

Tyler entered the house, then he darted into the living room.

"Why aren't you still at the party?" Sasha asked.

Tyler took his leather jacket off. "Jake didn't wanna stay out too late—he's taking his mom out for a birthday breakfast tomorrow."

Sasha gave Tyler a weak smile. "That's nice."

"Are you okay? You don't seem yourself."

"I told Cece the truth, and she hates me." Sasha caught her breath—if she wasn't careful, then she'd have another meltdown over her predicament with Cece. And she couldn't have that. She could only cry for so long. "And she left to go stay at a motel. You should've seen the look on her face—she probably wishes I was dead."

Tyler sat next to Sasha on the couch. "I'm sure that isn't true."

"You weren't there. I've never seen her so angry before."

"This might not mean much, but I'm proud of you for your honesty. Most people would've continued lying, and I'm proud to know you."

"Thanks."

"No secret you care about me more than my own mother."

Sasha sobbed. "Don't say that."

"Come here." Tyler spread his arms, inviting Sasha in for a hug.

A small gesture of comfort might not have been much, yet the offer was the only thing Sasha had. And she wouldn't hesitate with accepting it. Anything to let her know she wasn't alone might help her sleep better at night. She might've no longer had Cece and Dylan, but she still had Tyler, and that was something the universe couldn't steal from her.

CHAPTER 38

TYLER

Tyler and Jake entered the mansion the following afternoon after the party.

Sasha was sitting on the living room couch with a glass of bourbon, so Tyler didn't have a choice about chatting with Sasha. Fooling around with Jake would have to wait. Fortunately, Jake followed him without protesting.

"Don't tell me you still haven't heard from Mom?" Tyler asked.

"I tried her phone, but it went straight to voicemail." Sasha gripped her glass tighter.

Tyler raised his eyebrows. "Did you try her work?"

"She didn't show up today in addition to how she didn't call in sick," Sasha said.

Jake exhaled a breath. "I'm sure she just needs time to herself and will be home before dinner."

Sasha almost spat out her bourbon because of what Jake just said. "Please. I've got a feeling something is really wrong."

"Don't assume the worst." Tyler rubbed Sasha's back. "My mother has to return at some point."

No harm in telling Sasha what she wanted to hear, because Tyler would try anything once. If he were Sasha, then he would've wanted someone to humor him. Reality would settle in soon enough if Cece wouldn't return home.

Sasha sipped her remaining bourbon. "I'm not blind—it's obvious she hates me."

"You don't know that," Jake said.

"Can I get you anything?" Tyler asked.

Sasha giggled. "Shouldn't I ask you that?"

"Maybe it's my turn to take care of you," Tyler said.

"I'm not an obligation," Sasha quipped.

Tyler tucked his hands inside his jean pockets. "Sorry. Came out the wrong way."

Tyler wouldn't make a big deal about Sasha's outburst. Sasha proved herself long ago even before the night Mr. Parker died. Just being concerned about something being wrong with him after Mr. Parker made Tyler end his relationship with Jake proved Sasha was a good person. She didn't have to show interest, yet she had, and Jake would always remember that fact. The real Riley would've never done something like theat. Not even if Riley's life depended on it—the kindest thing Riley ever did for Tyler was not using their tryst against him in hopes of winning favor with his mother. Doing so would've been beyond despicable and would've made Tyler regret sleeping with Riley more than he already did.

"Don't worry about it—you're the least of my problems," Sasha said. "And I know what you meant."

Tyler continued looking at Sasha. In a perfect world, he would've known what to say. But nothing Tyler said would make the situation better. Only Cece's reappearance would, and if Tyler was honest with himself, then he didn't know when that was gonna happen. Cece not even calling out of work was more than a little suspicious.

***

Tyler and Jake continued kissing sometime later in Tyler's bedroom. Jake's hands remained on Tyler's cheeks before snaking down Tyler's body to his waist. And Tyler didn't stop Jake when he lifted his shirt off his body and tossed it onto the floor. Tyler deserved some pleasure in light of Cece's absence, and he seized this opportunity with Jake. Especially since he hadn't seen Jake all day because of his mother's birthday breakfast.

Jake pulled back after another beat. "Maybe we should stop."

"Why would we do that?" Tyler asked.

"Having sex doesn't feel right in light of what's going on. What if your mother is in trouble?"

"If she really is in trouble, then she has herself to blame. Sasha has been nothing but wonderful, and Mom's a fool if she can't see that."

"Not everyone likes being lied to."

Tyler squinted. "Is that supposed to be a dig at me because of how I kept the Mr. Parker situation a secret for so long?"

"I just meant the situation might take longer to resolve itself than you and Sasha like. But that's okay, because I'm sure your mom will reappear."

"She better," Tyler said.

"Were you putting on a façade for Sasha or are you really not worried something is up with your mom?"

If only Jake hadn't asked that question, because Tyler couldn't craft some neat phrase. Causing problems without a reason would only cause more drama, yet his intuition never failed him. So, if something about his mother's situation seemed off, then he should've at least considered the possibility. Any decent son would've done that—doing so was only fair, because no amount of fights changed how Tyler and Cece remained bound together because of blood. The only problem was getting to the good part of their relationship, because Tyler would've been damned if he let the universe rob him getting to the point in his life when it was acceptable to be friends with his mother.

Jake snickered. "I deserve an honest answer."

"The truth might might've been somewhere in the middle."

Jake tugged Tyler's arm. "It's okay to be scared—I promise not to judge. I'd feel the same way if I was in your position."

"Good to know."

"I'm serious. And if you wanna cry, then that's okay with me. Nobody will be the wiser to your venting."

"I'm good," Tyler said.

"I'm serious, Ty. Shoving your feelings aside isn't the healthy thing to do."

Tyler coughed. "I never told you this, but I wrote a letter re the Mr. Parker situation. It was a huge relief."

"Glad to hear it."

"Enough serious. You having your way with me with is the only thing I want."

"Don't say I didn't try." Jake pulled Tyler against his body. Then, he kissed Tyler.

Tyler closed his eyes while Jake's fingers brushed up against his cheeks. The following steps proceeded like a clock changing to the next minute, and soon Tyler's head thumped against his cotton pillow.

Jake leaned against Tyler's left ear. "Are you sure you wanna do this? Not too late for you to change your mind, because I won't think any less of you."

"I've never been more certain of anything." Tyler's body quaked while Jake's fingers linked with his. The sweet scent from Jake's cologne wafted through the air, tickling Tyler's nostrils—he'd never tire from having a boyfriend who smelled nice.

So, an afternoon and evening of fun wouldn't eliminate Cece's absence. Yet Tyler was still doing something for himself, and that was what counted.

***

Tyler and Jake strutted into Tyler's kitchen the following morning.

Sasha stood by the kitchen stove, pouring water into a mug. But the possibility of Sasha being clumsy and spilling water wasn't the issue. Sasha still wore the same clothes as yesterday, begging the question of Sasha not taking care of herself. Because that was the last thing Tyler should've witnessed after Sasha resembled a mom-like figure to him.

"Any news from Cece?" Jake asked.

"I didn't realize you stayed the night." Sasha placed the kettle on the middle of the stove, then whipped her body around. "But no. I don't know anything new."

"I'm sorry to hear that," Tyler said.

"I'm just gonna say it if you two won't." Sasha grabbed hair tie on the kitchen counter, then put her hair in a ponytail. "Something is wrong with Cece, and we gotta figure out what the hell we're gonna do about it. No matter how angry she was, she doesn't strike me as the irresponsible type."

Tyler's stomach lurched—he couldn't deny having the thought re Cece not calling out of work. So, Sasha might've been right. The only question was what they were gonna do about Cece's absence—if she really was in trouble, then she didn't have an infinite amount of time.

CHAPTER 39

RILEY

Riley didn't recoil from the draft while sitting in a chair behind the wooden desk.

The cold was a small price to pay for life going her way for once, because she'd received more bad luck over the years than she liked admitting. Like with how her mother had been a violent drug addict or how she had been denied her family's money because her parents hadn't expected identical triplets and she was born last. Or like when she slept with Tyler or Josh broke up with her. Or even when someone stole the money from her motel room back in LA. Any one of those events might've sent someone on a downward spiral. But not her. She always picked herself up and continued with her life.

So, Riley would revel in how kidnapping Vanessa and Cece couldn't have gone any better than it had.

***

The key turned in the lock.

Vanessa entered her home while Riley sat in the dark on the living room couch.

"I don't remember turning the lights off before my walk," Vanessa mumbled.

No use in Riley getting upset about Vanessa's suspicions. She'd snatch Vanessa soon enough in addition to how she'd be laughing at her grandmother's misfortunate.

Vanessa flicked the lights on, then screamed.

"What are you doing here, Katrina?" Vanessa asked.

Riley cackled. "The name's Riley."

"I'm not blind—your hair is longer and blonder than Lola's." Vanessa didn't move from her spot by the front door.

In a way, Riley respected Vanessa for not shuffling into the living room. A smart person would keep their distance after someone broke into their home. Although a smarter person would've ran out the front door, never looking back. Riley wasn't just playing a game, because there'd be real consequences she'd enjoy from kidnapping Vanessa and Cece.

Riley clapped. "Congrats, you're right! I'm Katrina."

"What do you want?"

If Vanessa wouldn't walk into the living room, then Riley would join Vanessa by the front door. She needed control of the situation before her grandmother fled. Riley wasn't about to let anything mess up her plans—even if there was only a small chance of that happening.

"That's a good question," Riley said after approaching Vanessa.

"Lola and her boyfriend are right behind me, and they'll return from dinner soon enough. So, you might wanna flee while you can."

Riley shook her head. "I don't think so. I saw them leave together—probably for a nice date night. Shame they didn't let you tag alone, although I don't blame them. I wouldn't want my grandmother joining me on a date."

"Excuse me?"

"I'm not going anywhere—not until I finish what I came here to do."

Vanessa snarled. "You haven't told me what you want."

"It's simple. You're coming with me, because I'm gonna kidnap you."

"Sending Sasha to prison for a crime she didn't commit was despicable," Vanessa said. "I don't know how you live with yourself."

"I was sold on the black market as a baby just because my parents, your daughter, hadn't anticipated three children."

Vanessa locked her hands together. "I'm sorry you went through that, but that wasn't Sasha's fault."

"You're the one who abandoned Sasha when she was in prison," Riley touted.

"I had to help Lola."

"You chose one grandchild over the other."

"If you won't leave, then I'm calling the police," Vanessa said. "This is my home, and I won't be bullied."

Vanessa stepped forward several yards, then Riley shrieked. Riley stormed over to Vanessa before grabbing her shoulders.

"You aren't gonna call the police or anyone else," Riley said, sweat rolling down her face. "If you don't come with me willingly, then this situation is about to get more violent. I'd hate for you to fall and break a hip."

"Bitch," Vanessa whispered.

"I heard that." Riley tightened her grip on Vanessa, then gave her a good shake. Vanessa's earring even fell off.

***

A door opened, snapping Riley out of her digression while she continued sitting in her chair by the desk.

Someone climbed down the ladder in the distance and footsteps shuffled.

Her friend's arrival didn't mean Riley was done with her moment of hubris, because she couldn't get over kidnapping Cece.

***

Riley hummed while looking at her watch.

She didn't have a choice with having patience even if she never enjoyed waiting around for people—couldn't go anywhere until Cece returned to her motel room.

The key clicked in the lock, then Cece turned the lights on. Riley even giggled from Cece biting her lip.

"What are you doing here, Riley?" Cece asked.

"How do you know I'm not Sasha?"

"You're wearing a different colored blouse than the one Sasha had on earlier this evening when we had our fight."

Riley smiled. "How observant of you."

"She told me everything." Cece walked to the opposite end of the room, then put her purse down on the table by the curtains. "And I have a confession to make. You outdid yourself, because I never imagined you'd do something as despicable as staging your suicide."

"Whatever."

Cece wove her arms together. "How'd you even know what motel I got? I've only been here a few hours."

Riley's cackled echoed through the room. Cece shouldn't have wasted time with her question. Riley always found a way to get what she wanted, because she deserved the best of everything. It was an unwritten law of the universe.

"I have friends in high places," Riley said.

"Doesn't matter. I want you to leave."

"We haven't even caught up yet. Aren't you interested in knowing what I've been up to the last several months? Come on. What'd say we grab a drink and reminisce for old times' sake? You can't have anything better to do tonight?"

"I'm not afraid to call the police on you."

"Don't be like this," Riley said.

"You never cared about me."

"You're the one who wanted a trophy wife."

"Doesn't matter—you need to leave!" Cece exclaimed.

"You can come out now," Riley hollered.

Josh came out from his hiding spot behind the curtain, then injected a syringe into Cece's neck.

Riley had never been more thankful for the brief time she dated a doctor and stole syringes full of sedatives from the hospital he worked at. Never knew when they'd be needed, but the important thing was Riley finally used one. Better this way, because Cece might've been younger and stronger than Riley's grandmother.

"Thanks, babe," Riley said.

Josh gave her a look. "No problem, but don't call me that ever again. We both know you didn't give me a choice with helping you."

***

Someone's laughter ended Riley's second digression.

Riley adjusted her posture in her chair.

"I never took you for the sitting around and doing nothing type of woman." Josh tossed the plastic bag onto the table. "Anyway, I got the burner phone as requested."

"Thanks." Riley sipped her Champagne from the glass in front of her on the table. The mixture of the carbonated, tart, and sweet flavors electrified her taste buds while Riley let the beverage linger in her mouth before swallowing it. Better to savor the flavor, because she deserved all the luxuries she got.

"Easy on the Champagne," Josh said.

Riley pointed her finger. "In case you didn't notice, you have a cellar full of Champagne."

"Doesn't mean you should drink it all."

"You have no living family, so nobody is gonna get suspicious. Anyway, please relax, because I don't need a buzzkill."

"Not sharing this place with anyone is nice."

"Yeah, I wouldn't wanna share a vacation home in the Catskills with anyone." Riley chugged the rest of the Champagne, then poured a refill.

Josh threw a gaze to the locked door a hundred or so feet away from him and Riley. "How are our guests?"

"I don't know—I haven't checked on them in several hours."

"I hope you at least gave them some water?"

Riley almost sneered at Josh's question. She might not have been perfect, yet Josh should've given her more credit. Giving hostages water was as simplistic as this type of situation got.

Riley waved the empty water jug at Josh. "I did."

Josh sat on the desk. "Good. I'd hate for them to die until you got what you needed from them."

"I know what I'm doing."

"Whatever you say," Josh said.

"Fine." Riley took another swig of her beverage. "I don't know what I'm gonna do, but I'll figure it out."

"Let me know what you decide—it's the least I deserve since I'm risking disbarment and arrest."

Riley still had to be mindful of her behavior towards Josh. His worrying might not have been her favorite thing, yet self-preservation remained her top priority. Like with how those diary pages couldn't be leaked. Nothing good would've come from that happening, so Riley would focus her mind on happy things. Like puppies. Or a beach. Or booze. She couldn't have gone wrong with any of those items.

Riley rose, then straightened Josh's tie. "You'll be the first to know my intentions."

"Good. But it'd be nice if nobody died."

Riley elevated her eyebrows. "Afraid to get your bad on?"

"I don't think I've gotta remind you how one wrong move might unravel the truth. You know. How you're really Katrina, not Riley."

"I know."

"As long as we're in agreement," Josh said.

"Go get a glass and pour yourself some Champagne," Riley said. "The fun is just beginning, and you'll need something to take the edge off."

"If you insist."

Riley's grin expanded while Josh poured himself a small glass of Champagne. Josh didn't know the truth yet, but Cece and Vanessa were gonna die. And that fact was okay. She'd have fun first, which was why she insisted Josh buy a burner phone. But she'd let him enjoy a glass of Champagne—or several—first She wasn't joking about how Josh needed to be a lot less uptight. No point in him living if he wouldn't enjoy himself a little. Especially since Riley had to put up with him for the foreseeable future.

CHAPTER 40

LOLA

Lola couldn't stop pacing in her grandmother's living room.

Several days passed since her and Preston returned from their date, discovering Vanessa wasn't home. And numerous thoughts swirled in Lola's mind, each worse than the previous. Even a five-year-old could've inferred something bad might've happened to Vanessa. The universe just wouldn't let her be happy. Allowing Lola not to worry would've gone against the natural order of life. Like when someone insisted Earth was flat. And Lola had a pretty good idea of who might've been responsible for the event. Riley, aka Katrina, must've had something to do with Vanessa's disappearance. She just knew it—even if she didn't have proof.

Preston squeezed Lola's shoulders. "You're gonna drive yourself crazy."

"I can't help it—it's not like we can go to the police."

Lola meant what she just said. Visiting the police wouldn't have accomplished anything, because they didn't have proof of foul play. One earring just wasn't enough no matter how much Lola wished they had more to go off of.

"There's something we could do," Preston said.

"We've already discussed what you're referring to, and it isn't an option."

"Sasha lives nearby and she might be able to help us, especially if her wife works at a hedge fund—money is power."

"Cece isn't technically her wife," Lola said.

"You know what I meant."

Lola pushed her hair back while sweat drenched her back. "Exposing Katrina and how I'm really Riley would be too risky."

"I don't think so," Preston said. "Sasha is a victim of Riley like you."

"She might be angry I didn't come forward sooner."

"That's a risk you're gonna have to take."

Lola gritted her teeth. "I can't—I'm sorry."

"Fine. But then you've gotta prepare yourself for how something terrible might happen to Vanessa. Like Riley killing her."

Lola almost slapped Preston. He shouldn't have been so careless with his words. Putting the idea of something terrible happening to her grandmother out there was bad enough, because the universe might've been listening. Yet Preston was right. She'd lose her mind if she kept walking back and forth. There was nothing left for her to do, because her life couldn't get any worse.

So, she didn't have a choice. She had to tell Sasha the truth.

Preston's Adam apple bobbed. "Say something."

"You win—let's go to Cece's."

Preston caressed Lola's shoulder. "You aren't alone."

"I know, I know."

***

Rain pounded against the ground while Lola and Preston stood by Cece's front door, waiting for it to be opened.

Preston gave Lola a small smile. "Everything will be fine."

"Thanks."

The door opened, revealing Sasha.

Lola continued standing by Preston, unable to speak. The day she never thought would arrive finally did—the day she got to see Sasha again.

"What are you doing here, Riley?" Sasha asked. "We both know you kidnapped Cece. Although I've got no idea why your hair is a darker shade of blonde and shorter that the last time I saw you."

Deep breaths for Lola. Confusion was only natural for Sasha, and Lola couldn't get angry if she wanted her sister's help.

"What are you talking about?" Lola asked.

"Don't play stupid. Cece disappeared, and you probably killed her." Sasha closed the door right as Preston used his arm to prop it open.

"There's something you don't know," Preston said.

Sasha's nostrils flared. "Doubtful. Riley is a terrible person, and nothing will change that fact."

Preston exhaled a breath. "She isn't Riley. Not exactly."

"What are you getting at?" Sasha demanded.

"Please let us come inside," Lola said. "It's time you finally learned the truth about how we're identical triplets. You've actually met her. Her name is Katrina, but she's gone by Riley the last seven years."

"What do you say?" Preston asked.

Sasha grunted. "Fine. But you better not be pulling something, because I'm not in the mood for your bullshit."

"Do you hate me?" Lola asked sometime later.

Lola and Preston sat on a living room couch across from Sasha and two guys—Tyler and Jake.

Sasha drummed her fingers against her knee. "No. But do you know much drama would've been avoided if you came to me sooner? I went to prison for a crime I didn't commit because Riley assumed your life."

"I'm sorry," Lola said.

Tyler shot Lola a glance. "Coming forward was brave."

Lola might not have known Tyler, but she appreciated his kindness. Some people wouldn't have believed the best in a stranger even if doing so was easier than assuming the worst in someone.

"Absolutely," Jake said.

Sasha giggled. "Tell me something. How'd you decide on Lola as your new name?"

"First name of my favorite singer." Lola paused for the longest time before clearing the uneasiness from her throat. "But do you think we're right? Does Riley have Cece and Vanessa."

"Probably," Sasha said.

Tyler whipped his head back and forth. "God. Awful doesn't even describe this situation."

Something beeped, then Sasha grabbed her iPhone from the living room table.

"What is it?" Lola asked.

"Yeah, don't leave us in suspense," Jake said.

Tyler let out a laugh. "We can't help you unless you tell us what's wrong."

"I just got a text from a blocked number," Sasha said.

"Lovely," Lola said.

"What does the message say?" Preston asked.

Sasha sneezed while her eyes remained glued to the iPhone. "Surprise, bitch. I kidnapped Cece and your grandmother. I'd reveal my identity, but something tells me you already know who I am. And if you go to the police, then I'll kill them. Kisses."

"Must be from Riley," Lola said.

Sasha nodded. "Agreed."

"What are we gonna do?" Tyler asked.

Jake chuckled. "We obviously can't go to the police."

Tyler elbowed Jake. "I knew that."

"We can't let them die," Lola said.

Sasha pursed her lips. "I know, but I'm lost like you. And if you got any ideas, I'll listen."

Lola didn't respond. Instead, her gaze shifted from Tyler to Jake to Sasha and then back to Preston. Once again, life reminded her of how cruel it was. Lola reunited with Sasha under the least ideal circumstances. And prayer was the only thing Lola could do for the moment—false hope was better than no hope, because Lola didn't know what she would've done if Vanessa died. Her grandmother must've had at least a good twenty-five to thirty years left, and a premature death would've been a tragedy. And Lola couldn't live with the outcome, because it might just kill her if it came true.

Diary of a Vigilante
By Shaun Curtis

I Am This Girl: Tales of Youth
By Samantha Benjaminn

Arthur: Shadow of a God
By Richard Denham

Dark and Light Tales of Ripton Town
By John Decarteret

Mixed Rhythms and Shady Rhymes
By Teresa Fowler

Thin Blue Rhymes
By various authors

Click Bait
By Gillian Philip

The Woe of Roanoke
By Mathew Horton

Weirder War Two
By Richard Denham & Michael Jecks

Broken
By Ivy Logan

Origins: The Legend of Ava
By Ivy Logan

A Storm of Magic
By Ashley Laino

Father of Storms
By Dean Jones

Arthur: Shadow of a God
By Richard Denham

King Arthur has fascinated the Western world for over a thousand years and yet we still know nothing more about him now than we did then. Layer upon layer of heroics and exploits has been piled upon him to the point where history, legend and myth have become hopelessly entangled.

In recent years, there has been a sort of scholarly consensus that 'the once and future king' was clearly some sort of Romano-British warlord, heroically stemming the tide of wave after wave of Saxon invaders after the end of Roman rule. But surprisingly, and no matter how much we enjoy this narrative, there is actually next-to-nothing solid to support this theory except the wishful thinking of understandably bitter contemporaries. The sources and scholarship used to support the 'real Arthur' are as much tentative guesswork and pushing 'evidence' to the extreme to fit in with this version as anything involving magic swords, wizards and dragons. Even Archaeology remains silent. Arthur is, and always has been, the square peg that refuses to fit neatly into the historians round hole.

Arthur: Shadow of a God gives a fascinating overview of Britain's lost hero and casts a light over an often-overlooked and somewhat inconvenient truth; Arthur was almost certainly not a man at all, but a god. He is linked inextricably to the world of Celtic folklore and Druidic traditions. Whereas tyrants like Nero and Caligula were men who fancied themselves gods; is it not possible that Arthur was a god we have turned into a man? Perhaps then there is a truth here. Arthur, 'The King under the Mountain'; sleeping until his return will never return, after all, because he doesn't need to. Arthur the god never left in the first place and remains as popular today as he ever was. His legend echoes in stories, films and games that are every bit as imaginative and fanciful as that which the minds of talented bards such as Taliesin and Aneirin came up with when the mists of the 'dark ages' still swirled over Britain – and perhaps that is a good thing after all, most at home in the imaginations of children and adults alike – being the Arthur his believers want him to be.

Broken
(Book I of The Breach Chronicles)
By Ivy Logan

BROKEN BUT NOT LOST

The dark shadow cast by an ancient prophecy shatters an innocent family, but all that is broken is not lost and will rise again.

Half-blood sorceress, Talia, had a unique childhood. It might have been bereft of dolls but not of love. Instructed in combat skills and trained to escape detection, she was schooled to face an unknown menace. Yet, when her family's worst nightmare comes to pass, Talia finds her protected life spinning out of control. Everything she believes in, and everyone she loves, is cruelly snatched away. Talia is forced to flee the attentions of a mad king and denied her supernatural legacy.

She chooses the path of retribution, devoid of love and friendship, but learns that sometimes love is received even if not sought.

'Broken' is a tale about Talia's coming of age, reuniting with her family and seeking vengeance. Most of all it chronicles Talia's rise from the ashes and her journey into finding herself again.

Read Talia's epic saga of love, sacrifice, friendship, and discovering the hero within set against a background of time travel and supernatural forces.

A Storm of Magic
By Ashley Laino

Being brought back from the dead is an impressive trick, even for magician Darien Burron. Now he must try and use his sleight of hand to swindle modern-day witch, Mirah, to sign her power away, or end up a tormented demon in the afterlife.

Meanwhile, sixteen-year-old Mirah is starting to lose control of her powers. After an incident at her aunt's Witchery store, Mirah is sent to a secret coven to learn to control her abilities. While away, Mirah meets up with a soft-spoken clairvoyant, a brazen storm witch, and the creator of dark magic itself. The young woman must learn to trust in herself before she loses herself entirely to the darkness that hunts her.

Weirder War Two
By Richard Denham & Michael Jecks

Did a Warner Bros. cartoon prophesize the use of the atom bomb? Did the Allies really plan to use stink bombs on the enemy? Why did the Nazis make their own version of Titanic and why were polar bear photographs appearing throughout Europe?

The Second World War was the bloodiest of all wars. Mass armies of men trudged, flew or rode from battlefields as far away as North Africa to central Europe, from India to Burma, from the Philippines to the borders of Japan. It saw the first aircraft carrier sea battle, and the indiscriminate use of terror against civilian populations in ways not seen since the Thirty Years War. Nuclear and incendiary bombs erased entire cities. V weapons brought new horror from the skies: the V1 with their hideous grumbling engines, the V2 with sudden, unexpected death. People were systematically starved: in Britain food had to be rationed because of the stranglehold of U-Boats, while in Holland the

German blockage of food and fuel saw 30,000 die of starvation in the winter of 1944/5. It was a catastrophe for millions.

At a time of such enormous crisis, scientists sought ever more inventive weapons, or devices to help halt the war. Civilians were involved as never before, with women taking up new trades, proving themselves as capable as their male predecessors whether in the factories or the fields.

The stories in this book are of courage, of ingenuity, of hilarity in some cases, or of great sadness, but they are all thought-provoking - and rather weird. So whether you are interested in the last Polish cavalry charge, the Blackout Ripper, Dada, or Ghandi's attempt to stop the bloodshed, welcome to the Weirder War Two!

Click Bait
By Gillian Philip

A funny joke's a funny joke. Eddie Doolan doesn't think twice about adapting it to fit a tragic local news story and posting it on social media.

It's less of a joke when his drunken post goes viral. It stops being funny altogether when Eddie ends up jobless, friendless and ostracised by the whole town of Langburn. This isn't how he wanted to achieve fame.

Eddie knows he's blown his relationship with rich girl Lily Cumnock. It's Lily's possessive and controlling father Brodie who fires him from his job - and makes sure he won't find another decent one in Langburn. And Eddie doesn't even have Flo to fall back on - his old nan died some six months ago, and Eddie is still recovering from the death of the woman who raised him and who loved him unconditionally.

Under siege from the press, and facing charges not just for the joke but for a history of abusive behaviour on the internet, Eddie grows increasingly paranoid and desperate. The only people still speaking to him are Crow, a neglected kid who relies on Eddie for food and company, and Sid, the local gamekeeper's granddaughter. It's Sid who offers Eddie a refuge and an understanding ear.

But she also offers him an illegal shotgun - and as Eddie's life spirals downwards, and his efforts at redemption are thwarted at every turn, the gun starts to look like the answer to all his problems.

www.blkdogpublishing.com